THE SONS OF WOODMYST

The Sons of Woodmyst

THE WOODMYST CHRONICLES BOOK II

Robert E Kreig

WHITEKEEP BOOKS

For Lee, my sister.

The Realm

THE FROZEN WASTE

THE CORE LANDS

BLACKROCK HAVEN

WINTERMARSH

IRONFIELDS

ERIMOOR

WHITEKEEP

BLACKSHORE

THE CANYONS OF TERRITH

REDLOCH

MALLOWHILL

LIGHTHOUSE

THE SEA OF SOLACE

STRONGHOLDT

MELAMWED

THE PILLARS OF MOHAA

CLEARFOO

HAVENCREST

KALIBARD

OAKBEACH

BROOKNESS

WINTERSPRING

THE FOREST OF ERUN

MEADOWMOOR

THE GREAT DIVIDE

WOODMYST

NEWHOLT

OSTFORD

DELLMOOR

OLDCASTLE

GRASSBEACH

BELBURN

PRYHOLT

GREYROSE

LUNKHUL FOREST

DWEAGAN

BARROWFIELD

THE SEA OF LUNKHUL

REDEDGE

LINPORT

BYVIEW

BUTTEREDGE

ROSEFORD

FREYMOOR

BELMORE

THE WESTERN SEA

THE EASTERN SEA

N
W   E
S

Prologue

Silently and stealthily, they moved over the snow-covered ground with determination. Their intent was malicious. Their prey was close by.

The night air was bitter, and the darkness was impenetrable. Everything worked in their favour.

Careful to keep the sound of their footfalls as quiet as they could, the band of thirty men moved towards the small cluster of crude houses. It was a small village still in the process of settlement.

Pausing, crouching upon the crest of a small ridge, they scanned the hamlet warily.

A large campfire sat smoking, slowly dying, in the centre of the clustered houses. The surrounding structures, with their snow-covered thatched roofs and walls consisting of stone, wood, and canvas, appeared welcoming. Friendly.

A few small pens had been fashioned from tree limbs in order to house small livestock. There were no horses from what the men could see; no carts and no well-established constructions of any kind.

It was apparent the small community had probably set up camp and erected their crude buildings before the snow fell. The only recent handmade object, placed after the deluge of white powder, was an enormous pile of firewood at the far end of the village.

Apart from the livestock in the pens, there was no movement in the settlement. The acrimonious frostiness assured them that most of the village men would be inside the warmth of their beds.

The defences were non-existent and their flanks unprotected. It was easy prey.

The men drew nearer and nearer, looking this way and that for a sentry. There was none.

One of them saw something move and signalled to another at something ahead, near the edge of the village. The other placed an arrow onto his bowstring and aimed carefully. The dog didn't feel a thing.

But the hound was seen as it fell silently upon its side.

An old man had been sitting behind his house praying to the gods when he saw the arrow pierce his dog. He instinctively crawled behind the pile of firewood to hide from the invaders. There he cowered and froze in fear.

The intruders entered the village like ghosts, unheard and unseen. Each took position outside the door of a small hut.

Waiting for the signal, they stood with daggers ready to push the doors open.

A nod was given.

The doors smashed open simultaneously, splintering and breaking onto the floors covered with skins of beasts.

Bewildered men raised their heads from where they slept as women and children screamed.

Before the men of the village could rouse themselves to challenge the intruders, daggers were plunged into chests and necks.

They bound and gagged the women. Girls from around ten to those of adolescent years also had their hands fastened and mouths covered. The younger girls and newborns had their throats slashed and left to bleed. The boys of all ages suffered the same fates.

One man gave a long whistle.

Many horses led by two men with torches and an enclosed wagon, driven by one man emerged from the trees and moved into the village, where the women were loaded onto the covered cart. A man threw a pile of blankets in with the women who screamed, cried, blubbered, and swore at the invaders.

Some marauders took what supplies they could from the little huts. They took grain, blankets and weapons from inside while others gathered the swine and goats and threw them into the wagon with the weeping women and girls.

Two men upon the ground approached the two on horseback and received the flaming torches. The men walked around the village lighting huts on fire before returning to mount their steeds.

All men still in the centre of the small collection of huts straddled their chargers and prepared to leave.

The women and young girls screamed and cried as they watched their homes burn with their men and sons inside.

One man gave a gesture with his hand and all men moved out of the village with the wagon in tow.

The flames intensified, and before long, the village was an inferno.

Listening to ensure they had gone, the old man cautiously made his way out from behind the pile of wood and watched as his new home burnt to the ground.

It wasn't long before the structures collapsed to the ground with loud crashes. Snow fell again, and he wrapped his wiry arms around his body for warmth.

He was glad he had kept his coverings on and the bearskin that he draped over his shoulders as the icy breeze blew.

Looking at his dog, he considered burying the poor beast, but ruled against it because of the weather. He was too old to dig a hole through the snow and then the hard ground beneath.

Instead, he pulled the bearskin around him tightly and started trudging towards the west.

He needed help and the best place for him to get that was from his closest neighbours.

The journey would take a day or so. With no food or weapons to defend him, he would need to take care.

So, warily, he made his way towards Woodmyst.

One

―――――――――

"Don't you dare," Tomas warned the young cow edging its way from the rest of the herd towards the grove. He sat atop his brown mare, attempting to prevent stragglers from leaving the rest of the cattle. Around him were five other young men on horseback trying to drive the heifers into a fenced yard near the base of the eastern hill.

The sun smiled down upon them from high in the sky. Its warmth welcomed as snow blanketed everything in sight and the air was bitterly cold. The men were rugged in thick skins as they drove the cattle from the open lands beyond the hill back to the security of the yard.

"Bring it back in," shouted Lor from his steed near the open gate to the enclosure.

"You just mind that gate," shouted Tomas. "Be ready to close it when I bring her in."

He moved the mare between the grove and the cow.

Staring at Tomas, she stamped her feet and lowered her head. She directed her sharp horns at his horse and put the mare in more danger than him.

He loosened the reins to allow his steed to move freely, just in case the heifer charged. The cow stood her ground. So did the mare.

The horse threw her head back and forth, stomping her hoof against the snow-covered ground in reply, stirring the white substance with her forelimb.

The challenge had been set.

A deep snort gusted from the cow's nostrils as she stepped forward one pace. The mare mirrored the action and took a step towards the challenger.

Suddenly the heifer bolted to the side towards the hill. It was her only passage to freedom. With her access to the grove blocked, and the village to the west and the river to the south hedging her in, she was going to try for the only way to escape.

Looking quite clumsy as she ran, the cow moved quickly past the fence-line that encircled the yard and climbed the gradual incline of the east hill. Kicking up snow and mud, she bolted up the embankment, leaving a deep trail in the snow behind her.

"Tomas," shouted another young man with a wide grin, "do you require assistance?"

Tomas steered the mare hard to his left and raced after the escapee, ignoring the remark.

The heifer attempted to pick its pace up, but the incline of the hill and her enormous form slowed her down. She wasn't made for running this fast for so long. A jog or a trot was more to her fashion.

The mare, however, loved to run.

She raced like an arrow after the cow and caught up easily. The mare didn't stop there. She kept running past the heifer and turned around only once she reached about halfway up the embankment.

Stamping her feet, the horse challenged the cow.

The heifer stopped. She was tired already. Breathing hard, thick ooze dripping from her nose and snow in her nostrils, she stuck out her tongue and swept it away. Her eyes moved to her left, where the grove presented an inviting avenue of escape.

The mare instinctively shifted her weight, ready to intercept.

Tomas smiled. "Just you try to get away, bitch," he hissed.

The heifer moved her eyes to her right and scanned the end of the ridge where the river flowed by. She then looked back at the man on the horse in front of her.

She surrendered.

With the grove as her only option for freedom, they limited her escape. The mare was too fast and the snow too thick to run through. Her winter weight slowed her down, and she was just too tired.

Slowly, she turned and trundled down the embankment towards the opening to the yard.

Lor, still seated upon his steed, held the gate open for her. The other members of the herd waited for her inside. She strolled in and moved into the large gathering of bovines.

"That was easy," Lor remarked as he closed the gate.

Tomas sidled up to his steed with a smile. "My horse is just too smart and too good," he replied.

"Well, it needs to be," Lor retorted. "After all, look at who its owner is."

"What do you mean, *owner?*" asked one of the other men. "It's not he that owns that horse. That horse owns him."

The men laughed as they turned their charges towards the village.

Small wooden cottages with thatched roofs adorned in snow and smoking chimneys enclosed a large patch of open ground. In the centre of this area was a stone hearth, blanketed with snow. No fire had been lit here for some time.

Most of the villagers preferred the warmth of their homes and the small fires they kept within to that of the town centre during the cold seasons.

Some shop fronts faced the town centre but, for the better part, remained closed. They could hear only a blacksmith beating his hammer on the anvil.

To the edge of the town was a new large stable. Tomas remembered the stable house from his earlier years, when he had first encountered his mare. It was large and catered to many steeds. This one was sufficient and could really only be said to be a good place to put horses up for the night. The pens were small and cosy.

One day, Tomas told himself, they would rebuild the stable house as it once was. A place fit for his mare.

He recalled when he first saw her. She was young then, but age was creeping upon her. Once, she could run through the snow without a hint of weariness. Now, she breathed heavily with such exertion.

One day soon, he would need to retire her and put her out to pasture with the other older horses.

But not today.

An older fellow, his long beard greying with age, stood by the stables, waiting for the young men to return. He hugged a thick cloak that draped over his shoulders and stamped his feet periodically to keep warm.

"Richard," Tomas called as they approached.

"Lads," he greeted them as he opened the door. "Bring those horses in before they freeze to death."

The men rode carefully through the narrow door and dismounted once inside. Leading the horses into their designated stalls, the riders turned them so they faced outwards, towards the centre aisle of the stables.

The stable was warm and inviting, with straw scattered across the hardwood floor and bags of grain piled neatly against the rear wall.

On either side of the interior were twelve small stalls, each now containing a steed. Ropes of varying sizes, leather bridles and iron horseshoes hung from nails hammered to the beams that separated the pens.

The horses nickered gently as their riders removed saddles. The men hung the reins upon the nails stuck into the beams and placed their saddles on the railings separating the pens.

Nodding their heads and swishing their tails, the horses waited impatiently for the men to rub them down with coarse-bristled brushes. As the rubdown began, most horses stood perfectly still until their humans drew the brush close to a hard-to-reach spot that a horse just couldn't get to on its own. A slight movement with a leg, or a lean towards or away from their groomer, enabled the brush to access the places that the steed so desired to be rubbed.

Richard found this behaviour in the horses most fascinating, seeing some similarities between the animals and their human counterparts. He watched with a smile as the mare lifted her leg for Tomas to reach behind her thigh.

"How long did it take for you to get her to do that?" he chuckled.

"She has just always done this," he answered. "I didn't have to teach her anything."

"She's a good horse, Tomas."

"She's getting old," Tomas admitted. It had taken him a long time to do so. He would ride the mare forever if he could.

"Have you chosen a new steed?" Richard asked, a hint of care in his voice.

Tomas shook his head as he brushed the mare's rear flank.

"I don't see the need to rush," the older man advised.

"I will need to choose by next winter," Tomas stated. "She won't be able to drive the cattle during another one. But you did fine today, didn't you, girl?" He rubbed her nose, and she rewarded him with a soft nudge.

Richard nodded and smiled. He admired the relationship the boy had with the mare as he grew up. With all that had happened to them, it was a wonder this young man before him had kept a level head.

After losing his father and mother, left to raise his sister on his own, Tomas had become a natural leader, involved in the restructuring of his village from day one. Richard had acted as a guardian, a guide, for all the orphaned children of Woodmyst. He had taught them how to farm and fish, passed on his skills as a tracker and warrior. He had no sons of his own, but the orphaned boys had all become his children.

But it was Tomas who had the ideas.

Tomas had directed the construction of the cottages and the stables very early on. Not long after the siege upon his village, he had established a camp for the survivors.

They used existing farmhouses dotted upon the pastureland, but the shelters could not cater for all the children and young women returned home by the Night Demons. Tomas instructed the mothers of newborns and adolescent girls to take the younglings into a selected house. The boys, over a certain age, would set up tents using what supplies they could muster.

Working hard every day for the best part of a year, the boys, with advice from Richard, constructed several cottages about halfway between the east hill and the ruins of Woodmyst. Families could pair up and share cottages for another year at most, as more cottages were built.

During this time, they tended to cattle and sheep, and re-established trade with nearby towns. They were glad to have such good neighbours as those who hadn't heard from the village came to investigate within days after the attacks. They donated grain and food to help get the band of orphans back on their feet.

After three full years, there were twenty new cottages, establishing a small community. Some others had moved in from larger cities, wishing to escape the hustle and bustle of crowds. As a result, Woodmyst now had a blacksmith and a few farmers who had set up fields just to the east of the settlement.

Richard believed none of this would exist without Tomas Warde's leadership. The orphans had asked Richard to be their chief, but he had refused the title in favour of that of mentor.

The inhabitants of the town, however, viewed him as their leader and so Richard had reluctantly taken on the role. He knew that one day Tomas would be chief, and he'd welcome the day when that would occur.

Now he watched the young man move around to the other side of the mare with the brush. He wanted to talk to Tomas, but not in the presence of the others.

"Tomas," he said, "when you are done here, come find me. I want to speak to you about a few things."

"Of course," Tomas replied.

"I'm going to my hut," Richard said. "My old bones need the warmth of the fire."

Richard strolled past the other men grooming their horses and bade them a good day before leaving the stable.

Tomas stared after him for what must have been too long from the mare's perspective. She nuzzled him to bring his attention back to her.

"All right," he answered her as he rubbed the brush against her coat.

***

He knocked on the door, which rattled loudly in response. The wind had picked up slightly and swept down from the mountains to the north and across the vast expanse of open land to the south.

Peering in this direction, he remembered a time when plantations stretched from just beyond the river all the way to the foothills of the southern ranges. Orchards comprising a vast variety of fruit trees and fields of vegetables and grain not only kept the large population of Woodmyst fed, but provided necessary resources for trade with other communities beyond the forest and mountains.

Now it was all but a wasteland.

The great flying beasts that were in league with the Night Demons had scorched the ground in that area, preventing anything from growing there for almost a year. Rain and snow filled the ground and eventually turned it into a marsh with a slow run-off into the river near where it met the forest. The wide stream, as a result, turned murky once it entered the tree line, forcing the people of Woodmyst to fill their water vessels and canteens from near the village before venturing into the woods.

The marsh had grown ground-hugging plants and mosses, but nothing of significant size or of particular use. It mattered little, as there was no means to access the southern region unless one was to head west for a mile into the woods, where they constructed a bridge for travellers venturing on the roads between the few communities this far east from Oldcastle. There, the river met the Sea of Lunkhul. Once at the bridge, one would need to backtrack on the opposite side of the river to get to the place where the orchards once grew.

Doing this proved pointless as the road to the south traversed the forest, only to come out from the trees where the forest met the southern ranges, bypassing the marshland altogether.

It had been nine years since that terrible night, but even now, if the south wind blew, the smell of smoke and fire drifted faintly upon the air.

The door opened with a long creak.

"Come in, Tomas," Richard invited him from inside. "The fire is warm and out there is not."

Tomas entered and felt smothered by the heat. He peeled off his bearskin and draped it on a chair near the door.

"Sit, sit," Richard insisted. "Becka has made tea."

"Afternoon, Tomas," a comely young woman chirped from the quaint kitchen to the rear of the room. "Would you like a cup?"

"Please," the young man replied.

Richard sat in a deep chair opposite Tomas and settled in with a long, exhaling breath. At that moment, Becka brought the tea, one cup for Richard and the other for Tomas.

First, she handed one to her husband who, after just settling into his seat, almost jumped back out again to receive it from her. "Thank you, my love."

"You're welcome." She smiled. Dimples formed on her cheek as she handed the cup of tea over. She handed the other cup to Tomas, who thanked her as well.

Secretly, Tomas envied the older man. Becka was easily the most beautiful woman in the village and only three years older than he was. Tomas remembered her as a young serve who worked in the Great Hall during banquets. He wasn't sure what other duties she had performed and never asked.

From his perspective, *that* Woodmyst was well into the past and what they were building now was a new beginning for all of them.

No serves.

No walls.

No Great Hall.

Becka and Richard had grown close over the past few years, as both rebuilt the community. He oversaw everything from construction and supplies while she distributed required provisions around the township. No one delegated them the responsibilities they had, they just performed them out of necessity. Someone had to do them.

Before long, they were working together more often, spending more time together at communal gatherings, and then living together with the blessing of all the people.

It simply made sense that they would end up with one another, even if he was old and she was only a handful of years out of her adolescence.

Perhaps sensing his thoughts, she sat near the men with her own cup and began the conversation before Richard spoke.

"So," she began, "when are you going to find a woman for yourself, Tomas?"

Richard almost spat his tea. "Becka. Leave the lad alone." He shook his head as he turned his attention to Tomas. "No, but seriously. When are you?"

"This is why you asked me here?" Tomas eyeballed the older man.

"No," he replied. "Not really. It was one thing I was going to discuss with you, but not the only thing. But think about it. I was able to find the love of my life. Me. Richard Dering."

"I understand." Tomas smiled.

"I don't think you do," Richard remarked as he pointed to himself, sounding as if he didn't quite believe it. "Me. Richard. Now with Becka, the beautiful. How?"

"You were both meant to be." Tomas lifted his cup and sipped.

"Well." Richard leant forward. "It's time for you to find a wife. You have a future here and you need to build it. We're talking about children and grandchildren. You can't make those with that mare of yours... although, some people are talking."

Now it was Becka who almost spat her tea.

"There are plenty of girls in the village," Richard continued. "More than there are boys. You could have two or three wives."

"No, thank you." Tomas chuckled. "I don't need that many children."

"We're a blossoming community just starting out," Becka joined in. "The more the merrier."

"Well, then!" The young man smiled. "If that is true, why haven't you two made a young Richard or Becka yet?"

"Not through lack of trying." Richard reached over to his wife, who took his hand lovingly.

"You two make my guts rumble." Tomas held his stomach, feigning sickness.

"Finish your tea," Richard instructed. "We'll take a walk in the ruins."

***

Clouds had formed at the peaks of the northern range. Their greenish tinge showed Tomas that snow was coming. The sun was low and, around this time of the year, it found itself below the horizon earlier than the warmer seasons.

By his side, Richard stood at the crumbling remains of the centre bridge in the ruins of Woodmyst. The bridge, now missing its bulk, once crossed the river, allowing access from the Great Hall to the southern gate.

Near to where he stood, he had slain a dragon. That act was one of the many memories that still haunted his dreams.

The Night Demons stole all the mothers of newborn babes and the children of Woodmyst and took them from the village. It was then that the dragon buried its head in the doorway of the Great Hall and spewed flames into the auditorium, incinerating all the women and the men who were too feeble to fight.

More an opportunity to go out fighting than using the situation to his advantage, Richard approached the beast from behind and plunged his sword into its side. The monster attempted to flee but crash-landed in cottages nearby.

To this day, he pondered how he'd achieved that victory. He did not understand dragon anatomy, but believed he had stumbled upon a weak spot that possibly no one had discovered before.

Peering around at the snow-covered stonework and the jutting rusted iron structures that once were the surrounding walls and Great Hall, he visualised the way things used to be. People would move about the streets as peddlers sold their produce from markets on the sides of the roads. Children would run and dive under stall markets and horses' legs as they played war games. Old men would ogle young serve girls as old women clucked their tongues and shook their heads.

He missed that.

"You will be chief one day, Tomas," Richard said suddenly. "Whether you like it or not."

"You're better at the job," Tomas argued.

"I never accepted the job," the old man replied. "Mine is to safe keep what is yours until you're old enough for me to hand it to you."

"Why me?" Tomas asked, peering towards the white expanse of the marsh. "Why not Lor or even one of the Shelley girls?"

"You know our traditions," Richard stated. "Women don't hold positions on the council."

"Perhaps things need to change," Tomas proposed.

Richard lowered his head and gave that some thought. The young man was right. They were starting again, which also meant that they could adjust or even rewrite laws and perhaps begin new traditions.

That he was right also gave credence to why Tomas would be chief someday.

"We should offer prayers to the gods and ask for their guidance in this," Richard suggested. As soon as he had allowed the words to pass over his lips, he regretted it.

"There are no gods, Richard," Tomas replied coldly. "If there were, this wouldn't have happened to our village."

Richard shook his head. "This was not the fault of the gods."

"It was the fault of my father," Tomas interjected. "The council members. All except for you. You have told me this story. Many times. Surely, if the gods were real, they would have allowed only those responsible to be destroyed. Instead, they let everything be consumed in flame. What sort of gods are these? There are no gods, Richard."

"Do you want revenge?" the older man asked. "Do you want to destroy the Night Demons for this?" Richard gestured to the surrounding ruins.

"No, of course not," Tomas replied, kicking the snow with his boot. "That would just make me the same as them. This was their revenge. Through it, in some twisted way, they proved they were better than our fathers."

"Why?" Richard wore a perplexed expression. "Because they were better tacticians? Because they were better fighters?"

"They weren't all better fighters." Tomas smiled. "You took down your fair share. No. It was because they didn't hurt the children. Not one scratch was placed upon a newborn or its mother. There was no bruise upon a young teen girl or child. They were careful with us. The Woodmyst children lived, while theirs did not."

"For that alone, I will be thankful to the gods," Richard remarked. "Even if you will not. I know that the gods have their eyes on you, Tomas. I know they surround you all the time. I know it in here." The older man held his palm against his chest.

Tomas looked up to the sky where a small flock of birds had darted from the forest and now made its way towards the new village. He followed them with his eyes as they flew past where the eastern wall once stood.

"Regardless," he said, "I still don't want to be chief."

The birds continued over the cottages and towards the east hill. Tomas watched them dart to the left in the grove's direction.

But his eyes quickly returned to the hill.

Something was there.

"Richard," Tomas breathed. "Do you see?"

The older man fixed his eyes upon the hilltop.

Upon the crest, staggered a lone figure. A man.

"Not again."

Two

"Someone upon the hill," Tomas called as he sprinted through the village.

Richard, feeling his age in the cold weather, had jogged behind him for some distance before his body failed him. Now he trudged into the township, puffing and panting as Tomas continued beyond the circle of cottages towards the hill.

Other young men peeked from behind their closed doors to see what the commotion was about. Lor, however, burst from his cottage with sword in hand and ran as quickly as he could after his friend.

The man on the hill staggered down the embankment towards Woodmyst. He stumbled and fell onto his side and rolled a fair way down the hillside.

Tomas, lifting his knees high to clamber through the thick snow, ascended towards the tumbling man. By the time they met, Lor had made it to the base of the mound.

The newcomer was face down, covered with white powder and breathing hard. Tomas rolled him over and helped him into a sitting position. He brushed the snow away from the man's face and cloak as Lor strode over to them.

"Thank you, young man," the visitor hoarsely. He was shivering violently and his leathery skin was taking on a tinge of blue.

"Don't speak," Tomas instructed him. "Help me get him into my house, Lor."

"Of course." Lor nodded as he lowered his blade.

Both young men lifted the stranger to his feet by placing their hands under his arms. Before long, they were slowly making their way past the fenced-in cattle and towards the township.

Several people had gathered near the edge of the village to see what was happening. Most of them remembered the siege, which began with one lone figure on the hill. They feared the Night Demons had returned to complete their task, and shared relief when they saw that there was no mutilated corpse left behind this time.

Still, they wondered why this stranger had appeared and what troubles he might have brought with him. Soft whispers and long looks followed as the two young men carried the individual in through the door to Tomas' cottage.

Richard and Becka followed the three men into the house and closed the door behind them, blocking out prying eyes. The gathering groaned and grumbled somewhat before dispersing and making their way back into the warmth of their own dwellings.

Lor and Tomas lowered the newcomer into a deep, cushioned chair by the fire. Richard helped the stranger out of his wet clothing while Becka found some blankets to drape over the cold man.

Tomas made tea for them all as the man clenched the blankets tightly, soaking in the fire's warmth as he continued to tremble.

"Don't worry, friend," Richard said, attempting to comfort the old man by the fire. "We'll have you all nice and warm soon enough."

"Killed them all," the man whispered. His eyes half closed from exhaustion.

"What did he say?" Lor asked from beside the door.

"I think he said that he killed them all," Becka replied, with a hint of panic in her voice.

"No," Richard, who was the closest to the stranger, said. "He said, 'killed them all'. You're safe now." He placed a hand on the man's shoulder.

"Took the women," the old man managed.

Tomas, gathering cups together, dropped one onto the wooden floor where it bounced loudly. A sudden memory came flooding back to him. As a boy, he'd sat in a cavern with a hessian sack over his head.

"What of the children?" he asked, staring blankly at the table.

"Taken," the man started.

"They took them?" Lor stepped forward, his excitement apparent.

"Took the girls," the stranger continued.

"It's them." Lor was convinced. "It must be them."

"Wait," Richard snapped. "Go on, friend."

"Killed the boys. Killed the babies."

"They're back, Richard," Lor said.

"No," Richard replied.

Tomas bent down and retrieved the fallen cup, placing it back onto the table with the others. The old man closed his eyes and drifted off into slumber.

"We need to wake him up and ask him more questions," Lor insisted.

"You'll do no such thing," Becka argued. "The poor man needs rest."

Richard peered at the old man's face. His skin was like leather, stretched tightly over his bony face. The lines around the stranger's eyes and corners of his mouth told Richard this was a man accustomed to smiling and laughing a lot over the years.

The room fell silent as the visitor slept. Tomas made tea for the three others and himself. He handed the steaming cups around, offering each of them a seat. After some time of watching the old man, Tomas looked to Richard.

"Are they back?"

Richard shook his head. "It can't be them," he replied.

"Why?" Lor asked. "How could you know that whatever happened to this poor man wasn't by the hands of them?"

"Because *he* told me they would not be back," Richard affirmed.

"And you believed *him*?"

Tomas scowled at Lor disapprovingly.

"I have little to say about the Night Demons, Lor," he said, his temper rising. "But they were honourable, much more so than our own fathers were during the Realm War. I believe Richard's word, and I believe their word. If they told him they would not be back, then they won't.

"Whatever this may be," Tomas continued, "it is not the doing of the Night Demons. They didn't kill children. We're living proof of that. We will give this man time to recover and then he can tell us his story."

***

Reading by the fire, Tomas sat in a chair across from the sleeping old man. He had stirred awake momentarily a few times during the night. Tomas had observed as the man's face twisted with fast spasms as dreams took him to unpleasant places.

A quick readjustment of his covers and a gentle hand on his shoulder from the younger man brought the stranger's troubles to a temporary close. And this was how it had been for most of the night.

The book he read was made of old parchment and contained stories of old wars and kingdoms that lived on only in such pages. Tomas read it periodically as he continued to watch the old man through the night. Once or twice, he had drifted off and sleep for a short period until the newcomer stirred, arousing Tomas from his slumber.

He'd pull the covers to the stranger's neck, place a soft hand on the shoulder and speak soothing words.

"It's all right, my friend," Tomas would whisper before sitting back into the other chair by the fire to resume reading from where he left off, only to drift into sleep again.

He had lost count of how many times this cycle had taken place.

The final time that he woke wasn't because of the old man's struggle with night terrors. It was because the water-fowls called as they summoned the sun to rise.

Tomas opened his eyes and stretched in his arms above his head. The old book fell upon the floor with a loud plop.

"Good morning, my friend," said the old man. His voice was still raspy.

Tomas looked across to the stranger, who was staring into the fire. The flames had died, leaving only bright embers to keep them warm.

"Good morning," Tomas replied. He leant forward to grab a metal poker that leaned against the stonework framing the hearth. Tomas introduced himself as he stirred the embers to revive the flames again. "My name is Tomas Warde."

The flames burst from the ashes with new life as he placed some wood in the fireplace.

"Antony Grenefeld," the old man replied. "Where am I?"

"Woodmyst." Tomas wanted to ask him where he came from and what happened. The information given by the old man the night before had produced more questions than answers. He opened his mouth to probe this Antony Grenefeld with queries. "Are you hungry?"

"Famished," Antony answered.

Tomas rose and crossed the room to the small kitchen behind the man.

"I have oats, water and cream," the young man stated. "How does porridge sound?"

"Terrific!"

***

After breakfast, Tomas dropped the used bowls and cutlery into a large soup pot full of water that was boiling on the stove. He then returned to the chair across from Antony, who was still rugged up with blankets in the seat by the fire.

"How are you feeling?" Tomas asked.

"Good enough, thank you," the old man replied. He pulled the blankets around him tightly. "I don't know where my clothes are."

"I apologise," Tomas said. "They're still on the floor in the kitchen, behind you. I'll get you some fresh ones to wear. Yours are soaking wet. Your boots are by the fire drying out."

Antony nodded as he returned his gaze to the flames.

The young man stood and returned through the kitchen and passed through a doorway to the side. It led to a small bedroom with a large cot in the corner and a wooden wardrobe against the wall.

He opened the wardrobe and fished out some suitable clothing for the visitor. When he had a neat pile of garments for Antony to wear, he carried them back to the living room and placed them on the chair he had slept in during the night before.

"I think these will be fine," Tomas said. "I'll place your clothing on the back of a chair by the stove. With luck, it'll be dry by the end of the day."

"I'm sure they'll be fine." The visitor smiled as he lifted himself from the chair. The blankets fell to the floor, exposing the old man. Tomas quickly averted his eyes and returned to the kitchen, where he retrieved the wet clothing from the floor and draped it over the back of a wooden chair. He then moved the chair from beside the table to nearby the stove.

"They're a bit loose for my frame," the old man stated as he patted his belly. "I think I must not have it as well as the people of Woodmyst."

"It wasn't always this good," Tomas replied as he grabbed two towels from the back of another wooden chair and used them to lift the soup pot from the stove. He placed the pot, still filled with boiling water, bowls and cutlery, on the kitchen table where it would cool while he talked with Antony.

"Would you like tea, Antony?"

"Please," the visitor replied.

Tomas placed a small pot onto the stove and poured in some water from a bucket that had been sitting upon the kitchen bench nearby.

"It will take a while," he said as he returned to the living room.

Antony was right. The clothes were loose for the old man's frame. Tomas didn't believe he was an overly big person. In fact, he thought he was quite average when he compared himself with other men of his age that he knew and had met. Perhaps the old man had been missing a fair portion of food for some time.

There was a knock at the door.

"Tomas," a voice called. "It's Richard."

He was early. The sun was barely visible above the horizon, and it was bitterly cold outside. The young man guessed Richard's curiosity about the stranger had got the better of him. As he opened the door and saw the lines under the other man's eyes, he assumed Richard had not slept too much, possibly mulling over the newcomer's words from the night before.

"Good morning, Richard." Tomas invited the man inside. "Becka is not with you?"

"Ah, no. I left her in bed. I probably kept her up with my tossing and turning."

"Richard Dering," Tomas said as he closed the door, "meet Antony Grenefeld."

The old man stood from his seat by the fire and shook the other's hand.

"I wish I could say it was a pleasure to meet you," Richard stated, "but from your words last night, I would be safe to say that it probably is not."

"Why?" Antony asked, as he sat back down. "What did I say?"

"Not much," Richard replied as he took Tomas' seat across from the old man.

"Tea, Richard?" Tomas called as he entered the kitchen again.

"Yes, thank you," he answered, and returned his attention to the visitor. "You said that some were taken, and that others were killed. It was difficult to find out exactly what you meant. From what I could gather, the men and the boys were all killed except for you and all the women and girls were taken away."

"I was praying," Antony started. "I was behind my hut and was praying near the firewood we had piled for the settlement. My wife and daughters were inside.

"Then they came. I saw little. Just shapes in the dark moving about. I hid, like a coward, behind the firewood."

"You had no choice," Richard assured him as Tomas poured the tea.

The old man sobbed. "They killed my dog and put all the women and girls in the back of a wagon. Then they threw our livestock on top of them. A few goats and pigs were all we had. I think they took some of our supplies, perhaps the grain. I'm not sure."

"I saw men going into the huts where babies cried, then I didn't hear the crying anymore. Before they left, they torched everything."

"They were men?" Tomas asked.

"Yes," Antony assured him. "What else could they be?"

"They don't kill babies, Tomas." Richard looked at the younger man. "Remember?"

Tomas nodded as he brought two cups of tea to the men.

"Who are you talking about?" Antony asked, wiping the tears from his old eyes as he took the cup from Tomas.

"That's another story for another time," Richard answered. "Right now, we're more interested in how we can help you."

"Can you bring my wife and daughters back to me?" the man begged.

"Ah..." Richard looked to Tomas for help.

The other held his cup to his lips and stared back to his friend.

"We don't have warriors here. We are farmers mostly. Apart from accommodating your immediate needs, Antony, I really don't know how much help we could be to you."

"What Richard means," Tomas interjected, "is that you will have a roof over your head and food on your plate."

"My family..." Tears formed again in Antony's eyes. "My people are a lost cause, then?"

Tomas turned to look out through a tiny window above the kitchen bench. Through the tiny portal, he could see the river flowing by and a few geese braving the icy water.

"I know you're upset, Antony." Richard placed a hand on the man's knee. "But the snow would have covered their tracks by now and there is no way of knowing where they intend to go."

Antony placed his face in his hands and wept.

"I'll go," Tomas offered.

"What?" Richard lifted his eyes away from the sobbing visitor and peered at the back of the young man's head. Tomas was still looking out through the window.

"I'll go," he said again.

"Didn't you listen to what I just said?" Rising to his feet, Richard left Antony by the fire and entered the kitchen. "The snow is deep and we are in the middle of winter. Your horse and perhaps even you will not last a week out there."

"We can't just let people come and attack other villages because we're afraid after our own experiences." Tomas turned to face the old man, still crying by the fire. "I'll go after them and try to bring them back here."

"On your own?" Richard shook his head as he pointed to Antony. "We don't know how many of these men attacked his village."

"I have my father's sword," Tomas reminded him, "and your breastplate."

"What makes you think I'll let you wear my armour?"

"You're not coming," Tomas informed him.

"Like hell, I'm not," Richard retorted angrily.

"You're a married man." The younger man met his friend's eyes. "She would kill me if I let you come. I'm more afraid of her than anyone else in this village."

Richard smiled and nodded. "Me too," he agreed.

"Good," Tomas continued. "Then you will stay and watch over the village, and I will wear your breastplate. Besides, you're getting too fat for it in your old age."

"You little bastard!" Richard embraced the young man, remembering he had raised them all since the siege. He also knew it was useless arguing with Tomas. Ever since he was a boy, he had proven to be stubborn and adventurous. There was no talking him out of doing something once he made his mind up about the matter. "You'll be taking others with you. No argument."

"Four," Tomas replied as they released from each other. "And none with women or children attached to them. And, not Lor."

"He will be angry," Richard told him.

"He's been meeting with my sister as often as they can," the young man informed the older. A look of surprise crossed Richard's face. "Nothing too serious yet. I've seen them cuddling by the river during autumn and they sit be one another whenever we all meet. I'm surprised you haven't noticed."

"She is only fifteen." Richard clenched his teeth.

"So, what of it?" Tomas replied. "There are some in this village who have married as young as twelve and thirteen. Your concern is that she is like a daughter to you. But *you* are like a father to both of them." The young man entered his bedroom and opened the wardrobe.

"Think of it this way," Tomas continued. "I am five years older than my sister. Your wife is only two years older than me. What does that make *you* in the light of all things?"

Richard hadn't thought of his relationship with Becka in that way. Age was simply something that never entered the discussion and no one in the village had openly talked with him about it before, until now. He suddenly felt ancient and disgusted with himself.

Tomas saw the look on his friend's face. "I didn't mean that in a bad way, Richard. You and Becka are meant for each other. I also believe with the same conviction that Linet and Lor are meant to be with each other as well. It simply makes sense."

Richard snapped back to reality and stood by the bedroom door. "What are you doing?" he asked.

"Packing," Tomas replied as he placed some clothing into a knapsack he had laid out on the bed.

"You'll need warm things to wear," Richard advised him.

"I'll be wearing most of my warmer garments," Tomas replied. "I'll pack changes of undergarments, socks and tunics, just as you taught me."

Richard watched him for a while before he nodded and turned from the door. "I'll call a meeting. We need to select the four others to accompany you."

"You mean *you* will select the four others." Tomas smiled. "I'll talk to Linet and Lor. Let me do that?"

The older man gave a sad smile and a nod. "Of course."

Three

"But I don't want you to go," Linet cried. She was standing in the middle of Lor's living room staring at her brother, who was sitting by the fireplace. Lor had moved from the room and stood in his kitchen with his arms crossed, clearly upset, as he stared at the wall.

"I don't understand," said another young woman sitting next to Tomas. "Why not wait until the snow has melted? We're right in the middle of winter."

"If this had happened to us, Sevrina," Tomas replied, "and it was you that had been taken from your house, wouldn't you want someone to come for you?"

She turned her face to the flames, silently conceding.

"I should go with you," Lor stated.

"Not only do you have a sister to consider, Lor," Tomas said. "But my sister likes you. And you like her. She may lose a brother, but I couldn't live with myself if she was to lose a husband before there was even a wedding."

The two lovebirds quickly looked at each other with the same question in their eyes.

How does he know?

"Everyone knows about you two," Tomas said, perceiving their thoughts. "Well, except for Richard. He did not know until I told him this morning."

Both Lor and Linet looked to the floor bashfully, not knowing whether to smile at the news or scowl at Tomas for what he was about to do.

Tomas stood and crossed the floor to his friend in the kitchen. He grabbed Lor by the shoulders and locked eyes. "Promise me you will marry my sister and you will do so this spring. Promise."

"I will." Lor allowed a single tear to roll over his cheek. "Of course I will."

Tomas smiled and embraced his friend. He then turned to his sister and held her tightly. She pressed her face into his chest and sobbed.

It seemed to her that he was making sure everything that needed doing was getting done. He was being overly cautious with his answers and he was choosing his words carefully. She wondered if he believed he would return to them or not.

His response to Sevrina's words was right. Someone needed to go after these marauders before they disappeared. Waiting until the warmer seasons would be too late. The women and children taken could well be dead by then, and she didn't want that on her conscience.

Being selfish and keeping her brother at home was not the right thing to do in this situation. She knew her brother well and saw he felt strongly about this quest. How could she to stop him? As if she could! This was Tomas Warde. Nobody could direct Tomas away from adventure and risk. Not even their parents could when they were children. No woman had ever come close to taming him. He was a free spirit, a creature that could not be caged.

"Now you are promised before witnesses," he whispered gently in her ear.

Linet couldn't keep it together any longer. She bawled because she was happy about her engagement. She wept because her brother was about to leave, perhaps for good.

Sevrina rose to her feet and clasped her hands together with glee. "We're going to be sisters," she laughed, an attempt to make a sad departure into a happy moment.

The two girls hugged in the middle of the room as Tomas opened the door.

"You best be back by spring," Lor warned him.

Tomas smiled, gave a nod, and closed the door behind him.

**

"Pickings are slim," Richard whispered to Tomas as they approached the fire in the centre of the village. They had piled wood onto the hearth at knee height and lit it with flint. The flames danced about inside the circle of stonework, emitting heat to all those men who braved the cold and stand about. "Too many are with someone or not willing to go with you in this weather. I can't say that I blame them."

"I understand," Tomas replied as they came to a halt. He counted twelve men standing around the fire. All of them looked willing. All of them looked young. Tomas suddenly remembered that he was only twenty, and considered to be an older member of the village.

"Do you know where you're going, yet?" Richard asked him.

"Northeast into the mountains," Tomas replied. "Antony told me how to get there. I know the way. Lor and I travelled out to where he described when we were younger. It was before Antony's people settled. There were no huts back then. It's deep in the Forest of Khun. There was a clearing with a river nearby; a good place to camp and plenty of game in the warmer seasons. I don't know what it's like during the winter."

Richard nodded as they drew nearer to the fire. He would have to admit that he had not been into the Forest of Khun at all. It was far into the mountains. Most of his travels eastward were to the villages and townships further south for trading. Tomas and Lor, however, had left Woodmyst for weeks on end as they explored new regions. It didn't surprise the older man that Tomas knew the place. Tomas probably knew all the different places around their region.

"So," Richard began. "From these fine men, I have selected four to go with you. They are eager to follow you and are at your disposal."

The younger man suddenly felt the weight of responsibility upon his shoulders. Internally, he questioned if he was ready to do something as encumbering as this.

"Who are they?"

"David Gyfford." Richard pointed to a tall, broad man with a bald head. He reminded Tomas of an enormous tree trunk. His thick, black beard ran from his ears to his chin, where it ended in a long plait bound in place with bands of twine. The man appeared to be an intimidating individual with a long sword strapped to his back, but knowing him from childhood, Tomas knew David to be a kind soul to those he cared about.

"Oliver Weston," the older man continued, moving his gesture to a muscular frame with handsome features. His long, blond hair draped over his neck and he carried two curved swords that once belonged to the Night Demons sheathed over his broad shoulders.

"Simon Bell," said Richard, motioning to a beefy individual with a thick black beard and long, dark hair. Tomas thought the man looked similar to a boulder covered with black fur. On his hip, he wore a long sword and dagger.

"Ivo Hamond," Richard announced finally.

A young man stepped forward, the hilt of a long sword sticking from beneath his cloak. He wore a hood over his head and was clean-shaven. Tomas thought perhaps the boy hadn't reached puberty yet and could not grow whiskers.

He carefully looked at each one of them and surmised that it was an excellent group. Tomas knew the men well. They had all shared a history together, living through the siege and rebuilding their homes to the current state in which they now lived. These were good men.

"Has Richard informed you of what you've volunteered for?"

They all muttered and nodded their affirmations.

"Good," he replied. "Gather your things, say your goodbyes and prepare your mounts. We leave as soon as we can."

The men disbanded and went their separate ways.

"Splendid speech," Richard teased.

"We don't have time for motivating conversations," Tomas replied as he started towards the stables.

Richard followed the young man through the village. "Perhaps not, but you could have told them how you were looking forward to working with them. Give them some sense of hope."

"Hope?" quipped Tomas. "How can I give them something I don't believe in? Whatever fate awaits us out there is what we will get. Pure and simple. Nothing more."

"So you're going to face death?"

"I'm going to try to retrieve some kidnapped people," Tomas corrected as he opened the stable door. "If death wants to show his ugly face to me along the way, I'll simply ram my fist into it."

***

The five men packed their horses in the stables. They loaded two more steeds with supplies; one rolled tent each, a small amount of flour and oats, blankets and ropes, as well as some basic tools for camping.

The men dressed each horse in a caparison made of thick canvas that draped from over the neck to the rump and down to the animal's knees. The clothing's intent was to keep the beasts warm and dry during the journey.

Hooves stomped excitedly as the men tightened saddle straps and fastened bridles. With knapsacks attached and other supplies such as canteens of water and pouches, the steeds seemed to know that a long journey lay ahead of them.

All the horses needed now were their riders.

David Gyfford, the giant of the crew, naturally had an oversized charger. His dapple-grey draught horse hadn't borne such a heavy load before and, although she was more than capable of carrying such a load, she stamped her hoof and snorted loudly in protest as the hulk of a man straddled her.

"Settle down, bitch," he commanded her. She tossed her head, flinging her mane around wildly.

"Not a nice thing to call your horse, David," Ivo Hamond, the youngest of the men, jeered.

"That's not her name," he replied before moving his gaze to the animal beneath him, "but she has always been one since she was a foal."

Soon, the men were ready. David and Tomas tied the packhorses to metal loops they had fastened to the front of their saddles with long pieces of rope.

Leading his two horses by the reins, Tomas steered the beasts out through the stable doors and tied them to a post positioned at the side of the building. He held the door open for the other men to ride their animals into the open. Once through, Tomas closed the door and returned to his bay mare. She eyeballed the other horse attached to her.

He gave her a rub on the muzzle and she rewarded him with a soft nudge and a friendly nicker before he lifted himself upon her back. She nodded her head excitedly, as she always did when Tomas took her out for a run.

But today was different.

They would not return before dusk as usual. They would be away for an undefined period. Tomas felt for the animals as he looked around to see if all were ready to depart. The steeds did not know what they were in for.

Neither did he.

With horses loaded, weapons at the ready and supplies at hand, the band of riders prepared to leave. They peered back to Tomas as they awaited his instruction.

"All set?" he asked. They nodded and mumbled their affirmations. "Let's be off then."

The troop moved steadily towards the hill.

No one had come to see them off.

No one had come to say farewell.

This was by their request.

They intended to return.

There were no reasons for goodbyes.

***

Kicking their knees high and sending a flurry of snow into the air, the steeds made progress as they climbed steadily higher upon the slopes that led deeper into the mountains. The sun, floating majestically in the sapphire sky, shone upon them from directly above.

The branches of the pine trees bowed heavily, laden with snow, occasionally dropping their load upon the ground with a loud thud. Ivo kept turning his head towards the sound, only to discover that nobody was there.

"Did he get away again?" Oliver Weston asked, seeing the younger lad looking this way and that.

"What?" Ivo turned his head to face the blond man upon a golden mare.

"The ghoul," Oliver replied sternly.

"What ghoul?" Ivo looked frantically into the gaps amongst the trees they had just entered.

A loud thump came from behind the travelling troop.

"That one," Oliver hissed, quickly glancing behind him as if to see who was there. "Did you hear him?"

Ivo looked back, then around him.

"You had better spot him before he gets you," Simon Bell called from his steed.

"Tomas!" Ivo cried.

"They're playing with you," the leader informed the young lad. "It's nothing. Just snow hitting the ground. Reach deep into the pouches on your saddle and find your balls. You're going to need them out here."

The men laughed loudly at the remark, all except Ivo, who turned red from embarrassment.

They moved deeper into the woodlands, sheltered from the bright sunlight. The smell of pine filled their senses as the steeds trudged onwards.

The forest was full of life. Small birds chattered as they flew about. Tiny squirrels scurried across the surface of the snow and clambered up and down the trunks of the surrounding trees.

The band of men had now entered the Forest of Khun, leaving the open plains and foothills behind them.

Four

Gnarled limbs and fingers stretched in all directions, looming above and around the five riders. The sensation was almost suffocating as they rode through the thick forest of bare trees. Dark trunks penetrated the snow, presenting an intense contrast of tone to their surroundings.

Heads low as they pressed on, the horses seemed to soak up the emotions from the bleak environment. They trudged forward, on and on, without a care, for there was nothing to care about.

There was nothing.

A harsh mist had formed just beyond reach, causing the black pillar-like trees to form shapes that appeared to move in the shadows. The phenomenon caused unease amongst the men, to which they responded by looking this way and that with an element of paranoia.

Now and then, the sun pushed through and formed an inviting yellow circle of light here and there. Soon, however, a cloud would blot it out and return the environment to a scene of doom and gloom.

Once in a while, the forest opened into small clearings where the jagged snow-speckled forms of pine trees jutted from the ground. Small birds fluttered about their branches and sang welcoming songs to the approaching men.

Cheerfully, the steeds' heads lifted and their ears twisted as the chirping drew their attention. The band of men pointed and called the birds by names, briefly arguing if they disagreed upon a species, whistling along to the calls if they could.

For a moment, the party was a merry bunch; man and beast alike. Then they moved back into the thick of the woods, where seemingly lifeless trees stretched their crooked arms in a menacing manner. It wasn't long before a grievous feeling crept upon them again.

The horses lowered their heads, their noses almost touching the ground. Shapes formed amongst the dark pillars in the mist. Terror sank her teeth deeply into the men as they trudged on.

And on.

Five

Snow had fallen.

A light, white blanket of powder laced the charred ruins of the small settlement. Dark beams of timber protruded through the clean surface in places, proving to the band of men that they had arrived at the correct location.

A thin road, not much wider than a wagon's breadth, ran through the centre of the village. Snow covered it with a thin veil that stretched from one end of the village to the other.

Two huts still partially stood in defiance, one on the left of the road and the other farther along and on the right. Burn marks scarred the edges of the windows, doors and flames had eaten the thatching on their roofs. Their walls, however, remained upright.

The pile of firewood behind which Antony must have hidden sat stacked at one end of the tiny village, with snow rested neatly upon its top. A few chickens came hobbling from among the trees to examine the newcomers.

"Well," Tomas said as he lowered himself from his mare, "I think this is it."

Simon Bell continued to ride his chestnut along the tree line to the left, scanning the ground and trees. The other men dismounted.

The giant David Gyfford and golden-haired Oliver Weston headed for the partially standing structure farther into the settlement on the right. Ivo and Tomas inspected the one close by and on the left.

"I think they went through here," Simon called. He had pulled his steed to a halt by the tree line at the far end of the township and pointed into the forest. "Some fresh marks are on the trunks here and something large has snapped low branches off in the woods. I would say it was a wagon."

"Good work, Simon," Tomas complimented.

As Simon turned his horse back towards the others, the men entered the charred structures to salvage what they could.

Ivo's gaze instantly fell upon the charred remains of a youngling. Blackened and void of flesh, the child's body lay on the ground, awkwardly twisted upon its side. Its empty eye sockets stared up at Ivo, grinning at him with a lipless smile.

"By the gods," he whimpered.

Tomas appeared unmoved. He looked to the remains of the child and then to the young man by his side.

There are no gods.

Stepping over the tiny corpse, he moved into a small room beyond the scene. He glanced up to see the sky staring back at him. Singed beams of wood stretched across from one wall to the other.

A pile of five hessian sacks rested on the floor. Each sack, if stood upon its end, would reach a man's waist. Some snow had fallen over the top one and collected around the one at the bottom of the stack.

Tomas brushed the frosty covering off the top sack and pulled his dagger from his belt. Stabbing it into the bag, he made a slit about the length of his finger and placed the knife back into its small sheath. With two fingers and his thumb, he reached into the slit and dug out some contents.

Oats.

They were wet and practically unusable. The three sacks beneath could prove useful.

He lifted the top sack from the pile and handed it to Ivo, who took it in both hands.

"Throw that outside," Tomas ordered. "Not near the horses."

Carefully stepping over the remains of the child, Ivo left the hut to discard the sack of oats.

Looking about, Tomas saw blackened pots, an iron stove with a pipe extending above the walls, and beams of timber over his head. On the floor, he saw the remains of the child amongst a mess of debris.

"We found a sack of flour," called Oliver. "Well, we found four. But only one is of any use."

"Good," Tomas shouted back as he stared at the smiling remains. "Bring whatever you can down here. Simon," he called.

"I'm here," the stocky man called from near the horses. He had just tied them to some nearby trees.

"Bring the shovel and a blanket." Tomas then thought about what other things David and Oliver might have discovered. "Oliver, did you find any bodies?"

"No," the other replied. "Just flour."

"Just the one blanket, thank you, Simon."

***

Taking turns to shovel through the snow and then deep into the cold, hard ground, the men formed a grave for the youngling in a patch of land near the tree line behind the hut where they'd discovered the body. They carefully wrapped the remains into a blanket.

David and Simon lowered the wrapped body into the ground, facing the body westward, as was their tradition in Woodmyst. Tomas shoveled dirt back into the pit.

"Shouldn't we say words?" Ivo asked.

"Words?" Tomas queried as he stopped shovelling and eyed the young man.

"You know," Ivo looked to each one of them, "to send this one on."

"You want to say words," Tomas remarked, "then say words. I want to put dirt back in this hole and set up camp."

Moving his gaze across the band of men before him, looking for support, Ivo found the others peering into the open grave in sheepish silence.

"None of us is an elder," Simon eventually put in.

"There are no elders," David remarked. "Not anymore."

Tomas resumed shovelling dirt into the grave.

"Perhaps we need elders again," Ivo suggested.

"Why?" asked Tomas as he continued scooping dirt onto the spade and dumping it into the pit. "So we can be told how Areang will accept this one back into her bosom of the earth? Perhaps how Haaen will guide their spirit across the sky. Maybe you like the part about how Gwendra, the goddess of life, grieves the loss of one of her children. Or, there's my favourite, of how Grolle will guide this one onward and be their carer in the next life.

"There are no gods, my friend," Tomas stated as he placed the last scoop of dirt over the grave. "There is just this. Existence. We live, then we die."

Tomas made his way back to the hut, leaving the others to stare blankly at the fresh mound of dirt. One by one, they moved off until only Ivo remained.

Perhaps Tomas was right, he thought. Perhaps there were no gods. But that was no reason to trample anyone else's beliefs into the dirt. Maybe it was naïve, as Tomas hinted towards in his tone, to believe in the gods. Maybe the naivety needed to believe in such deities was what some people needed to help them push onwards.

Tomas was arrogant and stubborn in these matters. But not everyone else shared his convictions. They understood why he hated the gods and what they represented.

Losing his father had hit him hard. His love of horses had come from Alan, as did his natural ability to lead. Alan Warde had taught his son almost everything he needed to know in survival, general living and the gods. But his father had kept a lifelong secret shame, a pact with the other council members of Woodmyst that resulted in the siege of the Night Demons.

For this, he despised his father.

His mother's death affected him the most. From his perspective, she was an innocent victim caught up in his father's past decisions. Killed by dragon fire; consumed by flame because of retribution.

Because of revenge.

For this, he blamed his father.

For this, he hated the Night Demons.

But his abhorrence towards the gods was vastly greater.

Keeping this in mind, Ivo closed his eyes and silently prayed for the youngling that just buried and for his friend who was in deep, internal pain.

***

They had cleared the floors of the two surviving structures and dumped the debris into piles on the side of the huts. They'd salvaged several items, including five large soup pots and two saucepans. Afterwards, they unfolded the large canvas rolls to use as tents, and stretched them over the beams atop the structures. Each canvas sheet they then fixed in place by threading ropes through steel eyelets along the seams and then pegging the other end of each rope into the ground near the base of the walls.

Fires in the ovens of both huts would soon brew heat into the temporary dwellings. The horses were unloaded and their gear packed neatly outside the hut where they found the youngling. They covered the equipment with another smaller canvas sheet before splitting the seven steeds into two teams.

Four went into the first hut and the other three to the other hut farther along the road. After fastening them inside the structures, the men gave each horse a feed of oats. The reason for the division of the steeds was lack of space; they wouldn't all fit in one hut together.

The men chatted idly as they worked. Some spoke about how they intended to grow corn, wheat, or barley when they returned home. Others discussed how they would tend to the flocks and herds, producing the best wool and meat for the village.

Tomas remained silent.

His mind was on the task ahead of them. He wondered where the wagon full of the village females was heading and why they had been taken. Other thoughts moved onto how they were going to liberate the women and just what they might need to do to the kidnappers in order to do so.

As the sun lowered in the west, the men gathered in the eastern hut. They had gathered snow and packed it into three of the soup pots they had found to melt over the hot stove. After some time, David removed two of the pots from the flames and poured the contents into two buckets that they had brought with them. They repeated the process several times; filling the pots with snow, placing them over the fire until the buckets were full. This would be their drinking water for the night.

They then used the five large soup pots to melt more snow; three heated on the stovetop in the western hut, two in the eastern hut. When the snow liquefied, they removed the pots from the heat and placed them on the ground near the horses where they could reach to drink.

Tomas wished they had found more of the large containers, or even a trough of sorts. The horses pushed each other away with their noses to get to the liquid. The pots were large enough to allow only one steed to drink at a time. It was frustrating to watch.

They used two saucepans to melt more snow, but this time brought the water to the boil and added oats from the well-preserved sacks they had found. Using a steel spoon Tomas had packed, they stirred these into a slushy substance like fine gruel.

"Bowls and spoons are in that bag," he said, and gestured to a brown satchel resting near Ivo, who was sitting with his back against the wall. The younger man reached in and pulled out five wooden dishes and four steel spoons. He handed them out to the other men, keeping one set for himself and one bowl for Tomas.

Tomas served the porridge to the crew. They sat in a circle on the ground, spooning the slop into their mouths. It was warm, filling, and tasteless.

"This would go well with some honey," David suggested.

"This would go well with goat shit." Simon smiled.

The men laughed loudly as the stars winked alive one by one in the sky and the last of the day's light faded.

***

Tomas and Ivo unrolled their blankets and prepared to sleep on the floor by the stove in the western hut. The four horses, tied up near the door, occupied most of the floor space of the front room. Tomas moved to the little area of the kitchen to bed down as Ivo took possession of the tiny storeroom where they found the sacks of oats.

"This is my first time out of Woodmyst since—" Ivo stopped mid-sentence as he pulled his blanket over him. He didn't want to continue.

"Since when?" Tomas asked as he placed a horse's caparison over the doorway to keep the wind out, fastening it to a beam above with some rope.

"Doesn't matter," Ivo replied as he settled down to sleep.

"Now you have me curious," Tomas said as he quickly patted his mare and crossed the floor to the stove. He placed some firewood into the hearth and used a long stick to poke the flames to life. A little more light flooded into the room, presenting an inviting orange glow against the walls and canvas above.

"Well," Ivo said, "I was just going to say that this is my first time out of Woodmyst since the Night Demons took us to the caverns. But I thought I would be better keeping my mouth shut about that."

"Why?" asked Tomas as he lowered himself into his bedding.

"Why what?"

"Why keep your mouth shut about it?" Tomas asked. "It's a part of our history. We should remember it."

He pulled his covers over his head and rolled onto his side. The wind whistled as it passed through the bare trees of the forest behind the hut. A soft flapping emitted from the canvas roof.

"Do you think we'll ever see them again?" Ivo queried.

"The Night Demons?"

"Yes."

"Nah," Tomas answered drearily. "They've moved on. Did what they believed they had to and left."

"Night Demons," Ivo whispered as he thought about the cavern they had taken him to as a child.

"I don't think they would like to be referred to by that name," Tomas mused. "That's something we called them. Who knows who they really were?"

The wind increased, and the whistling turned to gentle howls. The canvas flapped softly as the fire crackled in the oven.

"Voices," Ivo whispered.

Tomas listened to the breeze. The howls indeed sounded like voices calling in the wind.

"It's just the wind," he assured the other.

To Ivo, the voices continued to call gently as the wind blew.

It sounded as if they were men full of sorrow.

It sounded as if it were the weeping of the dead.

Six

A large pot of slosh dropped onto the ground in the centre of the ring. The women and young girls, chained to a metal loop attached to the wagon they had travelled in for the last three days, wept and held each other as all hope of freedom drained away from them. The long chain had clasps fastened to it at evenly spaced intervals. These were latched to the older females whose legs were large enough to fit into the iron cuffs.

The younger prisoners, too small to outrun their captors, remained untethered. They clung desperately to the older hostages in fear as their wide eyes darted from one ruffian standing nearby to another.

The barbarians numbered at least twenty, outnumbering the fourteen females in their keeping. Each man had a sword or axe. Some carried daggers on their belts and kept bows close by.

A chill wind blew through the camp as a group of men sat by a large fire watching as others moved the women out of the wagon. The few goats and pigs stuffed into the carriage with the prisoners kept in the covered cart and fed oats thrown onto the floor of the transport.

They dragged the prisoners onto the cold ground and placed them in a circle, the younglings crying and continuing to cling to the older ones.

One girl's eyes darted from one intimidating man to another.

Already, several men had performed unspeakable acts with some of the younger women. It was only a matter of time before they sought such play from the girls. From her and her sister.

"Eat," the largest one, their leader, barked as he pointed to the pot of slop. A deep scar stretched from above his left eye, across his nose, stopping at the right corner of his mouth. She hoped it hurt him severely when he received the wound that made the mark.

Some, who were beyond famished, crept on all fours to the metal container and dug their hands into the stew before shovelling it greedily into their mouths. She did the same, attempting to avoid standing out.

Reaching back, she grabbed her younger sister and drew her into the crowd of women. The girl resisted at first, but then she saw the hungry eyes of one man. His hair looked greasy in the firelight, glistening in the dark as he stared at her, boring his eyes into her.

She knew what he wanted, and she didn't want him or his long bony fingers anywhere near her. She cringed to her sister's side and tried to bury herself beneath the larger girls and women around her.

"Stay close to me, Joanne," the older girl whispered softly as slop fell into her long auburn hair. "That one likes the little girls. He is filth."

"Where's Mama?" Joanne asked, terrified.

"Over the other side," said the older girl. "She is too far from us. Stay close to me and do what I do. Understand?"

"Yes, Emily," the younger replied.

"Now eat. It doesn't taste good, but you'll need your energy. We don't know for how long we'll be trav—"

Suddenly, she felt her hair pulled from behind, and she was on her feet.

"You talk too much," slurred the greasy, thin man as he heaved Emily away from the others.

"No," Joanne stood.

A woman nearby grabbed her and held her to the ground, placing a hand over her mouth.

"Shhh, child," the woman commanded.

"Emily," an older woman called from across the group of prisoners.

"Get down and eat," barked the hulking mass of the leader.

"That's my daughter," she cried. "Please."

The leader pulled his sword from its sheath and strode over to her.

"Please," the woman kept calling, tears streaming from her eyes.

The leader took one swipe with his blade straight through her neck.

Silence and stillness seemed to last forever as Emily watched her mother breathe her last breath. Her head fell to the snow slowly.

A shrill scream suddenly filled her ears. All the other prisoners kept their faces to the ground. Joanne remained hidden beneath the woman chained beside her. It was only then Emily realised the scream she heard was hers.

The slimy man bent over, fiddling with the lock on the clasp attached to Emily's leg. It came loose and dropped to the ground before he gripped her by the arm and dragged her away from the others.

Her screaming had stopped as reality kicked back in and she realised he was taking her towards his tent. She knew what would come next. Struggling to free herself only made him grip her tighter and tighter.

Glancing around for help or a way out, she saw trees surrounding all sides of the camp with a steep embankment falling away into the darkness near the tent.

"First," the slimy man began, "I'm going to have fun with you. I've been watching you for a long time. I think about you at night, I do. You don't know how many times I wanted to come and give you what I got."

She kept darting her eyes about, landing them upon the sheathed sword and then the back of his belt. There, she saw a means of escape. It would mean leaving her sister.

But what choice did she have?

"After that," he continued. "I'm going to tie you up in my tent and go back for your little sister. What is she, ten? Eleven? Doesn't matter. After I'm done with her, she'll be all woman. What do you think about tha—"

The blade of the small dagger he had placed on his belt near the small of his back sank deep into his greasy hair.

She pulled it back out. Blood flowed over his face as his muscles contorted around his mouth. He moaned softly as his eyes rolled around in their sockets.

Plunging the blade into his back over and over and over again, she made sure he was dead and on the ground before unbuckling his belt and taking the sword for herself. As she left the tent, she looked over her shoulder, tempted to run back for her sister, or at least to take the head of her mother's murderer.

Twenty men gathered around the fire, laughing and watching the chained women and girls eating gruel from the large pot. If she were to take her sister, they would be upon her in moments. She would not survive.

One of them, sitting upon a log by the fire, looked over to her.

"Hey," he shouted, pulling his sword as he stood. Other eyes suddenly flashed in her direction. Several men were instantly on their feet and running towards her.

Instinctively, Emily turned and ran for the embankment. She didn't know how steep it was or for how far it fell, but what other option did she have?

Running as hard and fast as she could, she held the belt and sheathed sword tightly under her arm and the bloodied dagger in the other hand.

The barbarians drew closer and closer. Her weakened state worked to their advantage. She so desperately needed proper food and water.

It was too dark to know what was below her, but she leapt into the air over the embankment and dropped away from her pursuers. She fell for what seemed a long time before she crashed into a deep pocket of snow.

Then she tumbled and tumbled over and over.

Giddy from the spinning, she finally came to a stop some distance away from the top. She wasn't ready to get up and run, but her will to survive was too strong to stay where she was. The voices of the men above reverberated down the steep slope towards her as they debated who would go after her.

Carefully, she stood up and reached a hand out to steady herself. Her fingers found a tree trunk. She leant against it for a moment before wading through the snow into the shadows of the trees.

"Let her go," the leader shouted to the others. "It's dark, cold, and she is barely wearing enough to protect her from the elements. She'll be dead by dawn if she isn't already so from that fall. Get back to the fire. All of ya!"

It could have been a ruse to get her to drop her guard and relax. Instead, she pushed on and headed as far away from the camp as she could.

She placed the belt around her waist and tightened it beyond the notches punched into the leather. It was too big for her. Draping the belt over her left shoulder, buckling the belt on its widest setting, she could hang the sword against her right hip.

Pushing low branches aside and ducking beneath those too thick to manipulate, she eventually came to a small stream. She knelt on a soft patch of snow, placed her lips against the cold water, and drank.

When she had her fill, she peered around for shelter. There was no way she could continue to walk all night. Perhaps if she could find a hollow or space between the surface-roots of a tree and then place pine branches over her, she might have some protection from the weather.

She followed the river downstream, looking for pine trees to steal limbs from, but found none. Only the bare, twisted branches of dead trees presented themselves as she moved.

Rubbing her sleeves with her bare hands and feeling the damp soaking into her boots, she feared the barbarian leader's words were true. She wondered if she would last the night.

As the wind blew, gently calling with a howl across the night air, she pressed on. The cold penetrated her thick coverings and chilled her to the bone.

She desperately needed to get out of the wind.

Continuing for what seemed like hours, she trudged and pushed through the thick snow. Her boots took in more moisture and her skin felt numb.

Eventually, as she followed the stream, she came upon a shallow, but steep rocky embankment. Finding a crevasse of sorts, she tucked herself tightly into the cleft and shivered herself to sleep.

***

Slowly, her eyes opened, greeted by the morning. The sun had not lifted its head above the horizon yet, but the sky already donned a clear blue canvas that spread as far as her eye could see.

She had her knees tucked under her chin and her arms crossed over her chest. Moving slowly and painfully, her leg muscles extended out from the rocky cleft into which she'd folded herself. A sharp ache made its way along her thigh and into her spine.

Forcing herself onto her feet, she stretched her arms above her head as she stood on her tiptoes. A soft cracking emitted from beneath her armpits and elbows.

A thick mist had formed in the region near the stream that bubbled by gently. Lowering herself to her knees, she drank. She then looked around for a suitable place to perform other duties that her body required.

Sometime later, the young woman set off, continuing to follow the stream. She felt tempted to return to the camp. There, she planned to hide and keep watch from a safe distance. Her chief concern was for the welfare of her younger sister, Joanne.

Common sense won the internal struggle and urged her to continue away from danger. She hoped she would discover another community that could help her. Perhaps some soldiers might rescue the prisoners from those horrible men.

A small sense of pride came over her and a smile formed as she thought about the previous owner of the sword hanging on her side. She was glad she killed that filth. How many other girls had he victimised in such a way as he intended for her and Joanne? He deserved to die.

But now poor Joanne was exposed. There was no one to protect her. The monstrous leader of the barbarians had murdered their mother. Their father was missing when the invaders attacked their village, and there was no sign of him during their abduction. Now, she felt she had abandoned her little sister as she wandered the forest towards potential freedom.

Joanne was all alone in the clutches of the savages.

Her smile disappeared, replaced with a terrible ache in the pit of her stomach. She started to sob as she trudged on.

It got too much for her.

She leant against a tree and dropped to her knees.

Oh Joanne, she thought. *I'm so sorry.*

Tears streaked down her cheeks as she bawled uncontrollably. Part of her was angry with herself for leaving her sister. Another part of her suddenly felt the weight of what she had almost fallen prey to and was thankful to be alive and untouched.

She let herself go with her emotion as she knelt in the snow by the little stream.

The sun kissed her neck as it lifted slowly above the horizon. The warmth from the light felt like a loving embrace, telling her she would be all right, as if someone were watching out for her.

The sound of a horse snorting brought her back to reality.

She wiped the water from her eyes and peered around to find the source of the sound.

Standing on top of a nearby ridge in front of her, she saw five horsemen with two packhorses.

Fearing the worst, her heart pounded, and she lifted herself to her feet. She turned to flee back the way she had come from.

"Get her," she heard a man shout.

Three of the horsemen gave chase. She knew she had no chance of escape. They would catch her, take her back to the camp and make her face the leader of the thugs. He would either take her head, as he had her mother's, or let his men have their way with her.

She didn't want either option, so she pulled the sword from its sheath and stood her ground. Turning to face the pursuers, she gave a great cry and held the sword high.

The horsemen pulled to a halt and dismounted.

"Now hold on, girl," a tall, bald-headed man soothed. "We're not here to hurt you. You can trust us."

She swung the sword towards him. It sliced through the air harmlessly. Still, he kept his distance.

Another man, with long golden hair, reached for his sword. She instinctively turned the blade towards him.

"No," the first said to him. "Look at her. She's terrified. Keep your sword away."

They weren't attacking her. She didn't understand. She darted her eyes from one to the other, mistrustingly.

"It's all right, miss," said the third, a stocky man with a bushy black beard. "We have food and blankets. Please lower the sword."

"Y-you're going to rape me," she stammered, almost tearful. Her body was still cold and weak. Fear had settled in and she really thought she was going to be killed. "I won't let you."

The men looked absolutely surprised and appalled by her words, knowing she must have seen the worst in men to be in such a state.

"By the gods," said the stocky man with the black beard. "What did they do to you?"

She broke down and howled as tears welled in her eyes again. The sword was heavy and dangled from her hand as the blade touched the ground.

The bald man saw a chance and took it. He rushed in and took the sword from her, wrapping her into his arms as he did so. He handed the blade to the blond man.

"It's all right," he assured her. "We are not those men. We're here to help you."

The words rang true in her ears. Sudden relief swept over her like a strong wind.

With a long sigh, her sadness, torment and happiness flooded her body and wanted to be free all at once.

Held by the big man in his warm, welcoming arms, she cried and cried.

She felt safe.

For now.

Seven

With the tents erected and a fire set, the auburn-haired girl slept inside as the five men sat on logs around the hearth. A small pot of water sat steaming atop a tripod that sat neatly over the flames.

"This is going to slow us down," Oliver said as he reached towards the heat with his bare hands.

"It's unexpected," Tomas admitted. "But what other choice do we have? We came to rescue them, not leave them to the elements." He glanced over at the horses tethered to some trees close by. They were digging through the snow with their hooves and munching upon the growth beneath the surface.

"Should we take her back?" Oliver asked.

"That'll slow us down even more," Simon replied. "We go all the way back just to turn around again?"

"I meant just to her village."

"She wouldn't survive on her own," Tomas informed him. "There are no supplies and no shelter. How long would she last?"

"She stays with us," David told them as he stroked his plaited beard.

"And where does she sleep?" Ivo questioned. "We can't all fit in one tent just so she can have the other for herself. And what about bedding? Did anyone consider the bed sharing problem?"

"I'm not sharing my bed with any of you," Oliver was quick to say. "No bloody way."

"David seems to have taken a fancy to her," Simon quipped. "Perhaps he'd be willing to blanket down with her."

"No way," he replied, shaking his head. The men all turned to him with confused expressions. The girl was beautiful. How could such a remark insult a man such as David? It made little sense.

49

"What?" Simon asked.

"Ay, I admit she is a gorgeous lass," David said, "but I have a woman I've been seeing back home. Plan to marry her, too. There will be no lying with women on this journey or any journey hereafter."

"I was merely jesting, David," Simon informed the other. "No need to take offence."

"Wait…" Ivo furrowed his brow as the men returned their eyes to the flames. "Have you all gone dense? Did you not hear what he said? David is seeing someone? Who? When did this happen? How did you keep this to yourself without us knowing?"

The large man felt all eyes upon him again. The men around the fire would not let this one go.

"I don't tell you everything I do, Ivo Hamond," David replied. "Do I inform you when I take a shit?"

"No need," Oliver smiled. "The entire village knows when you take a shit."

The men erupted in laughter.

"Because you're loud and you stink," Ivo giggled.

The laughter eventually subsided, and their thoughts returned to the auburn-haired girl.

"Where will she bed down then?" asked Oliver.

"You three will take one tent," Tomas said to Ivo, Oliver, and Simon. "David and I will take the other tent with our guest."

The bald giant was about to protest, but the youngest of the troop spoke up.

"Makes sense," Ivo said. "She trusts you, David. It might make her feel safe if she sees that you're nearby."

"Then it's settled," Tomas stated. "On to other matters. I want two of you to continue tracking. Find the place where she got away from them and gather what you can from the site. Do not engage if they are still there. I want to know numbers, any insignia that tells us where they are from. Bring back supplies. Do what you can to help us get this task done. Any volunteers?"

"I'll go," David replied instantly.

"No," Tomas replied. "I want you here in case the girl wakes up. Ivo was right when he said she trusts you. It must be two of you three."

"I'll go," Ivo said.

"Me too," Oliver put in.

"Why don't the three of us go?" Simon asked. "I'm the better tracker."

"Who says?" Oliver challenged.

"I do," Tomas countered. "All three of you will go on ahead. I want you back before dusk."

***

The three riders tracked the progress of the barbarians' covered wagon by spotting broken limbs and scrapings over the bark lower on the trees of the forest. The thugs seemed not to be too concerned about being followed.

"They're fools," Ivo remarked. "A simpleton could follow their trail."

"They think their numbers will be enough to frighten others away," Simon replied.

"Too bad if an army was on their tail," said Ivo.

Oliver grunted, agreeing with Ivo.

"Too bad we're not an army," he added. "But, you're right. They're reckless."

Eventually, the tracks faded, covered in snow that had fallen over the previous day and night, leaving the men to focus solely upon what markings they could find on the trees. This proved time-consuming in places where the forest thinned out and the spaces between the vegetation spread open.

The three hunters would broaden their search and manoeuvre their steeds in wider circles until they found scratches on the surface of trees, or freshly snapped branches that once hung too low for the covered wagon to pass under.

The smell of smoke drew them onwards and eventually reliance upon the markings left by the cart was unnecessary. The scent of burnt wood grew stronger and stronger.

Carefully, they moved within view of a large clearing. It was empty apart from a smoking fire and a body lying near the hearth. They stayed hidden among the trees as they scanned the site carefully.

At one end, to their right, was a steep embankment that dropped away out of view. The thick forest encircled the clearing, obstructing any vision of threats that may be close by.

Oliver held his finger to his lips; *keep quiet.* He then gestured to his left. The others understood. They were going to circle the clearing to see what might lay in wait in the forest before they risked entering.

It took a long time. The riders were careful, quiet, and on edge. The slightest sound caused them to stop, listen, and look. Expecting the worst, they moved hands immediately to the hilt of their swords.

Nothing.

Continuing forward, keeping an eye and ear out for danger, the men came into view of the embankment on the opposite side of the clearing. The barbarians had surely moved on.

"Back here," Simon called as he drew his horse back towards the way they had come. "I noticed this as we were riding."

He pulled his horse to the side of a thick tree trunk. There were marks at his shoulder height.

"So, they left the clearing this way," Ivo said as he inspected the tree's trunk.

"Not just that," Simon said. He gestured into the woods. "Look."

The men followed his signal and saw tracks on the ground where the snow seemed a little thicker.

"We should follow," Ivo suggested.

"No," Simon replied. "We know which way they went. What we don't know is how long ago and how many of them there are. We'll check the clearing and find what we can here."

"Simon is right," Oliver stated as he looked at the clear sky above. "We've already passed noon. They could be miles away."

Ivo conceded, nodding his head.

The three riders turned their horses and entered the clearing. They directed their steeds to the fire, where they dismounted and tethered the animals to a log lying nearby.

Instinctively, driven by their curiosity, they approached the figure on the ground. It belonged to an older woman and had no head. Simon looked around for the missing body part.

"We should bury her," Ivo suggested.

"Of course," Oliver replied, staring at the corpse.

"I found the head," Simon announced as he pointed to the fire.

There, amongst the smouldering ashes, sat a charred skull, smiling back to them. Smoke trickled out through its empty eye sockets as the embers about it emitted a harsh reddish glow.

"Ghouls," Ivo hissed as he thought about what sort of people could do such a thing.

Oliver moved over to the hearth and removed the skull, placing it gently on the ground by the body. He then pulled his sword from its sheath and started digging into the ground with his blade.

The other men didn't hesitate. They followed Oliver's lead and joined him in preparing the grave.

After they buried the woman, the men returned their attention to the ground surrounding the fire and the expanse of the clearing. There were places of ground so frequently trampled by both man and horse that soggy earth had broken through the snow. Simon did a quick evaluation of the area, with the others observing him as he moved about.

"I think we're dealing with about twenty men here," he told the others. "Maybe ten prisoners. They killed the woman over there where we found her. But someone else was killed near the drop." He pointed to where the embankment disappeared from view. "I saw some blood on the ground there. I believe tents were set up near that spot and most of the horses were tethered over there as well."

"Do you think our auburn beauty might be responsible for the blood you found?" Ivo asked.

"Possibly," Simon answered. "She is carrying a sword and dagger she would have taken from one of them. I don't believe they would simply hand it over. She probably escaped over the ledge there. It's pretty steep but the snow would ease the fall."

"I wonder why they didn't go after her," Oliver questioned as he strode towards the embankment to look over the side.

"Too dark?" Ivo suggested. "Maybe they didn't notice she was gone."

"Maybe they thought she would die out here and left her to her own devices," Simon submitted. "Who knows?"

Oliver looked to the sky and noticed the sun creeping lower, making its way to the horizon in the west.

"We should return to camp," he said as he turned towards their steeds.

***

The return trip was quicker, as there was no need to search for trails left upon the trees or ground. Upon arriving, the three riders saw Tomas and David cooking something in a soup pot over the fire. There was no sign of the auburn-haired girl.

The smell of stewing meat filled the three men's nostrils with an inviting aroma. They dismounted their horses and removed the saddles as hastily as they could before tethering the beasts to the trees near the other steeds.

"What's for dinner?" Ivo called.

"Chicken and potato stew," David replied. "What did you find out there?"

"A campsite," Simon said as he sat by the fire, reaching his hands towards the heat. "They left some time ago. It wasn't pretty."

"Did you find her?"

The men all turned to see the young woman standing beneath the open flap of the tent in which she had been resting. Deep, dark lines under her eyes showed she needed more sleep. Her dirty, torn clothing reminded the men she had been through a traumatic time. The sight of her softened the men's hearts, prompting them to remember why they had come on this journey.

"If you're asking about a certain woman," Oliver said, as he dropped his saddle onto the ground by his golden steed, "then yes." He kept his gaze on her as he strode over to the fire and took his place upon a fallen log. "We buried her. Ivo here said some words. She was known to you?"

"She was my mother," the girl answered, a lump forming in her throat.

"Then I am sorry for your loss." Oliver turned his attention to the fire.

"It would appear that you got to one of them," Simon probed.

"Filthy scum," she replied as she crossed the snow-covered ground to sit by the fire, next to Tomas. "He raped some women, the youngest ones. I'm glad he's dead."

David poked at the fire and placed another piece of wood over the flames beneath the tripod that cradled the pot.

"What's your name?" Tomas asked.

"Emily," she answered, peering into the flames. "Emily Grenefeld."

The men quickly shot glances to one another. She didn't notice.

"What happened, Emily?" Tomas delved.

Lifting her eyes, she looked around the circle at each of them. Her vulnerability and fear were still apparent. Here she was, surrounded by more men. So far, they had treated her well, but she still had her doubts.

"They came at night while we were sleeping," she began. "They dragged us through the cold and threw us into a wagon." Tears welled in her eyes as she spoke.

"They killed all the men and the boys and the babies." She cried, but pushed through the emotion and continued her tale.

"They gave us blankets and then threw the goats and pigs on top of us. I don't know what happened to my father. He wasn't there when they took us from our hut. I assume he is dead too." She wept bitterly. "One of them killed my mother by cutting off her head, and now they have my sister. I fear for her after what I saw them do to other girls her age."

"We need to kill these brutes," Simon affirmed.

"Agreed," David grunted.

"Your father is Antony Grenefeld?" Tomas asked her.

"Yes!" Her eyes lit up. She wiped the tears away and stared at Tomas expectantly. "How do you know?"

"Antony is fine," Tomas informed the girl. "He found his way to our village and is staying in my house. He was the only one to make it out. If you wish to be reunited with him, I can send you back with one of these men."

The four men looked at each other before staring at Tomas with questioning looks. None of them wanted to return home; not now when they were closing in on their quarry.

Tomas saw their expressions. "You promised to obey my commands out here, did you not?"

The men reluctantly nodded or grunted their replies in the affirmative.

"Good," he continued. "Then the lady decides."

"I'm not leaving," she insisted, to the men's relief. "They have my sister. If you're going after them, then I'm coming with you."

"It's settled then," Tomas announced as he rose to his feet, pulling a rag from his pocket and a wooden spoon from a plate by the fire. Using the rag, he lifted the lid from the pot and stirred the contents.

"So," Emily ventured. "What are the sleeping arrangements?"

Eight

Early in the morning, as light filled the sky, the men packed the steeds and prepared to continue on their way. Emily felt out of place as she watched the men work together. She wanted something to do, but the crew was sufficiently able without her.

She sat by the fire and poked a stick into the embers, breathing life into flames. Taking the lid from the pot sitting above the hearth, Emily placed a handful of clean snow inside and stirred the contents. There was still a small amount of chicken stew lying at the bottom.

"Good idea," David called over to her as he tied a tent roll onto one horse. "We'll need a hearty breakfast before we move on."

She smiled, feeling a little more useful.

"How far will we travel today, Tomas?" Ivo asked as he tightened his saddle strap to his black charger.

"I intend to find these brutes today," Tomas announced. "I want eyes on them. I want to know how many they number and how many prisoners they have taken."

"Will you rescue my people?" Emily asked.

"I can't say for the moment," Tomas replied. "We simply do not know enough about these men to act. What we do know is they outnumbered us."

Simon nodded as he held a handful of oats up to his chestnut steed. "Sounds like a night assault to me."

"Aye." Oliver smiled. "A real hunt."

"More like a slaughter," David replied, stone faced. "That is if we do it right."

"Let's not get ahead of ourselves," Tomas interjected. "We need to see what we're up against first."

They gathered around the fire and emptied the stew from the pot into wooden bowls they carried in their saddlebags. Tomas offered his to Emily and ate directly from the pot.

Using handfuls of snow, they cleaned cutlery and plates as best they could, then packed them away and loaded them onto the horses. The men mounted their steeds and Emily the bay mare, riding double with Tomas. She draped a thick blanket around her shoulders before wrapping her arms around his waist.

Tomas tethered the lead rope from one packhorse to the iron loop on his saddle. He then turned his attention to David upon his draught horse, which held the rope to the other packhorse. The bald giant had pulled his hood over his head.

"Are your ears getting cold?" Oliver asked.

"I don't think there's a part of me that isn't cold," he replied.

"Then, why shave your head at the height of winter?" the blond man questioned.

"Because it makes me look so pretty," David smiled.

The leader of the troop glanced around to the other men. They all appeared ready to move.

"We're not racing off, gentlemen," he began. "But we will move at a steady but quick pace to try to catch up to these swine. If you find you are drifting back and can't keep up, give us a whistle. David and I will lead."

They started forward, entering the thick forest of leafless trees once again. Snow crunched under the heavy hoof falls as the horses trudged through the thick ground cover.

"So," Ivo said, "what do you think we'll be eating tonight for dinner?"

"By the gods, boy," Simon chuckled. "We just had breakfast."

"I know," the younger man replied. "It's just that we have only one chicken and some oats and flour."

"Don't forget the potatoes," Oliver quipped. "You can't forget those."

"If we catch up to our quarry," Tomas put in, "there will be no cooking tonight. We can't risk the aroma of food or the smell of smoke reaching our target. We need the element of surprise and subterfuge. I'm sorry, lads."

Ivo's countenance dropped.

Simon drew his steed closer to the young lad. "It's one day," he said. "You can survive. Besides, the amount that you consumed from that chicken stew should last you a week. Drink plenty of water."

The horses set into a steady jogging pace, kicking snow high in all directions as they continued to follow the trail left behind by the covered wagon. Simon occasionally called out which direction to turn the horses, remembering the trail to the clearing from the previous day.

It wasn't too long before they were in the clearing where the marauders had camped. Tomas pulled the horses up to the charred circle where the fire once burned before scanning the site with his eyes. He could see the fresh patch of earth where the three men had buried Emily's mother the day before.

Before he knew it, she slid off the mare and ran to the grave. The men felt empathy for the girl as she dropped to her knees and sobbed, placing a hand on the tilled ground.

Tomas lowered himself to the ground and approached the grieving woman. He crouched beside her and instinctively wrapped his arms around her shoulders. She leant into him and bawled uncontrollably.

"Her name was Alice," she managed.

Tomas had no words to comfort her, so he held her tighter against his chest. He vaguely remembered his own mother. It had been so long ago since he had last seen his parents. Like Emily's, his mother had been the innocent victim of an overpowering force.

Tomas didn't recall a time where he had ever mourned for his mother. He remembered only ever harbouring anger and hatred towards the Night Demons and the gods for taking her from him. But now, as he held Emily in his arms, he felt the need to cry.

He allowed the tears to fall upon his cheeks as she burrowed her face deeper into his chest, continuing to weep.

***

The trail left by the barbarians led deeper into the forest. The ground seemed to be gradually descending more and more as they progressed through the gnarled woods.

There were moments where the trees thinned, unveiling the panorama of a wide blue ocean to the east. The forest still obscured the seaside from view, but they knew the journey to the edge of the water would still be a day or two away.

Winding tracks, still prevalent in the snow, continued down the mountainside.

Emily held tightly to Tomas' waist as he and David navigated their chargers and the packhorses beside a steep embankment. The tracks they followed, hemmed on one side by thick shrubbery, drew dangerously close to the edge.

"Surely they could have chosen a far better place to travel," Ivo called as he peered over the side.

"As far as we know," Oliver replied, "this may be the best place to take a wagon."

The land ultimately widened, presenting a gentler slope to descend upon. The trees changed from gnarled, leafless pillars to the familiar tall pine trees similar to the ones near Woodmyst.

Snow still blanketed everything in sight, but the covering became thinner and thinner as they proceeded down the mountain. The sparser forest exposed open ground except for a thick cluster of trees here and there.

The riders felt a sense of relief as they pressed on. The lifeless trees upon the mountaintop enclosed them so tightly that they felt shut in. Down here, where the hills rolled a lot more softly and parts of the ground flattened out, the sky opened up and the horizon held a better view.

The trails left by the barbarians spread apart upon the open areas. The five riders similarly widened their cluster and breathed a little easier. A grove of pine trees drew them back together until they ventured through to the other side, where they would spread out again upon the fields of snow.

Pausing momentarily, the riders found an area that gave an unobstructed view of a large seaside village in the distance. There was a port to the north of the settlement where several ships lay moored. One vessel, dark and large, was sailing away from the harbour as the troop watched.

Smoke streamed from chimneys of the tiny buildings that lined the streets, causing a haze above the village. It looked inviting, but it would still be a few hours before they could reach the township.

"We won't catch up to them today," David stated.

The shadow of the mountain range was creeping towards them as the sun sank below its jagged peaks.

"Agreed," Tomas replied. "My guess is that they would have made it to the village by now. We'll set up camp near those trees."

The group looked to where Tomas was pointing. A small thicket of pine trees clustered together a little farther down the embankment, forming a hollow that could provide protection from the wind that might sweep down from the mountains.

"Can we set a fire and cook some food?" Ivo asked.

"Thinking with your stomach again," Simon laughed.

"I believe we can," Tomas answered. "We'll cook another chicken and use some of the flour and make some loaves for tomorrow's journey."

"Sounds good," Emily whispered in his ear. Her soft voice and the warmth of her breath sent a feeling like fire throughout his being. He had never felt such a sensation before and was uncertain what it was. She rested her chin upon his shoulder, "I'm famished."

He nodded, dumbstruck for a moment, before he turned his mare towards the trees.

***

The fire was lit, and the bird was plucked and positioned over the heat of the flames. After some time, they placed a few potatoes directly into the hot embers. Oliver placed a small pot of snow on the coals where it gradually melted and heated, sending a plume of steam into the air.

"Tea?" he called. They all replied in the affirmative. Oliver busied himself with preparing the beverage as the others started mixing flour and snow with their hands until they had formed thick dough. After breaking the mixture into fist-sized portions, they placed the dough into the hot embers and left it to bake.

"Why do you always drink tea?" Emily asked as she rolled a ball of dough in her hands.

"We drink water too," Ivo replied.

"I mean," she said, "that usually most men would drink mead."

"Or cider." David chuckled. The others grunted tiny laughs.

Emily felt she was not part of the joke.

Tomas saw the lost expression on her face and explained. "Wood-myst came under siege many years ago," he explained. "Mead and cider were about the only drinkable liquid consumed by the men in our village. Tea was a woman's drink. Water was a mere necessity.

"We lost our plantations in the attacks and, as a result, we lost the produce that was used to make the cider and mead. Our carer, Richard, decided not to ever allow mead back into the village again. He was, and still is, under the impression that the warm fermented cider and barrels of mead hindered our defences."

"The drink caused you to lose?" she asked.

"No," Tomas replied. "Our people would have lost, anyway. There were too many of them for our fathers to stop. It's more the idea that we got soft. There were no proper warriors left in the village. Wood-myst had become a place of farmers and peddlers, mostly."

"If our fathers had been focused," Simon interjected, "and not drinkers of fermented liquids, perhaps the fight would have lasted longer. That's my opinion of the matter."

"In other words," Tomas continued, "we trained with weapons from a young age and know our strengths and weaknesses. We also know how to farm and build, but we are ready to fight and defend what we care for. One thing that we have never done, and have sworn never to do, is taste any intoxicating drink which may hinder our senses. This is why we drink tea."

"Either that," David chuckled, "or the barrels of mead are just too heavy for Richard to load upon the wagons by himself and transport all the way from Oldcastle. So he made up the rule, *no mead in Woodmyst*. After all, tea is packed more densely and is much lighter to carry."

"You idiot," Oliver snorted as he threw a handful of snow across the fire, hitting the other on the shoulder.

"What?" The bald giant laughed.

Nine

Before the sun was up, David rose from his bedding and checked the horses by giving each of them a loving rub on the nose. They greeted him with gentle nickers as he whispered to each of them.

He then returned to the fire and rekindled the fire by poking a stick into the embers. The flames reignited before he placed the pot, stuffed with fresh snow, onto the tripod over the heat. After putting another piece of firewood in place, he sat down to stir the coals again.

"You're up early," Oliver whispered as he emerged from his tent.

"I didn't sleep too well," the giant admitted.

"Scary dreams?" the other asked as he scratched the scalp beneath his golden mane.

"I'm thinking there are too many of us in that tent," David said.

Oliver took a seat beside him and peered into the dancing flames.

"Tomas making his moves?"

"On the contrary," David replied, "he has been an absolute gentleman. In fact, I don't think he perceives her intentions."

"Perhaps he thinks it's too soon," suggested Oliver. "After all, she just lost her mother and her sister is still out there with those brutes."

"Perhaps." The bald man scratched at his plaited beard. "Or perhaps he's been on his own for so long that he forgot what it's like to have affection thrown his way."

Oliver shrugged.

"What are you two talking about?" asked Simon as he strode over to the fire.

"Good morning to you too, sir," David quipped.

"Good morning," he replied as he sat beside Oliver. "You appeared to be in a deep discussion."

"David didn't sleep well," Oliver replied. "The love birds in there kept him awake."

"What?" Simon turned his eyes upon the tent that still housed Emily and Tomas.

"No," David snapped. "It's not like that. It's just that… Well, you know… There's a sense of something brewing between the two."

"Only," Oliver interrupted, "he thinks Tomas does not know that the girl has fallen for him."

"By the gods." Simon turned his eyes back to the fire. "Glad you're in there with them and not me. Must be tense."

"You have no idea." David sighed.

"No idea about what?" Ivo asked as he stepped through the tent's opening.

"Tomas and the girl are forming a bond." Simon giggled.

"Shhh!" David stood up and pointed to his tent, not more than a few feet away. "They're just in there. Don't let them hear you."

"You could see that coming a mile away," Ivo replied as he sat down by Simon. "Is the tea ready yet?"

"David doesn't think Tomas has noticed the girl's intentions," Simon stated. "And, no, the pot hasn't heated yet."

"Maybe someone needs to talk with him," Ivo suggested. "Not me though."

"Talk to who?" Tomas asked as he appeared from the tent.

A sudden silence fell upon the campsite as the men shot quick glances from one another and into the flames.

***

They set off directly after breakfast. Snow had fallen during the night, lightly covering the tracks left by the barbarians. Soft depressions on the ground were all that remained of the trail.

They often lost sight of the tracks or confused them with other lines and lumps made in the ground cover, forcing the troop to backtrack and try another lead. The wagon appeared to have taken wide detours around any clustering vegetation, preventing the familiar markings left upon tree trunks as they passed by.

All the men had to go on, as far as tracking their quarry, were the grooves in the snow.

"They're heading for the port," Oliver informed the others.

"We don't know that," David replied. "As far as we know, they could be in that village."

Oliver shook his head as they continued to ride on. The trail was heading to the east, but gradually creeping northward. If the trail kept moving in the direction it was turning, they would ride past the village and to an area where ships moored and large warehouses stood.

"We're heading that way," Oliver pointed. "The village is over there."

"The trail could turn back," Simon called. "But I have my doubts too."

"What does it matter?" asked the bald giant. "They go this way, they go that way. We go after them."

Oliver looked around to each of the riders. One of them must have been thinking the same thing as he was.

"They are heading for one of the ships," Oliver said.

"To go where?" Emily called. Her voice baring a tone of fear beneath the question. Tomas lowered his hand to his waist and gently touched her arm.

"Don't worry," he assured her. "Ship or wagon, we'll get her back."

A quick journey through a small forest gave them an opportunity to find clear markings left by the horse-drawn cart. The proximity of the surrounding trees had protected the ground from the previous night's weather. Hoofprints and wagon tracks wound tightly between the trunks of the tall pines, leading the troop through to an open plain that looked upon the seaside.

Directly before them was a harbour with tall ships and broad wharves. Large timber warehouses lined the shore where a boardwalk, extending from the structures met the jetties where the moored ships rested.

Many carts and horses crossed the ground before them, moving products from the warehouses to the village and beyond. The trail left by the barbarians was lost.

The seaside village lay to the south, a short way from the port. It was a large community, much bigger than they believed when they had spotted it from the high ground.

It was full of bustling people who moved quickly, whether on horseback or on their own feet. Tomas understood these were the kinds of people looking for the best deal. Peddlers, merchants and scum were the usual variety in places like this.

Honesty would be scarce here, particularly from a businessperson or a scribe. He directed his horse towards the warehouses. If he were to get answers or help, it would be more likely to come from a man unafraid of little dirt and sweat.

The riders approached the warehouse positioned nearest to the village. Tomas noticed that most of the action took place away from the wharves. Men were loading carts, directing them away from the warehouses before signalling another waiting in line to approach.

An old man sitting on the edge of the closest jetty, smoking a pipe as he fished with a rod, eyed the troop as they approached. David saw the man watching them as they drew nearer.

"There." The giant pointed with his chin. "That one has been watching us for a while."

Tomas found a quiet place by the wharf to pull the horses to a stop. He helped Emily to the ground before dismounting. Handing the reins to Ivo, he instructed the men to wait for him and keep watch.

Both Emily and Tomas walked towards the old man. He was the only person they could see that wasn't engaged in some rigorous activity. They hoped he wouldn't mind being disturbed, so they advanced cautiously and with a smile.

"Good morning," Tomas called politely as his boots met the wooden surface of the jetty. Emily tucked her hands under his arm and pressed herself against his side, giving the impression that they were indeed a couple.

"Morning, young ones," the old man replied, pulling the pipe from his mouth. "How can I be of assistance?"

"We're seeking information about some travellers," Tomas replied.

"Horsemen?" the elderly angler probed. "Wagoners?"

"There were horsemen and a wagon," Tomas answered.

"There are plenty of those, as you can see," he informed the young couple. His line gave a sudden jerk. "Ooh!"

The old man yanked the rod sharply before lifting the line out of the water. On the end, hanging by its teeth, was a large silver fish twisting and flipping in the air as the fisher lifted it to the wharf's surface.

The man opened a large basket sitting on the jetty next to him. He rose to his feet and lowered the fish onto the wooden boardwalk.

"They were a large group, correct?" he asked as he bent to one knee.

"At least twenty men," Tomas responded.

The old man tugged at the line near the fish's mouth with his bony fingers. The hook came free, and he put the fish into the basket.

"The first for the day," the angler stated, gripping the pipe between his teeth, allowing a puff of smoke to escape his lips. He closed the basket, where the new occupant continued to flop and flip inside, and reached into a pouch on his belt where he retrieved a large, wriggly worm. He pierced the worm through its end by the hook and slid it upon the tiny metal object like a sock over a foot.

"The wagon was full of people?" the old man asked as he lowered the line back into the water.

"Yes," Emily replied, her hands gripping Tomas' arm tighter.

"There was more than one wagon?" He sat back down on the wharf's edge.

"No," she said. "Only one."

"You misunderstood, my dear," he said, pulling the pipe from his mouth and puffing out more smoke. "I was telling you that there was more than one wagon. There was also more than one group of men. You say twenty. I say, more like fifty."

"Fifty?" Tomas clarified.

"That's right." He placed the pipe back into his mouth. "Some made a couple of trips, too. They unloaded farther along the port into a large black ship that sailed out yesterday."

Emily's countenance dropped. "Sailed out?"

Tomas instinctively looked at the ocean. "Do you know where to?"

"Nope," the old man replied. "But it can't be too far."

"What makes you say that?"

"They only unloaded whatever they had in the wagons, and that's all," the angler answered. "The sea is wide between here and Ananduil, the lands to the east. They would need plenty of food and water for a journey like that. There were no supplies taken from any of the warehouses here."

"How can you be sure of that?" Emily asked. "This is a busy place."

"I own the warehouses," he replied. "My accountants inform me of what goes out and what comes in. That ship left nothing and took nothing."

"Then you must know where it was going?" she pressed.

"I own the warehouses," he replied, "not the docks."

"Who do we speak to about the traffic on the docks and the possibility of contracting a ship?" asked Tomas.

"It doesn't work that way." The old man puffed smoke into the air. "The docks are open to anyone. First in, first served. There is no keeper. Your ship, the one you seek, showed up just before the other ships came into port for the winter. No captains would be willing to take you anywhere until the worst of this season is over. I can assure you of that."

Tomas looked around at the busy workers in the warehouses. "If no ships are moving," he began, "why so much activity?"

"Do you see them loading or unloading the ships?"

"No," he replied.

"Everything is being transported by land up and down the coast," the old man informed them. "From what I hear, the ports up north are all but frozen in. I don't know how far your ship intends to travel that way, but it can go only so far before it hits ice."

Emily sobbed.

"They're gone," she whispered.

Tomas wrapped his arms around her tightly.

The old man observed the exchange between the two with deep consideration.

"Took something from you, did they?"

Emily nodded. "My sister."

The old man peered over to the band of men that had arrived with the young couple standing near him.

"You don't have enough to go with you," the warehouse owner advised. "You'll need more men."

Tomas glanced at his friends and then back to the old man. He was right. Going up against twenty men was going to be a task. Fifty or more might be impossible.

"People talk in villages like this one," the warehouse owner stated. "Many visitors from far and wide always share tales. Might I advise you to visit the tavern and share your tale? Do you have money?"

"We have some food," Tomas replied. "Nothing of real value. We'll continue on our way."

"No, you won't." The old man stood up and dug into his pocket, where he retrieved a handful of gold coins. "Take this."

"We couldn't," Tomas objected. "We don't know you and have done nothing to earn it."

"Sometimes," the warehouse owner said, "you need to accept a gift from strangers. Your horses need a place to shelter and the six of you could benefit from a comfortable bed for at least one night. Someone in that tavern may know where that ship has gone and you need all the help you can get."

"What is your name?" Tomas asked as he took the coins.

"Reynard." He smiled. "Reynard Merys."

Tomas shook the man's hand gratefully. "Thank you, Reynard."

Emily wrapped her arms around the warehouse owner's neck and kissed him upon the cheek. He blushed beetroot red as a great smile spread across his face.

"You make sure to mention my name to the innkeeper at the tavern," he said. "Tell him your story. His name is James Halle. He may be able to give you some advice as well. Good luck."

Ten

The tavern was warm and cosy.

A large inviting fire blazed in the corner, sending heat to every corner of the room. Tables and chairs stood neatly placed about the area, offering many pockets for small groups of four or five to gather.

The floor and beams were dark hardwood and dull white panels, stained by tobacco smoke, lined the walls. Windows, bordered by dark timber frames, opened from the front wall. Light from the outside world streamed into the room, enticing the troop to venture further in.

"Quickly," called a burly man from behind a large bench positioned near the far wall. "Close the door. You're letting the heat out."

"Sorry," said Ivo, as he followed the others into the establishment.

The bench sat parallel to the back wall, across the floor from the windows, and stretched almost from one end of the room to the other. It was adorned with wooden panels that obstructed their view of the large man's legs.

Behind him, upon the wall, were shelves containing mugs, glasses and bottles of varying and strange shapes. Some carried labels in languages, both familiar and bizarre. Halfway along the wall behind the bench, framed by shelving, was a door leading to another room. A sweet aroma emanated from the unseen area, drawing the group closer to the bench.

"Tavern's closed until the late afternoon," the man informed the newcomers.

"I apologise," Tomas replied. "Reynard Merys sent us. You wouldn't be James Halle at all, would you?"

"I am he." He nodded politely. "What would Reynard be sending you here for, then?"

"A room or two, we hope," Tomas answered. "A place to keep our horses and belongings. Just for the night."

"I suppose you'll want some food also?"

"Please." Emily smiled.

James Halle smiled back. "I'll have your horses fed and watered, fresh sheets on your beds, food and drink in your bellies all day for two gold pieces."

Tomas reached into his pouch and produced the required payment. The innkeeper took it and placed the coins into his pocket.

"Sleeping arrangements," Halle began. "Our rooms accommodate two people. Given that you two are together, I can give you a room with a double bed."

Tomas looked to Emily and felt his face growing hot.

"We're not together," he informed the man. He then turned to see the other men behind him stifling giggles and looking away. "We can pay extra for another room for you," Tomas suggested to the girl.

"I'm not staying by myself." Her eyes widened anxiously.

"Oh." Tomas scratched his cheek, thinking of a suitable solution.

"Might I suggest," the innkeeper interjected, "that you take another room with two beds instead?"

Tomas nodded. "Yes, please."

"It'll mean two of you lads will need to share a bed," Halle informed the others.

Oliver glanced over to David and batted his eyes suggestively.

The larger man shook his head and growled, "Fuck off."

"Behind you then." Halle pointed to a door midway on a wall next to the bench. "Go through there and turn left. I'll meet you in the corridor." With that, James Halle disappeared through the door behind the bench.

The troop entered the corridor and followed the directions given to them by the innkeeper. Seven doorways lined the passageway. There were four on the right, three on the left, and one at the very far end of the walkway.

Halle appeared through an open access immediately on their left.

"This is the kitchen," he announced. "Staff only. The three rooms on the left are for my family. Washroom is at the end. Your three rooms will be these."

He opened the door across the passage from the kitchen. Inside was a small room with two beds, one to the right and the other to the left, and a window with lace curtains overlooking a yard to the side of the tavern.

"This room, that one and the one next to it," Halle said, and pointed. "The doors latch from the inside for added security while you sleep. We've had no trouble, but some travellers get a little itchy when staying in a strange place. Can't say I blame them."

He entered the room and gestured the troop to follow. They crowded as best as they could near the door as the innkeeper continued explaining their accommodation to them. He pulled the curtains away from the window to expose the yard beyond. There was a large stable across the way with its doors open. A young man was inside, moving bundles of straw with a pitchfork.

"Your horses and supplies will be safe in our stable," Halle informed them. "My son is out there now, as you can see. He'll take care of your animals."

The innkeeper shuffled towards the door, forcing the troop to make a gap for him to pass through. "The missus will put fresh sheets and blankets on the beds for you. In the meantime, put your stuff in here. It'll be perfectly safe. Only family and paying guests are allowed in this section of the tavern.

"I'll quickly go and tell my son to prepare the stalls. After you've got your horses settled, I'll have some toast and stew ready for you, if that's to your liking?"

"Thank you." Tomas shook the man's hand. The other men of the group followed suit.

The innkeeper disappeared back into the kitchen, leaving them to themselves.

"Right," Tomas announced. "I'll sleep here."

"Ivo and I will take the next room," David stated.

"What?" Ivo quizzed. "Why me?"

"Those two snore," David said, pointing to both Oliver and Simon.

"I haven't heard them." The younger man raised his brow.

"That's because you sleep like a dead man," Oliver replied. "And I don't snore."

"Yes, you do," Simon replied. "You've been keeping the entire Forest of Khun awake with your night beast noises for the entire journey."

"I'm in here with you," Emily stated before any of the snorers could get in before her.

"We thought that would have been the case." Oliver smiled as he edged towards the door. "Besides, you two lovebirds need some time alone."

"What?" Tomas snapped, looking at the door. The man had disappeared. The others chuckled as they withdrew from the room to place their belongings in their overnight dwellings.

The two remaining travellers stood awkwardly in the small chamber. Emily gestured to the bed near Tomas and then to the one near her.

"Which one do you prefer?" she asked.

"You choose," he replied sheepishly. "Pick the more comfortable one. I can sleep on a rock if I have to." He started for the door.

"Where are you going?"

"You'll be fine," he assured her. "I'm just going to tend to the horses. I'll be right back. I promise."

***

With the horses cared for, they sat down at a table to devour a hearty breakfast of stew and toast. James Halle, the innkeeper, had offered them mead or warm cider to wash the feast down, but they declined in favour of tea and water. Complying to their wishes, finding it odd that men would turn down a good drink, the innkeeper served the warm beverage, also placing a jug of water with six glasses on the table.

"You're an unusual crew," he said as he pulled a chair from another table over and plonked himself at the end of their party. "Where are you from? What are you doing here?"

"Mmph," Tomas grunted before lifting a glass of water to his lips. After a quick mouthful, he replied, "we're from Woodmyst."

"Woodmyst?" Halle quizzed, furrowing his brow. "You couldn't be. That place is written in legend. They say dragons destroyed it."

"It was," Simon answered. "Two dragons and a bunch of... Well, we don't know what they were. Warriors of some sort. But we survived."

"How?" The innkeeper carefully peered to each one of them. "You would have been children."

"They spared us," Tomas stated. "And we've been rebuilding ever since."

"Amazing." Halle shook his head. "It's a shame you don't drink. I guarantee, the men that come in tonight will want to buy you barrels of mead once they hear you survived Woodmyst.

"I'm not kidding," he continued. "Travellers come from all the way along the coast as far as Dweagan, and they still talk about the end of Woodmyst. But why are you here?"

"Where is here?" Simon asked, his mouth filled with toast.

"Here?" Halle's eyes widened. "Ah, Oakbeach. This place is called Oakbeach. I have no idea why. I've never seen an oak tree anywhere in this area. Only pines grow around here. But I'm rambling. My apologies. You were saying?"

"Her village was attacked." Ivo pointed to Emily with his spoon as he continued to focus on the plate of food before him.

"What?"

"They took the women and killed everyone else," she told the innkeeper. "My father got away and made it safely to these men."

"And you?"

"I escaped from their camp one night," she replied. "These men found me the next morning."

"And now we're tracking the bastards," David finished.

"You followed their trail here?" James Halle asked.

"That's right," said Tomas. "Reynard Merys told us they sailed out already. He says they headed north."

"You plan to go after them?"

"They have women and girls in their possession," Simon put in.

"They have my sister." Emily sobbed. Tomas gently put his arm around her.

Slowly moving his eyes across the table to each of the men, finally landing his eyes upon the young auburn-haired girl, James Halle contemplated the story he had just been told.

"You're going to need more men," he finally said. "And more equipment. At least one wagon and some horses. I may be able to help with some of that."

***

The tavern filled quickly as the dockworkers made their way towards the village, stopping on their way home for a refreshing drink or two. The men were loud and crude in speech. Their laughter was rough and their size threatening.

Tomas considered taking Emily back to the room, away from the men. That was until one of the large men in raucous conversation bumped the table the troop were sitting at, almost spilling their water jug. The man immediately turned and apologised, "Sorry sirs and lady."

"Quite all right." Tomas smiled. The man returned to his conversation as his companions gave a remorseful wave to the troop seated nearby. Mead was spilled and pipes were smoked as the night wore on. The revellers were in no hurry to return to their homes after a long day's work.

An older lady, quite round in the middle and wearing a cheerful expression, made her way across the room towards the table. The men gathered about the tavern respectfully moved out of her way as she drew nearer.

"Finished your meal, dearies," she said, and grinned.

"Thank you, Anya," Tomas replied, having met her earlier. "It was delicious."

"Well, I'm glad you enjoyed it." She gathered the empty plates on the table into a neat stack and placed the cutlery on top. "I've put some extra blankets in your rooms, just in case it gets colder tonight."

With that, she lifted the plates and started back across the room. James, the innkeeper, stood behind the bench with his son, tapping a spoon against an empty glass to get everyone's attention. The loud conversations and laughter continued, oblivious to the man's attempts.

"Quiet everybody," he called. The noise seemed to get louder. "Please, everyone."

"SHUT IT!" a screeching voice bellowed from the middle of the room. A heavy silence filled the tavern as all eyes fell upon Anya, holding the stack of plates and smiling joyously. "My husband would like to say a few words."

"Thank you, my love." Halle peered around the room. "Gentlemen, I need your help. We have strangers in the tavern with us tonight. Survivors of Woodmyst."

Sudden gasps filled the room as a few eyes moved on to the troop at the table.

"They need help," the innkeeper continued. "The young lassie with them is from a village that was attacked and the women taken. The ship carrying the women left one of our docks yesterday. I'm asking if any of you would help this lady and these men to find the bastards on that vessel and help bring the women home."

"Where are they heading, James?" asked a man across the room, out of Tomas' view.

"They went north," called another man close by. He was older than most of the others, but built robustly. "I saw the ship you're talking about. It seemed a bit queer that a large ship like that would head towards icy waters while the rest of us have moored here or farther south for the winter. Now I know why.

"They had a full crew," he continued. "At least fifty men. More than the five... Sorry, my lady... six of you can handle by yourselves. I'll accompany you. I'm only working on the wharves until the weather clears. Then my ship, the *Adelandria*, and I will head south. I can't speak for my crew, but you have me at your service. Besides, another night on that moored ship and I'll go mad. Captain Dakmel Tarkin."

He gave a polite bow and extended his hand. Tomas stood and shook it gladly.

"A pleasure, sir."

"Somebody needs to watch your back, Captain," shouted another voice. "I'm coming too, if only to make sure my place on that ship is safe."

"Aye," shouted another, then another. Soon, more than half the room was volunteering to join the troop.

"Looks like you have my crew also," the Captain smiled. "Counting you, this gives us around twenty men. Mine's a small ship."

Tomas glanced over to his friends at the table. They all smiled back with glee.

With luck, the crew's confident offer wasn't simply the mead talking and would still be valid in the morning when it was time to leave.

***

Later that night, Tomas stared at the wall, lying upon his side as Emily undressed for bed. With his blankets pulled over his shoulder and his knees tucked up, he formed himself almost into a ball. He had pulled three of the thick coverings over himself, as the only clothing he wore was his drawers.

The candle sitting on the bedside table beneath the window caused his shadow to dance before him. It was almost hypnotic, watching the light flicker and the soft sounds of the auburn-haired girl undressing behind him.

He tried so desperately not to think about her as he closed his eyes. He could still feel the smooth skin on her hands that held him for most of their journey around his waist. The gentle sound of her voice as she whispered in his ear, riding together through the snow, still sounded in his mind. When she smiled, soft lines near the corners of her lips would form.

Everything about her was intoxicating.

He flicked his eyes open to stare at the wall again. She was in his head, no matter what he did.

The light suddenly extinguished, and the momentary sound of Emily climbing into bed filled his ears. Within moments, it was quiet again.

"You can turn now," she whispered.

"I'm all right," he lied. With his mind filled with thoughts about her, he found his body had tensed up. He stretched his legs out slowly.

"Can you hear that?" she asked.

Tomas suddenly tensed again, thinking the worst.

"What is it?"

"I think I can hear someone snoring," she replied.

Tomas focused his hearing and, sure enough, he could hear two men snoring further down the corridor. *At least someone is getting rest.*

"So cold," she said after a while.

"You've just gotten used to sleeping in proximity to others," Tomas explained. "These bedrooms are a little bigger than most people get to experience. Quite luxurious."

He heard her shuffling about under her covers, followed by soft pitter-pattering on the floor. His blankets partially lifted from him as she slid into the bed and snuggled against his bare back, replacing the covers over them both.

Now, he really felt tense.

"That's better," she stated. "Don't you think?"

"Mmm," he agreed nervously.

"Good night." She closed her eyes as her hand moved around to his chest.

"Night," he replied as he stared at the wall with no hope of getting her out of his head now.

Eleven

Rising early, Tomas slipped out of bed without waking Emily. He dressed quickly in the dark and left the room, softly closing the door behind him.

Flickering light emitted from the kitchen door, where a lantern hung from a ceiling hook in the middle of the room. Tomas popped his head in through the door to see both James and Anya Halle preparing breakfast for the troop. Bacon sizzled on a hot plate over the stove as Anya mixed eggs and James sliced some bread.

"Good morning," Tomas said politely.

"Good morning," they chorused.

"First up?" the innkeeper asked.

"I thought so, until I saw you two hard at it."

"Well," James said as he slid the knife back and forth through the crusty loaf, "you're the first of your crew."

"Is anyone using the washroom?" Tomas asked.

"Willem is tending to your horses," Anya replied. "It's all yours."

"Thank you." He turned towards the door at the far end of the corridor.

"By the time you get back," Anya said, "I'll have a pot of tea on the table for you. Your breakfast should be ready shortly after."

"Thank you again." He smiled before returning his attention to the washroom.

Inside the small room, a bucket of water sat on the floor. On a table nearby was a large bowl and some folded towels. Next to the table was a short wooden box that stood almost as high as Tomas' knees. It had a closed hatch door with metal hinges to its rear. The door was square and roughly the size of a seat. Beside the box was a pile of parchment stacked neatly on the floor.

Tomas lifted the hatch, leaning it against the wall, exposing a round hole. He understood the functionality of such a device, but he had never seen a privy before. In Woodmyst, one would simply find a tree out of the view of others, or use a chamber pot of sorts in the privacy of their homes.

He peered through the hole to see a deep hole laced with white powder. It wasn't snow, as snow couldn't reach this far under the tavern. He surmised it was ash from the fireplace. He also saw fragments of sawdust and straw on the edges of the deep hole. Whatever was in there didn't smell pleasant.

"You only live once," Tomas said to himself, as he latched the door shut behind him before removing his trousers.

Soon after, he was sitting by the fireplace in the tavern, staring into the flames, as he sipped his tea from a small white cup. A white porcelain pot with a spout attached sat on a tray in the centre of the table with five matching cups positioned around it. The aroma from the kitchen filled the room. Tomas couldn't help but think the forthcoming meal certainly smelled much better than the privy.

He hoped he'd remembered to close the lid.

"Good morning," David called as he entered the room.

Tomas turned in his chair and lifted his cup. "Morning."

"Have you managed the privy yet?" the bald giant asked as he sat across the table from the other.

"An interesting contraption," Tomas replied.

"We should think about building them in the village," suggested David as he poured some tea from the pot on the table into a cup.

"I have the feeling that it's much more complicated than simply digging a hole in the ground," Tomas replied before he sipped from his cup.

"But it's by far much better than squatting in the woods or emptying a bucket of shit in the morning."

Tomas almost spat his tea as he choked back his laughter.

"I'm so glad you stayed with us," Agnes announced as she brought Tomas his breakfast. In her hands was a plate of steaming bacon, scrambled eggs, and toast with fresh butter spread across its surface. "It gave me a chance to dig my tea set out. Isn't it pretty? One of the ship's captains gave it to us years ago. He said he purchased it all the way in Dendoodah."

"Dendadia," James called from the kitchen, correcting her mispronunciation.

"It's very nice," David replied as he inspected the pot, adorned in pearl white with tiny blue flowers encircling the lid. The cups were decorated with similar adorning around the lip of each piece.

Tomas almost laughed again as he watched the bald giant, build like a walking tree trunk, carefully scrutinise the dainty tea set. It just didn't look right. He shovelled a fork full of eggs into his mouth and started cutting the bacon into smaller portions as the other gently turned the pot around on the tray to see the fine work of the flowers.

"Very nice, indeed."

***

Draped in their caparisons and loaded with supplies, the innkeeper's son led the horses from the stable and into the yard. Tomas, standing by the gate with the others, counted the steeds twice as the boy approached and came up with an extra animal each time. A cream steed, laden with saddle and bedroll, walked between the two packhorses.

"I think you've loaded someone else's horse, boy."

"My father is giving our mare to the young lady," the youngster replied.

"No." Emily took her eyes from the horses to James Halle, who was leaning with his elbow against the fence. "You can't do that."

"Of course, I can," he replied, standing to and wrapping his arm around his wife. "She's mine and now she's yours. Besides, she doesn't get used for anything apart from some recreational riding. The poor beast spends most of her time in the yard or locked up in the stable. I insist you take her. I will be offended if you don't."

Emily smiled and hugged the man, kissing him on the cheek. She repeated the gesture with Anya, who smiled cheerfully.

"You take care of yourself out there, dearie," she offered.

"Captain Tarkin will be waiting for you near the *Adelandria*," Halle informed them. "He's a good man and has knowledge of the north. It would do well to pay attention to his advice."

Tomas shook the innkeeper's hand and thanked him for his help. Each of the men did the same before mounting their chargers and preparing to leave. With a wave, the party left off and headed toward the wharves.

It wasn't long before they had ridden past the warehouses where they had met Reynard Merys and on to an area near to the docks. Many horses, saddled and loaded, gathered at the end of the boardwalk that ran along the edge of the wharves. Tomas quickly counted thirty steeds; three bore equipment, while twenty-seven wore saddles.

One man was standing at the side of the farthest warehouse. He gave a sharp whistle, calling Captain Dakmel Tarkin to the deck of a ship moored nearby.

It was a larger vessel than Tomas had expected to see. It appeared that the good captain was being modest when he had spoken of his ship the night before.

The dark hull was wide and long, with fifteen square gun ports lining each side. Attached to the bow was the carving of a beautiful maiden with flowing golden hair, dressed in a royal blue gown. On either side of her, etched into large gold plating were the words, "The *Adelandria*."

Three tall masts sprouted from her deck and reached high into the air. They had removed all rigging except for the shrouds that stretched from the sides of the deck up to observation posts near the top of the masts. They reminded Tomas of giant spider webs.

Towards the stern was the wheelhouse, which stood at the back of the quarterdeck. Beyond this, overlooking it all, was the poop-deck cabin fitted with a skylight on top. The ship was a monster, large enough to fit the entire population of Woodmyst in twice over.

"Good morning," called the captain.

"Morning," Tomas called back, keeping his eyes on the *Adelandria*. "Tell me again why you don't want to take this with us."

"The waters are freezing over," the captain replied as he climbed down a rope ladder to the dock below. "Icebergs the size of mountains will be all over the ocean as we creep north. And this ship, as strong as she may be, is not the most manoeuvrable when put in a tight spot. She will hit the ice and then she will sink. I don't want to risk that. She stays here with a few of my men while the rest of us accompany you on your quest."

"About that," Emily ventured. "Why did you volunteer so quickly? Was it the mead?"

"I have my reasons, young miss," he smiled as he approached. "One of which is an individual who calls himself *The Sovereign*."

"The Sovereign?"

"I think he's responsible for what happened to your people," Tarkin answered as he came to a stop beside her. "Not to mention many people and many villages on both sides of this sea for many, many years.

"I'd be lying if I said that I didn't have an interest in finding him," he continued. "The fact is, most of my crew have been victims of his acts in some manner or form. We have been hunting him for a while now."

"Then you know where to find him?" David quizzed.

"Sadly…" The captain shook his head. "No. We know he is north. But we are not sure where. It was your story that brought me to thinking that the ship heading north is most possibly linked to him in some way."

"But you're not sure?" Tomas asked.

"No," he replied. "We're joining you on a hunch."

"Why take such a risk?" Simon inquired. "We're total strangers."

"My ship isn't going anywhere for a while," Tarkin answered. "What else can I do except sleep on the *Adelandria* and get drunk on mead at the inn? I'll be broke in a month."

"Whatever the reason," Tomas said, smiling. "I'm glad to have you along."

***

Steering their horses along the road, the mass of riders kept close to the shore. The village of Oakbeach and the warehouses by the wharves grew smaller as the distance between them and the band of travellers increased.

The land inclined as the area between the road and the water rose, revealing rocky outcrops that eventually turned into steep, stony slopes that dropped away to the sea below. The rocky surface was a harsh, dark grey. It appeared smooth in places, like flowing mud, frozen in place for eternity.

Tomas understood flowing molten rock that once spewed from the mountains to their west had formed the land about them. Such information had been shared through stories and songs for as long as people existed in the lands near the mountains. He remembered hearing about rivers of fire that swept towards the seas, leaving a wide trail of black rock behind that spread in all directions as far as the eye could see.

The contrast between the dark stone and the white snow that surrounded it was a spectacle he admired. How nature provided such amazing moments of wonder and beauty was something that produced awe from deep inside Tomas.

Slowly, the road wound to the left, away from the water and towards the woods that covered the slopes leading towards the northern mountains. The horses instinctively followed the path with little direction from their riders.

Tomas and his men led the company with Captain Tarkin alongside. He glanced around and found that five women who rode just behind them were separating Emily from their group.

"You have women on your ship?" Tomas asked the captain.

"They're excellent sailors and magnificent warriors," Tarkin replied. "Don't worry about the lady. She'll be perfectly safe with them."

Carefully weighing each of them with his eyes, Tomas moved his gaze over the women that followed Captain Tarkin. Their appearance was beyond exotic. Each had smooth, dark skin and piercing green eyes. One of them locked onto his gaze and smiled sweetly before looking away.

Each wore a curved blade on her hip and a bow slung over her shoulders.

"Are they related?" Tomas asked the captain.

"No," he replied. "But they are from the same island. Far to the south where the weather is warm all year round. I think one of them likes you."

"It would appear I have a woman," the other replied.

"About time you owed up to it," Simon blurted out.

The women giggled. Tomas quickly looked back to see Emily smirking.

"Only one?" Tarkin asked.

"Do I need more?" Tomas asked sarcastically.

"I guess not," the captain chuckled. "I, on the other hand, have one in every port I've visited."

"Even back there?" Ivo shot a thumb over his shoulder, pointing back towards Oakbeach.

"Every port I've visited," he said, and smiled.

"I think I may become a sailor after this adventure," the younger man admitted wryly.

The women giggled again.

"I love your hair," one of them said to Emily. Her accent was thick and her voice husky.

"I've never seen such colour upon a woman."

"And so beautiful and brave," another stated. "I would never have picked you for a warrior."

"I'm not a warrior," Emily admitted.

"How is it that you are with these men if you aren't a warrior?" the first asked.

"My village was attacked," she replied. "These men are helping me to find what is left of my people."

"Still," the first woman said, smiling, "you are beautiful and brave nonetheless."

"I am Karlena," said the second woman. "This is Rhydra and these others are Sharek, Rhyodia and Akasati. We are from Erilia."

"I've never heard of this place." Emily shook her head.

"It is a large band of islands far to the south," Rhydra informed her. "The beaches are white and covered in sand as fine as powder. The water is a deep blue and the trees are always green. It is paradise."

"Why leave your home to sail with Captain Tarkin?"

"Our village was also attacked, when we were still little girls," Karlena explained. "Our homes were burnt and everyone was slaughtered. We hid away. The men who destroyed our home called themselves Prophets of the Sovereign."

"Captain saw the smoke from his ship and came to assist," Rhydra continued. "But he was too late. Everyone was dead except for us. We begged him to take us in, and he did. We became his cabin wards, and he trained us to fight."

"It would appear the captain has been searching for this Sovereign for a long time," Emily stated, eyeing Tarkin as they rode on. She wondered what exactly the man had experienced for him to harbour such resentment towards an individual he had never seen.

"Since before we met him," Rhydra replied. "But you have nothing to fear. We will protect you and help you find your people."

Emily smiled, gratefully accepting the Erilian warrior's offer.

***

Later in the day, when the sun slowly made its way behind the mountain peaks and the shadows grew longer upon the ground, the troop sought a suitable place to set up camp for the night. A large clearing, surrounded by leafless trees and blanketed in deep snow, lay near to a stream that trickled gently over smooth, dark stones.

They erected tents into a circular formation and gathered the horses together at one end of the area. They constructed a rope fence around the steeds as some of Tarkin's men measured feed carried by one of their packhorses into buckets before distributing it to the animals.

Soon enough wood was gathered for two fires, one in the centre of the circle of tents and the other near to the makeshift corral in order to keep the beasts warm during the night. They piled the timber near the tents where the men could easily get to it.

The sky changed colour, from a soft blue to pink and purple. Two of Tarkin's men appeared from the woods as the fire crackled into life. Each had a bow and quiver slung over his shoulder as they carried four rabbits in their hands.

"No sign of anyone out there, Captain," one called to Tarkin as he approached the fire, "except for these poor bastards."

"Silly buggers got in the way of our arrows," the other said, and smiled.

"Well done, lads," the captain replied before turning to another man. "Bring up some flour, a deep pot, and some of those large potatoes. We'll make some bread and a stew."

Tomas stroked his mare on the nose before carrying his saddle to his tent. As he approached the camp, he noticed one of the Erilian women instructing Emily in swordplay in a secluded place to the side of the clearing. He slowed his pace inconspicuously to watch the young women in action.

The first thing he noticed was the clothing Emily wore. She had exchanged her long garments for a pair of trousers of the same fashion as those worn by the Erilian women.

At first, he worried the men in the troop might ogle her, as the attire she wore was tight around her legs and buttocks. It almost appeared as a second skin. He then realised that he, or she, had nothing to be concerned with. The other women would look out for her. And if that failed, his blade was ready to stand in for her.

The attire, he surmised, wasn't for the benefit of men's eyes, but more for the fluid motion needed in battle. He watched on as the women manoeuvred and practised handling the blade, like a well-rehearsed dance.

The Erilian thrust and swung her thin, curved blade through the air with ease. It was almost hypnotic. She displayed grace and control, unlike anything that Tomas had ever seen.

He supposed the blade helped her to achieve such movement. It was skinny and shorter than his sword. His first impression was that it could not cut through a stick of butter because it was so thin. Tarkin, however, had told him that the Erilian women were formidable warriors.

Watching her as she flung the blade about her, so rapidly that it blurred in his eyes, he determined the sword was well suited to her needs. His blade was long, thick, and heavy, made for hacking flesh and crushing bone. Her blade was made for slicing and cutting.

The Erilian handed the sword to Emily, who almost dropped it when it, before grasping it tightly.

"It's so heavy," she mentioned as she gripped her other hand around the hilt.

Tomas smiled and lowered his face to the ground as he continued towards his tent, carrying the saddle in his arms.

"Feel the weight," the Erilian woman instructed. "I think we will need to work on your strength."

Tomas placed the leather seat inside his tent flap and continued to the fire where most of the men had gathered, seated upon fallen logs placed deliberately around the hearth. Some were mixing flour with snow to make dough, while others cut potatoes and rabbit flesh and placed the portions into a large pot of water sitting over the flames.

"There's another pot of water on the other side of the fire," Tarkin informed him as he rolled a ball of dough into the embers near the edge of the flames. "It should be hot enough for your tea."

"I think I'll wait," Tomas replied. "Can I help with anything?"

"Grab some flour and make some bread, if you don't mind," the captain suggested. "We'll need enough for tonight and perhaps some to bite upon during our journey tomorrow. Fist sized balls, straight into the coals."

Tomas grabbed a handful of snow from the ground before digging into the sack of flour by Tarkin's feet. He glanced around the fire to see his own village men seated nearby and conversing to the crew of the *Adelandria*. It was a good sign to see the men getting along so well.

"Your woman is not a warrior," Tarkin stated. "She doesn't know one end of a sword from the other."

"I don't know her that well," Tomas replied. "But if I were to guess, I'd say she was more of a farmer than a fighter."

"Don't worry," the captain nodded. "Rhydra is an excellent teacher. She'll have young Miss Emily using a blade as if it were a part of herself before you know it."

Tomas glanced back towards the two women to the side of the clearing.

"I hope it happens before we meet up with that ship and its crew." Tomas frowned as he rolled his ball of dough into the glowing embers.

***

Tomas spent most of the night conversing with the captain, unintentionally distancing himself from his men and the girl. His eyes moved over the flames to where the others sat, engaged in conversations of their own with other members of their troop.

David and Simon were laughing with several men directly across from Tomas. No doubt the men were comparing tales of tavern fights and nights with wild women. Oliver simply shook his head as he listened, knowing full well his friends' stories were extremely exaggerated.

Ivo seemed to have a better time seated amongst the ladies. He frequently smiled, and they giggled in reply. Tomas couldn't help wondering what level of disappointment the young man would experience once he realised all the Erilian women were bound to Tarkin.

Occasionally, his eyes locked on to Emily's. She smiled sweetly from her place near Ivo before looking away bashfully.

"Tell me," Tarkin asked, "what exactly happened to your village? What is the story of Woodmyst?"

Fire and smoke suddenly filled Tomas' thoughts.

"Have you ever heard of the Night Demons?" he asked.

"No," the captain replied. "Can't say I have."

"It was the name we gave the creatures that attacked us," Tomas told the other. "They left a body for us to find at first. The next night, they lit torches in the woods. As many as the stars in the sky. In the morning, they vanished. The next night, they came back, and we sent scouts in to spy them out. They killed the scouts."

Other conversations around the fire grew silent as more ears tuned into Tomas' tale.

"Eventually, they attacked," he continued. "There were many of them. Too many for our men to defeat, but Woodmyst fought back. Some had their spirits dashed to pieces during that time. Still, they fought. Even at our lowest point, our men fought. Then the dragon came.

"It circled the village on the first night that it appeared. Then the second dragon came."

"After the fields were burnt," Simon put in.

"That's right." Tomas nodded. "They took me from the stables as they stole the horses. The Night Demons, that is. They tied me up and sat me right on top of that brown mare I have over there. Then they led me blindfolded to a cave."

"What did they do to you?" asked a man seated near Oliver.

"Nothing," he answered. "They kept me prisoner but showed me kindness. Meanwhile, they had killed my father and most of the other men in Woodmyst. They took the other children and the young mothers from the Great Hall before letting one of their dragons burn the building with the elderly and our mothers still inside.

"Everyone was killed except one man and the youths of the village," Tomas continued. "Richard, the only man to survive, said it was revenge for something my father and the other council members of Woodmyst did during the Realm War. He doesn't talk about it much and I never push him for information."

Tomas scratched his chin. "I've always wondered. How did they know which village to attack? How did they know that the men they were seeking vengeance upon were in Woodmyst? Why didn't they just go after those men instead of destroying an entire village of innocent people?"

He looked across the flames at his men. The twinkle of tears welling in their eyes glistened in the firelight.

"Even though they allowed the children to live, I hate them," Tomas admitted. "They are truly an evil breed of beings."

"What did they look like?" Tarkin asked as he stared quizzically into the fire.

Tomas shook his head. "Grey skin, shaped like men with large yellow eyes."

"Yellow eyes?" The captain raised his brow.

"You know of these creatures?" David asked.

"I have heard of them," Tarkin replied. "Some call them the Dragon Keepers. It is said they live in the north, far from here; beyond the mountains and an ocean of ice. Thousands of them.

"The stories tell of sightings of these creatures in secluded places, hidden from the world of men. The Realm War invaded many of these places, forcing the creatures away. Rather than fight back, the Dragon Keepers simply gathered together and disappeared before too many men could see the creatures themselves. The stories remained just that. Stories."

"But why were they called Dragon Keepers?" Simon asked.

"Well," Tarkin continued, "the stories say that they bred dragons and raised them. Some people said they saw the creatures near to where dragons roosted. Mind you, they were just stories that were mostly shared in taverns and no one could guarantee any truth in them."

The captain turned his gaze to Tomas. "That is, until now. I have a feeling you have had a very close encounter with the Dragon Keepers. The only answers I can offer to any of your questions about how and why they did what they did are these. First, dragons are excellent trackers. That's probably how they found your village and the men they believed committed whatever deed they held a grudge about. Second, they are not men and don't think or act the way we do. Apart from that, who knows how their minds work?"

Tomas peered into the flames and thought about the captain's words. They didn't bring any comfort, nor did they truly answer the questions that had plagued him ever since the siege upon his home. He still detested the Dragon Keepers for what they had done to his father and even more for killing his mother. He also knew his fellow village men shared his hatred. That feeling alone would always remain an everlasting scar placed upon them by the Night Demons.

It wasn't long before Tomas felt weariness creep upon him. He turned in for the night. Bidding all around the fire a good evening, he made his way to his tent and lifted the flap to enter.

After lowering himself to his bedding, he removed his boots. A gentle movement behind him caught him by surprise.

"I was wondering how long you were going to be," said Emily's familiar voice from the darkness.

"I thought you would have bedded in the Erilians' tent," said Tomas.

"They belong to the captain," she replied.

"I know," he agreed. "But surely they have a tent for themselves."

"They don't take turns," she giggled. "They all sleep with him at the same time."

Tomas furrowed his brow. He found the concept of so many women at one time quite exhausting.

"Are you sick of me sharing your bed?" she asked.

"Quite the opposite," he answered as he slipped under the blanket and sidled up next to her.

Twelve

Tomas suddenly found himself awake. He was sitting upright and listening intently before he knew it. Something had brought him out of his slumber.

Soft breathing from nearby informed him that Emily still slept soundly. He touched her bare skin with the back of his hand as he replaced the covers he had inadvertently peeled away as he stirred awake.

It was still dark.

Pitch black.

He cocked his head, scanning for any unfamiliar sound.

A horse snorted a sound of disapproval.

Carefully exiting the bedding, attempting to leave Emily to her rest, Tomas rose to his feet where he quickly and quietly dressed.

A thud and several cracking noises, as if someone stepped upon twigs, reverberated from the woods near to the camp.

Tomas threw his bearskin over his shoulders and opened the flap of his tent. He stealthily stepped outside as he lifted his sword from the ground near to where he had been sleeping before lowering the tent flap back in place behind him.

The snow-covered ground appeared luminous in the moonlight, shining like smooth silver. The trees surrounding the camp stood like dark pillars. Some reached towards the star-filled sky with gnarled limbs while the pines pointed directly above themselves with frosted needles.

The snow crunched noisily beneath his feet as he crept around the tent towards the horses. They stood with their heads high, ears twisting this way and that. The sounds had upset them enough to have them a little on edge.

THUD! CRACK, CRACK, CRACK!

Tomas snapped his head around. The sound came from his left.

THUD! CRACK, CRACK!

This time, it came from the woods beyond the makeshift yard where they tethered the horses.

THUD!

To his left.

THUD! CRACK, CRACK!

Behind the horses again.

Dismissing the chance it came from built-up snow dropping from tree branches to the ground, Tomas raised his sword. Creatures, human or other, were out there moving about.

Several horses, including his brown mare, thumped their hooves against the ground. Others moved slightly from side to side. It was clear to Tomas that they wanted their bonds untied so they could retreat from the unseen visitors.

Their behaviour made Tomas believe that perhaps some predators were surrounding the camp. Possibly it was wolves or bears in hope of an easy meal of tethered steeds and sleeping men.

Tomas was not about to let that happen.

A sharp hiss from behind him made him spin on his heels and face the camp. David was creeping towards him, sword levelled in both hands and bald head shining in the moonlight. His head turned towards his left as he scanned the edge of the trees for any movement to accompany the sounds emitting from the forest.

More thudding and cracking sounded from behind the horses and farther to the left. It was as if the sounds were deliberate.

Tomas moved to the trees behind the horses and crouched, positioning himself between the steeds and the source of the sounds. David kept his eyes on the area to the left, where the noise increased.

"Come on, you bastards," he breathed, vapour rising from his lips in the frosty night air.

The clatter also picked up in the area before Tomas. Whatever was out there was still unseen and a fair distance from him, but they weren't afraid to let anyone know of their existence.

THUD! CRACK, CRACK, CRACK! THUD! CRACK! THUD! CRACK!

Louder and louder.

Closer and closer.

Tomas lowered his brow and peered deeper into the darkness beneath the trees.

Where are you?

He could barely make out black forms of tree trunks and smooth snow with his limited vision.

The noise, an almost violent din, was filling his ears.

His heart raced as his hands tightened around the hilt of his blade. His muscles flexed as he readied himself for battle.

The unseen were not animals on the prowl.

These beings were taunting on purpose.

Oliver raced up to his side, sword in his hands.

"Who are they?" he asked, keeping his voice low.

"I don't know," Tomas answered. "Where are the others?"

"Simon and Ivo are with David," the blond warrior answered.

THUD! CRACK, CRACK, CRACK! THUD! THUD! CRACK!

The racket continued to increase in front of the men and to their left, but sounds were now exploding from the area to their right as well.

Louder.

Faster.

Closer.

"What devilry is this?" called Captain Tarkin as he and several men bolted from their tents.

The clamour filled the night air, bouncing in all directions. It was becoming difficult to determine from where the sound originated.

The horses stomped and snorted.

The men raised their weapons and moved their heads this way and that.

THUD! CRACK, CRACK! THUD! THUD! CRACK, CRACK, CRACK!

Silence.

All stood motionless for what seemed an eternity as they waited for something, anything, to happen.

Nothing.

The men exchanged glances, sharing confused looks, each hoping the other had answers.

"What just happened?" Oliver eventually asked.

Tomas shook his head as he slowly raised himself to full height. He lowered his sword and walked back towards the horses, stopping to rub the nose of his mare, which nuzzled him gently, softly nickering in response.

"I'm tired." Tomas yawned. "I'm going back to bed."

Oliver stood his ground, sword raised, wide-eyed and ready for action. "I don't think I'll be going back to sleep ever again."

***

Tomas opened his eyes to a brighter environment. Emily pressed against him and still slept soundly. He recalled a different image of her when he returned to the tent after the night's adventure only hours before.

She was awake and sitting with the covers pulled up to her chin. The quivering in her voice as she asked him what was going on told him of her fear. He lied to her, assuring her that everything was fine as he held her tightly to his chest. There she stayed until they both drifted back to sleep.

Tomas left her in the tent as he ventured out to the fire where several of the men had remained during the rest of the night. Amongst them sat Oliver and David, who both sipped steaming liquid from tin cups.

"Water's hot," David said, pointing with his cup to a large pot sitting over the hearth, keeping his eyes upon the dancing flames before him.

Oliver lifted a small wooden box from the ground near his feet and handed it to Tomas. Grabbing an empty tin cup that was resting on a stump, Tomas sat down and balanced the items on his lap.

He opened the small box. Its lid was simply a square piece of cork jammed into the opening in order to prevent the contents from spilling out. Dried tea leaves, crushed into tiny fragments and compacted tightly sat inside the wooden vessel.

Tomas lifted a tiny amount of the sweet-smelling herb between his fingers and dropped it into his cup. He lifted the pot from the fire and carefully poured the steaming water into his cup. He replaced the pot over the flames before he took his dagger from his belt to stir the brew.

"Did you sleep at all?" he asked while he nursed his beverage, waiting for the contents to mix.

"Not a bloody wink," Oliver replied.

"I don't know how you did it," David put in. "That frightened me to the core. How could you sleep after that?"

"I was tired," Tomas answered as he lifted his cup to his lips.

"A few of us took a walk out there when the light first appeared," said David.

"What did you see?" Tomas turned his eyes towards the other. "Any tracks?"

"There were some," he replied. "But they didn't lead very far. They covered them over and seemed to stick to rocky areas once they got a certain distance out."

"They left towards the north," Oliver added. "The way we just happen to be going. Do you think it might be the ones we're chasing or just a mere coincidence?"

"They couldn't be the ones we're pursuing. They're sailing on the sea," Tomas replied.

"They could be in league with them," David suggested.

Tomas cocked his head with a slight frown. *Could be.*

"Good morning, gentlemen," said a voice from behind them. Tomas turned to see Tarkin approaching, still buckling his belt.

"Morning, Captain," the men around the fire returned.

Tomas stood up and was about to offer tea to the captain.

"No, no," Tarkin gestured the other to sit back down. "I can make my own tea, thank you."

Tomas returned to his stump as the captain crouched by the fire to prepare his beverage.

"Rough night?" Oliver asked.

"Before or after that racket?"

The men gave Tarkin a curious look.

"I have a number of women in my tent, gentlemen," he smiled. "The words *rough night* could have multiple meanings."

Soft laughter and chuckling erupted around the hearth.

"We should wake the others soon and be on our way before the sun gets too high in the sky," the captain suggested as he found a stump of his own to sit upon. He then turned his attention to one of his men sitting nearby. "Is there any bread left over?"

"Yes, Captain," replied a burly man with a long scar that stretched from above his left eye, along his cheek, disappearing beneath a dark bushy beard. He reached into a hessian bag, retrieved a fist-sized roll of bread and tossed it to Tarkin. "There's still some stew in the soup pot."

"One bowl, please Jeremy," said the captain through a mouthful of bread.

"Actually..." David raised his eyebrows. "Make that two, thank you."

"Three," another of Tarkin's men called.

"Better dish up enough for all of us," the captain instructed. "We have a long day's journey ahead and we'll need our strength."

"We should see to the horses also," Oliver put in. "They'll be the ones carrying the load during this journey."

"Good point," Tarkin admitted before turning his attention to another of his men. "Get some of the dried oats to the animals."

The man immediately left the warmth of the fire and retreated to a nearby tent. It wasn't long before he re-emerged with a large sack hoisted over his shoulder. Tomas watched him as he strode towards the horses tethered at the edge of the camp.

Before long, all the men gathered by the fire had eaten and were dispersing to pack for the ride. Some men had the dangerous task of waking the others, who had been sleeping soundly as the light in the sky grew brighter and brighter.

Tomas took the responsibility of rousing Emily out of her sleep. She resisted and complained by moaning and groaning, turning away from him on her side as he breathed her name and gently shook her shoulder.

"It's time to get up," he said.

"I am," she managed. He almost laughed.

"We need to move," he said. "We need to find your people."

Suddenly, her eyes were wide open.

"My people," she breathed as she sat upright, seeming to remember where she was.

"There's food and hot water by the fire," Tomas informed her. "Dress and make yourself ready. I'll pack our tent."

The captain allowed those he jokingly regarded as *lazy layabouts* to eat their fill as the others loaded the steeds. With tents and bedding rolled, and saddles buckled, the riders mounted their chargers.

It was time to move out.

**

As they entered the woods, Tomas turned to the captain and suggested they take a look at the area where some men found tracks left by the strangers during the night. Tarkin agreed, mainly because he wanted to feed his curiosity about who could make such a commotion.

The troop wove the horses through the thick growth as they made their way towards the north. David directed the others, pointing to churned places in the snow. He and the other men with him earlier believed these were signs left by the visitors.

Tomas noticed that most of the tracks were near to, or upon areas that were rocky and hard where the snow cover was at its thinnest. It would appear that the noise-makers either knew the area well or had luck on their side concerning where they placed their feet.

Indeed, it was difficult to track them.

The trees thinned out as they continued moving north. The dried and dead, twisted limbs became fewer and fewer, giving way to green pines spattered with fine, white coverings of snow.

The ground gently sloped from their left towards the sea out of their view to their right. The land appeared untouched, unfarmed, unknown to human hands.

Small birds fluttered about in the limbs of the pines, singing welcoming tunes as the sun climbed higher in the eastern sky. The sweet, inviting scent of the leaves had all the riders at ease as they happily navigated the forest, almost forgetting the intruders from the night before.

Tomas smiled as he looked over to Emily riding beside him. Her face beamed as she peered about her, soaking up the beauty of the scenery. Her auburn locks shone as the sun kissed her hair.

She turned her gaze to him and returned his smile. He looked away bashfully and rested his gaze upon the back of his mare's head.

What's wrong with you? Say something to her.

They ventured over a small ridge and into a tiny clearing.

The horses stopped dead in their tracks as all members of the party stared at the lone figure standing in the centre of the open ground.

It stood upright, arms stretched out from its sides.

A blank face with hollowed eyes stared back towards them.

Dressed in ragged clothing; a wide-brimmed hat and long tattered coat.

Tall.

Thin.

It didn't move.

It didn't breathe.

It just stared as its coat softly waved in the gentle breeze.

Fear and confusion now replaced the carefree feeling that had enveloped the travellers only moments ago.

Tomas stared intently at the figure, cocking his head to the side.

With a kick, he moved his mare forward. She didn't hesitate.

"Tomas," David protested as the other unsheathed his sword and continued towards the tall shape.

It didn't flinch, recoil or run.

It stared back with its deep, dark holes where its eyes should be.

The others watched silently as Tomas drew nearer and nearer to the figure. Ivo almost cried out as he watched Tomas put his blade away and dismount from the brown steed.

"What is he doing?" Tarkin asked.

"No bloody idea," Oliver replied, pulling out his sword and preparing to race in to help his friend.

The other men of Woodmyst did the same. Their blades were at the ready in their tight grips. They were not about to let their leader fall.

Tomas, perceiving their thoughts, signalled for them to relax.

He walked casually up to the lone figure and reached behind it.

It didn't move. It simply kept staring at those who watched from a distance.

With a heave, Tomas lifted the figure off the ground.

It was attached to a thin post stuck in the ground.

"Scarecrow," he shouted to the riders.

Thirteen

Captain Dakmel Tarkin nursed the head of the scarecrow in his hands. His thumbs pressed into the hollowed eye sockets as he scrutinised the handiwork of its creators.

It surprised him how much attention the makers of the scarecrow paid to the finer details of anatomy. They had formed the head by stuffing the small hessian bag with straw before using twine to mould the cranium into shape. As remarkable as this was, it was but only one marvel that contributed to making this figure complete.

With the coat, hat and other clothing removed, they saw the body covered with a skin of hessian sacks, coursely sewn together. Karlena, one of the Erilian women, used her dagger to slice the counterfeit skin open from neck to crotch.

Tightly packed straw spilt out from the belly as she used her hands to widen her cut at the figure's chest. Someone had fashioned woven twigs and thin branches into a set of wicker ribs.

"By the gods," Ivo gasped.

Karlena used her dagger to slice the fabric skin along the arms to reveal straw muscles and wooden bones, similar to real bones found in an actual person.

"Why go to so much trouble?" she asked.

Tarkin shook his head. It made no sense.

David took a handful of the straw from the stomach of the scarecrow and held it in front of his mare's mouth. She immediately turned her head away, as if it smelt repulsive.

"What's wrong, girl?" he asked, trying again. She kept swinging her head away, declining the offer.

"Try my mare," Tomas suggested, watching the exchange closely.

The brown mare eyed David as she also turned her nose away from his handful of straw.

"Something is not right," he said, turning back to the other men gathered around the scarecrow.

"Burn it," Tomas instructed. "Burn it all. Straw, wood and clothing. The horses sense something foul about this thing and my gut tells me to pay attention."

"You heard him," Tarkin said to his men.

One man pulled two flint stones from his pocket and scraped them together near the figure's stomach. The straw caught the spark and was ablaze almost immediately.

Several other men gathered the bits and pieces removed from the scarecrow and placed them on top of the flames. The fire burnt rapidly, engulfing the figure and its belongings within moments.

***

Speaking remained at a minimum as they rode on, sharing confused looks. Fear had manifested in the eyes of some of the younger men. With the night bringing terrifying sounds from an unseen foe, and the morning presenting the strange hessian figure, the riders were feeling less than excited about their journey.

Tomas suggested they ride closer to the coast, to within view of the water. He felt that the familiar sight, smell and sounds of the ocean might lift the spirits of the *Adelandria*'s crew members.

The men of Woodmyst instinctively placed their horses around Emily, protecting her from any more surprises. The ship's crew encircled them, creating a barrier around the young woman and her five escorts.

The thunderous sound of waves crashing against rocks arose to their right as they steadily rode together. The trees were still thick in places around them, allowing a momentary view of the liquid horizon as they pressed on.

The sun had crept high in the sky as white clouds with a greenish tinge collected above the mountains to the west. Tomas had been watching the vaporous gathering for some time and didn't like what he saw.

"Bad weather is coming," he said.

Simon looked towards the ocean where blue skies stretched as far as he could see.

"You're losing your mind," he grunted.

"Look at the mountains, you moron," Ivo pointed out.

Turning his head to his left, Simon mumbled to himself as he watched the clouds slowly heading their way.

"We may need to shelter the horses," Tomas called to Captain Tarkin.

"There is a small fishing village to the north," he replied. "I've only been there by sea, but I'm certain it isn't too far. We should get there by nightfall. Perhaps I should send one of the lads to go ahead of us and see if they will let us spend the night there?"

"Send two," David suggested. "That way, they can watch each other's backs. Who knows what was taunting us last night or who put that wretched scarecrow up for us to find. Could be the very people at this village you speak about."

"Or they may not be from the village, but could be watching us even now for an opportunity to attack," Oliver put in.

Tomas nodded. "You'd better send two."

The captain turned to the nearest two riders and instructed them to go ahead. Instantly, the riders dug their heels in and their steeds kicked up snow in all directions. The others watched them as they disappeared into the trees, leaving only the fading sound of hoof falls.

Emily moved her gaze to Tomas and back to the spot where the riders had vanished.

"I'm afraid," she admitted.

"You?" he asked with a hint of surprise in his voice.

She looked at him quizzically. He smiled wryly as he turned his face towards her.

"You could survive an attack from a band of marauders," he re-minded. "You killed one and escaped. You then spent an entire night exposed to the elements and survived. How could you be afraid?"

"Aren't you?" she asked.

"Not really," he lied, hoping to bring her some ease.

She smiled back at him. His words worked for now.

The sun slowly made its way across the sky and fell behind the dark clouds gathering to their left. Shadows grew longer, and the air felt colder as the riders drew further on their quest.

Eventually, they came upon a rise that looked down upon a quaint seaside village of five huts and a large stable to the northern edge of the town. A long timber jetty stretched from the side of one of the tiny houses, over the waves that crashed upon a pebbly shore.

Light from candles or a fire flickered through the windows of this hut, inviting the troop to venture closer. There was no sign of the two riders the captain had sent forward. A quick scan of the village gave the impression that there was no sign of any living soul.

Neat fences, fashioned from wood, and painted white, surrounded each of the cottages. They had small gates built into them, parallel to the doors of the dwellings.

Tarkin pulled his horse up to a gate and tethered the beast to the fence nearby. He glanced around cautiously, noticing that the men of Woodmyst already had their hands resting upon their sword hilts.

The captain pushed the little gate in. It opened with a rusty squeak as he stepped into the yard.

The snow had thickly covered the area, concealing what Tarkin be-lieved was a path and tidy garden that lined the boundary of the prop-erty.

He reached for a bronze-coloured knocker attached to the door and tapped it three times. Voices inside informed him that someone was present. Footsteps drawing nearer told him they had heard his rapping.

The door opened with a loud creak and revealed the two riders Tarkin had sent earlier.

"Captain," one of them said as they stepped to the side of the doorway in order to allow their commander in.

"Gentlemen," Tarkin replied. "Where are the occupants of this home?"

"It would appear that we are the only occupants of this home," one man answered. "In fact, I think we are the only occupants of the entire town."

"Any clues to their whereabouts?" the captain asked as he signalled the other riders to stand down.

"None, Captain," the other man said, noticing some others dismounting their steeds. "You might want to take the horses to the stable and settle them in before the weather hits us."

Tarkin turned towards the west where a large band of dark clouds crawled across the sky.

"We've got meat cooking," said a man in the doorway. "We found some pigs in the stable and butchered one. We didn't think they'd be missed, considering no one is here."

"Good thinking, lads," the captain said, nodding. "We'll see to the horses and you see to the meal."

***

The stable was a welcome sight for Tomas. It reminded him a little of the stables that once stood proudly in Woodmyst before the Night Demons destroyed it all.

Several large stalls lined each side of the interior. They held fresh straw and troughs for water positioned along the back walls of the stalls.

Seven pigs occupied the first stall on the right, lying on fresh straw; they raised their heads momentarily to see who it was that interrupted their rest.

Tomas led the brown mare past them and to a stall about halfway along the structure. Emily followed him, placing her horse in the same pen.

Tomas unloaded the horses and propped their saddles on the barrier between their stall and the one next to it. Ivo and Oliver used that one for their steeds.

"Give your horse a rubdown," Tomas instructed Emily as he removed the mare's caparison. He folded it roughly and draped it over his saddle before moving his hands over the beast's back where the saddle had been pressing.

Emily followed suit and rubbed her cream horse with her fingers. The steed nickered gratefully, bringing a smile to the girl's face. Tomas found the corners of his mouth involuntarily rising as he watched her.

"Dig your fingers in a little," Ivo instructed her as he tended to his own animal in the pen behind her.

Suddenly, he felt something strike him gently against the side of his head. His mare had hit him with her muzzle.

"Hey," he chuckled. "What was that for?"

She snorted and stomped her foot.

"I didn't know you were the jealous type," he whispered in her ear.

"The ladies are fighting over you, are they?" Simon whispered from the stall behind him.

David chuckled as he unbuckled his saddle, lifting it from his chestnut beast.

Tomas shushed him.

"Have you," Simon said softly, "you know, lain with her yet?"

"Now is not the time for this kind of talk, Simon," Tomas rebuked. "She might hear you."

"Oh, you haven't." He shook his head. "Two nights in bed with her and you haven't been to bed with her. What is wrong with you, brother? Did the Night Demons tie a knot in it when they had you in the caves alone?"

"I'm going to kill you," Tomas whispered as he shook his head, trying not to laugh.

"That's it," Ivo said to Emily as the young lady rubbed her fingers across the animal's coat. "See, she likes that."

Tomas looked over to her. She fixed her eyes upon him, a great, cheeky smile on her face.

She had heard them.

***

Captain Tarkin instructed several of his men to fan out and search the village for any sign of life or for evidence as to the whereabouts of the missing villagers. The men knocked upon doors politely before opening them and venturing inside the houses. Inside, they found folded clothing in drawers, food tidily packed away in pantries, firewood neatly stacked by the hearths.

"Nothing here, Captain," a man called from the door of a cottage.

Tarkin stood near the centre of the small community, his brow creasing as the words hit him hard.

"Nothing over here, Captain," another said from a hut behind him.

"Nothing, Captain," yelled another from farther away.

The words repeated again and again as he hoped to hear some good news. A person hiding in a cupboard perhaps, or at least a sign of struggle. The word 'nothing' made him feel absent, at a loss, confused.

What the devil happened here?

"Keep searching," he commanded. "Look for something, anything that may tell us where these people are."

"They might have just gone to a warmer climate for the winter, Captain," a man standing in the door of a nearby cottage suggested.

"They might have," Tarkin agreed. "But we can't know that for sure. Find me something to support that idea."

The captain turned towards the house with the jetty attached to its side. He strolled back through the door, where a welcoming aroma flowed from the kitchen and into the rest of the house.

In the front room, a large table stood. Mugs, plates and cutlery sat neatly at one end, all appropriated from the surrounding houses. The Erilian women sat upon deep-cushioned chairs that lined the room.

Karlena, curled up in the chair closest to the door, stood up as Tarkin closed the door behind him. She motioned for him to sit in her place.

He did.

She then placed herself on his lap and curled her legs underneath her before resting her head against his chest. He stroked her hair soothingly as she closed her eyes.

"Did you find anything?" she asked.

"Nothing," he said, repeating the word again.

***

The meal was both filling and delectable.

"You boys have outdone yourselves once again," Tarkin, sitting in the chair nearest to the door, congratulated the two men who had been slaving in the kitchen for most of the day.

"Thank you, Captain." They smiled, quite happy with themselves.

"You're quite welcome," Tarkin replied. "In fact, it is we who should thank you. You deserve to rest. Tomorrow will be an early rise, so I suggest you take a bunk in one of the huts near the stable. I'll clean up tonight lads."

"Aye, Captain," they said before gathering their sheathed swords that leaned against the wall in the kitchen. Tarkin heard the door open and close behind him as the men left the cottage.

"The fire-places are alight in the other buildings, aren't they?"

"Aye, Captain," answered the burly man with a scar stretching down the side of his face.

"Thank you, Jeremy," Tarkin replied. "I guess it's time for everyone to get some sleep."

The men filed out of the cottage, heading for a bed in a nearby hut they had claimed for the night. The Erilian women stayed seated as Tomas, Emily and the men of Woodmyst rose to their feet to follow the others out the door.

"Not yet," the captain instructed. "Please sit back down."

Jeremy remained by Tarkin's side as the last of the crewmen closed the door behind him. The captain reached his hand out to the other, who placed a thick, leather-bound book into it.

"What's this?" Ivo asked as he sat back down in his chair by the table.

"That will be all, Jeremy."

"Aye, Captain," the husky man said before opening the door and walking into the chilly night air.

"Jeremy found this tucked deep in a dresser drawer inside one of the cottages," Tarkin informed the gathering as he nursed the book in his hands. "He read a little of it and believes it tells us some of what happened here."

"I don't understand." Emily shook her head.

"It's a journal," the captain told her. "It was kept by one of the womenfolk of this village. I waited until my men had dispersed before telling you about it. They are a superstitious bunch and they take a lot to heart. They don't need to know the contents of this book."

Tomas looked over at the book in Tarkin's grasp. The red binding was tattered and worn from use. The pages looked yellow in the lamp's light that filled the room.

"What's it say?" he asked.

"Can you read?" the captain quizzed.

"We are an educated group in Woodmyst, yes," he replied.

Tarkin handed the book to Karlena, who was sitting in a seat beside her captain. She strolled across the room and handed the item to Tomas, who took it carefully in both hands, treating it like a delicate treasure.

He opened the pages carefully and found sketches of flowers, trees on a hillside, and one of the jetties with a small fishing boat moored to it. The drawings were beautiful, with attention given to finer detail.

Scribed in ink between the pictures, written messages flowed across the pages. Tomas imagined someone sitting at a writing table with quill and ink, dedicating their time to perfecting this artwork of words. He had never seen such exquisite writing, not even from the calligraphers that made the shop signs in Oldcastle.

"Do you recognise the words?" Tarkin asked, referring to the language inside the book.

"It is the same as we use," Tomas replied.

"Find the picture of the tree line with a figure of a man standing among the trees. It's about three quarters into the book."

Tomas carefully closed the book and reopened it at roughly where the captain said. He opened it at pages with writing. Carefully, he turned the leaves of parchment until he came upon the sketch.

They drew the trees tall and dark. Between them were thick sections of black ink, shadows between the trunks. There, right in the centre of the page, was a tiny figure. The outline appeared to be a man.

"The next page," Tarkin informed him. "The entry starts on the next page."

All eyes fell upon Tomas as they waited for him to turn the page. They looked to him longingly, with their curiosity eating at them. Watching. Waiting. Willing him to read the contents of the book to them.

"Read it," Tarkin implored the other.

Tomas glanced around the room to see all faces directed towards him. He swallowed hard and turned back to the pages in his hands.

"I saw him again last night," he began. "He was in the woods outside my window, just staring at me. I was so frightened that I found it hard to breathe.

"I closed the drapes and called Colin. By the time Colin made it outside, the man was gone.

"I know he will return. He always does."

Tomas took his eyes from the page and looked at Emily. Her eyes were wide and her posture rigid.

"Read on," the captain instructed. "Please."

"I don't know if I should," Tomas replied.

"Please," Tarkin begged.

Tomas turned back to the book and breathed a deep sigh.

This morning we were told that all five children went missing from the Khomfer's house. I know this man took them. He must have.

Colin told the Sheriff of what I saw. When he asked if my husband had seen the man also, he told them that only I had.

They accused me of seeing things and of letting my petty fears get the better of me.

They searched the woods all day and could find no trace of the children.

I know he took them.

He was there again last night.

This time, he was nearer to the stable. I wasn't certain if it was the stable or the houses close to it that had his attention.

That was until we discovered the Khomfers had vanished.

I told the Sheriff myself of what I had seen.

He took my words a little more seriously and set a watch for tonight.

The search found nothing again.

Surely there would be traces of struggle.

The house was neat and tidy. It is as if the Khomfers just left during the darkness of night.

I didn't see him last night, to my relief. Hoping that perhaps he has moved on and will leave us alone. Then we heard the news when we gathered near the stable.

The Sheriff is missing.

Godfrey, the butcher's son, found a word etched in a tree near the edge of the woods.

WITCH.

Colin offered to stand watch tonight. The other men volunteered to stay with him.

We are all afraid.

I've offered for all the women and children to stay under our roof together.

I'm not sure if that makes us safer, but it might make us feel a little more secure.

He's back.

There are others.

Many others.

The children are crying.

Our words do not comfort them. Perhaps they sense the fear in our voices.

I don't know what else to do except write this down before I hide this journal.

Colin and the other men have gone out to confront them.

I'm so afraid.

Tomas looked at the writing of the last entry. Rushed and messy, unlike the others. He turned the page to see if there was more, knowing there wouldn't be.

The remaining pages were blank.

Silence filled the room so thickly that it almost deafened him. All were staring at him and almost jumped in fright as he snapped the book shut.

"What do you think?" Tarkin asked.

"There are more questions than answers here," Tomas replied. "She mentions a man in the woods. The word *WITCH* engraved on a tree, indicates that one individual may be responsible. Then there are many of them. Either she was confused and letting her fears get the better of her, or there is more happening out here than we bargained for."

"I'm leaning towards the latter," the captain admitted.

"This is the first time in a long time that I feel the need for a strong ale," David quipped.

***

Tarkin had informed Tomas and Emily that they had made a room up for them at the back of the house. He and the Erilian women would occupy a room towards the front. The other men of Woodmyst had taken a cottage closer to the stable and had left Tomas and the captain alone in the sitting room after the women retired for the night.

Tomas helped the captain tidy the kitchen and plates as best they could before bidding each other good rest and retiring to their rooms.

The door opened with a soft creak as Tomas entered the bedroom. A lantern burned on a dresser by the door, illuminating the room with a soft orange glow.

Emily was in the bed, awake and waiting for him.

He closed the door gently behind him. "Trouble sleeping?"

She peeled the covers away, revealing herself to him.

"I heard what they said, Tomas." She lowered her voice. "In the stable. I know you want me. Sleeping next to you has shown me that much at least."

He soaked in the vision of beauty before him. His loins burned with desire. Every urge inside him wanted to take her in his arms.

"I want you, Tomas," she admitted.

He undid his shirt, fumbling with the toggles in his haste.

She rose to her feet and came to him, kissing him gently as she removed the shirt from him. He did not know how she did it so quickly, and he didn't care.

She crouched and unbuckled his boots and belt.

With his clothing removed, there was only one more thing to do.

With a quick breath, he blew the lantern out and climbed into bed.

He kissed her on her mouth and neck, moving his lips to her breasts. She moved her thighs around him, pulling him into her with her legs.

There, as he kissed her lips again, she received him.

***

Snow fell gently upon the ground as the dark clouds above moved out towards the sea. A chill wind blew down the contours of the land from the mountain peaks towards the shoreline.

Eyes watched the darkened village from the woods.

Fourteen

After a hearty breakfast of leftover pork on toast, the troop saddled their steeds and set off once again. The snow was thicker upon their path because of the clouds that had passed overhead during the night.

The air felt colder and their breath appeared thicker as they exhaled into the cold surrounding them. Most of the horses plodded on with their heads a little lower, unhappy about leaving the warmth of the stable.

Simon, using his skills as an observer, noticed that two of the troop members held their heads a little higher than usual. Strange looks exchanged between the two culminated in embarrassed smiles and giggles. It was like watching two children trying rather unsuccessfully to keep a secret.

He shook his head before pulling alongside Tomas.

"Everyone knows," he said.

"What?" Tomas turned his face to the other.

"About last night," Simon clarified, shooting a glance over towards Emily. "Everyone knows."

"How?" Tomas lowered his voice to a hoarse rasp. "We weren't being too loud?"

"Compared to the captain and his Erilian women?" Simon smiled. "No. The looks you are sharing with her now have told everyone. It's no secret. At least not one worth keeping, my friend. Embrace it. I don't think there would be a living soul that knows you that wouldn't give you their blessing."

"Thank you, Simon."

"Does this mean she's your wife?" he queried. "According to our traditions?"

"I'm not sure," Tomas replied. "Depends upon her traditions, I suppose."

The beefy man slapped his large hand on Tomas' back, almost sending him flying from the mare. With a hearty chuckle, he turned his horse to join with Oliver, who was riding nearby.

Several crows circled above them, calling loudly as they disappeared and reappeared behind a rise in the ground ahead of the riders. A thick patch of trees stood together, bunched tightly on top of the ridge.

Something hidden from view had the attention of the birds. As the travellers ventured closer towards the top of the crest, the din of the fowls grew unbearable.

The riders carefully navigated through the thick cluster of trees. Twisting this way and that, they attempted not to catch any of their cargo on protruding branches as well as not to hit their heads on the lower limbs.

Emily lowered herself and hugged the neck of her mare, allowing it to do most of the steering for her. The horse instinctively fell in line with Tomas' steed as they moved around the countless obstacles blocking their path.

All the while, the calls of the birds grew louder and louder, filling the air so thickly that the sound almost penetrated their ears and chests.

"By the gods," David called out loudly. "What in blazes is going on over there?"

Tomas turned to see Emily still embracing her steed's neck as they pressed on. He returned his eyes to the path ahead and could see the trees thinning out before him. Several crows gathered on the ground while others zipped through the air excitedly.

The birds hopped out of the way as the horses approached, allowing the travellers to pass by. Oliver noticed blood dripping from the beaks of those gathered on the forest floor. He surmised these had just enjoyed a feast.

A lump formed in his throat as he rode into a large patch of open ground.

He pulled his horse to a complete stop as his gaze fell upon a large tree in the centre of the clearing.

Its gnarled limbs twisted awkwardly in all directions like broken fingers on bony hands.

But that wasn't what caused him to stare in wide-eyed horror.

The bowed limbs dragged down towards the ground by the weight of macabre adorning.

He felt his stomach churn as he stared at the blood-soaked snow beneath the tree. Deep puddles rippled and sloshed as the crows bathed in the thick crimson pools.

Streams of red had flowed down the trunk, now slowed to a trickle.

The blood trail expanded along each branch where ropes were tightly bound.

Each cord was fixed to the feet of over thirty poor souls, skinned and gutted. Their entrails dangled from the open wounds and dragged across the ground far below.

Oliver's eyes fell upon one particular figure, small like a child. It swayed and rocked unnaturally as several birds clambered through the torso's cavity, picking at the flesh inside.

The pork, toast and tea he had for breakfast suddenly wanted to be free. Leaning to the side, away from his horse, he let his stomach's contents escape.

The silence from the other riders was almost as deafening as the crows' squabbling. Noticing that they weren't moving, Emily raised her head to look about her.

"What's happening?" she asked as her eyes fell upon the sight before them.

"No, don't look," Tomas said quickly.

He was too late.

Her scream pierced the air, frightening the crows away from their banquet and into the sky.

***

Tomas felt empty as he watched several of Tarkin's men climb the tree to cut the bindings before carefully lowering the bodies. Other men risked being stained with blood by standing beneath the carcasses, taking them into their arms in order to lay them in rows upon the ground.

"We can't bury them," Tarkin said from atop of his horse. "We don't have time and the ground is too hard."

"We just leave them?" Emily asked sadly.

"What choice do we have?" he questioned. "The men with your kinfolk are sailing further away the longer we tarry. We can't help these people, but we can try to help those you know who may still be alive."

She lowered her head, tears welling in her eyes as she looked upon the skinned bodies of men, women, children and babies lying in the snow.

"I'm sorry, young Emily," the captain breathed. "But we must be going."

He steered his steed away as his men mounted their chargers.

"He's right," Tomas told her. "It's not ideal and I too would prefer to give these people a better farewell than this. But he's right."

"I know," she conceded. "It doesn't make me feel any better."

He reached across to her and rubbed her neck.

"Come on," he whispered. "Let's go."

She nodded and drove her horse towards the gathering riders on the northern edge of the clearing. The Erilian women congregated in a smaller group, waiting for her. Karlena eyed Tomas quizzically, concerned for the girl. Tomas nodded to her as he remained behind, waiting for his men to muster around him.

"Is she all right?" Simon asked.

"She's upset," Tomas replied, his eyes still fixed upon her as Karlena silently greeted her. The female warriors surrounded her with their steeds before moving northward after Captain Tarkin and the crew of the *Adelandria*.

"Understandably," Oliver stated. "I think we're all a little upset after seeing this."

"I don't think we have seen the worst of it yet," David added.

Tomas moved his mare forward, keeping his distance from the group ahead of them so that he and his men could talk.

"How can you get worse than this?" Ivo questioned. "An entire village slaughtered."

"We've seen this before," Simon told him. "Remember. Our entire village was slaughtered too."

"This is a little different," David put in. "No infants were killed by the Night Demons. This is far more sinister."

"I agree," Oliver nodded. "This has a feeling of dread, unlike anything I've felt before."

"This is dark magic," Tomas told them. The others looked at him for more. He drove onwards, entering the woods again and continuing to keep his distance from the larger gathering. "We need to be cautious. Look out for one another. Keep each other safe. Don't let anyone get inside your head. We are dealing with a witch."

***

The sound of crows cawing grew fainter behind them as they pressed on. The men of Woodmyst closed the gap between themselves of the Tarkin's men, eventually weaving their way in and amongst the group.

Tomas re-joined the captain at the lead of the troop, giving Emily a quick look that asked her if she was all right.

She nodded.

"Do you not trust me, Master Warde?" Tarkin asked as Tomas pulled alongside.

"Sorry?" He lifted his brow and turned his face to the captain.

"Your men seemed to be in a deep conversation with you," Tarkin replied. "I'm wondering, is it because you don't trust me?"

"I don't really know you," Tomas admitted. "I'm learning to trust you, Captain. You must understand, my people have been through a lot. Trust is something we usually reserve for those who live in our village. But if you must know, I told my men to be cautious and to watch out for each other. I sincerely believe we are in danger."

"I understand." Tarkin nodded. "You're simply looking out for your people as I would mine. A lack of trust among a band of men like ours, however, would give a great foothold to what we may face out there. Particularly a witch."

Tomas cocked his ear. He and Tarkin were more in sync concerning their predicament than he had first thought.

"You know about witches, then?"

"I've had dealings with one or two," the captain admitted.

Tomas looked to the other for more information. The captain quietly entertained a memory before engaging in conversation again.

"Well?" Tomas asked impatiently.

"I've sailed from one side of this land to the other and beyond," he began. "In the far west, during the last days of the Realm War, I was a deckhand on a small frigate. We were engaged in battle and quickly became cannon fodder. The ship didn't sink right away, but washed up on the rocky coast near Blackshore. Only three of us survived.

"A young woman, perhaps fifteen or sixteen, found us and dragged us somehow to her house. She cared for us and nursed us back to a healthy state.

"When she left us alone, at least for a few hours every day, we would squabble and argue about her. Who was going to have her? Who was the better man for her? Stupid things young men got into fights over and old men have started wars for.

"We turned on one another so fiercely that one of the others found a knife and gutted the other right in front of me. He turned on me next and dug the blade into my chest, just deep enough to leave a scar.

"I fought back, gained control of the blade and buried it in his neck. I had never seen so much blood before that day.

"Unbelievable how three men who knew each other so well could turn on one another so violently over a woman." He shook his head as he remembered the faces of his crewmen. "I turned away from the sight in disgust and threw up all over the floor of the house.

"And there she was. Standing by the fireplace, watching with a wide grin on her face and hungry eyes staring at the blood.

"We thought she had gone. We heard the door open and close. But the more I think about it; I don't think she ever left.

"I tried to get up, but she jumped on top of me and held me down, saying I was the one and that she needed my seed. She was strong, and I struggled to get free.

"I got the knife back into my hands, to this day I still don't know how, and I plunged it into her chest." He frowned as he spoke. "By the gods, she was beautiful. Such a shame."

Tomas stared at Tarkin for a long time as the horses plodded on and as the captain remained in deep thought.

"I've had an encounter with another, not long after I found the girls," Tarkin said. "They warned me of her straight away.

"The witch was an exquisite creature. She used seduction like you wield that sword of yours. We were transporting food and supplies from Dweagan to an island in the southern seas.

"When we arrived, several of the women ran out to the wharf to meet us. We thought for a moment that we were kings, if you know what I mean. Then they told us that a witch had taken up roost and taken all the men from them.

"She had eaten them, Tomas," Tarkin hissed. "Can you believe that? Someone eating another person?"

Tomas' mind flashed back to the stories that Richard had told him about the elder's experience during the Realm War. He recalled the word *cannibals* used to describe the old council members of Woodmyst, including his own father.

Then came the image of the men that he once looked up to, milling about some campfire as they ripped into the flesh of a small tribe of swamp dwellers. Although the victims were not human, Tomas couldn't help but feel appalled by the thought that his own father could have stooped so low.

That one act had brought about the destruction of the entire township of Woodmyst by dragon fire and blades of the Night Demons.

"I know there are savages out there who crave human flesh," Tarkin admitted. "Still, the idea ties knots in my stomach.

"We agreed to relieve the island of their pest and set off to slay the beast. But she was no beast, Tomas. She had dark skin, long hair and was so beautiful.

"I don't know how she did it..." The captain shook his head. "But every man dropped his weapon on the ground when she stepped out of her cabin. We were..."

He searched for the word, looking here and there as if for a sign on a tree that could help him.

"Bewitched," Tomas offered.

"Bewitched." Tarkin nodded. "If it wasn't for Sharek, who smacked me with a long stick over the head, we would have become her next meal.

"The other men with me remained in a trance," Tarkin said. "That little girl saved my life."

Tomas glanced over to the Erilian woman. She was tall, well built and anything but a little girl now.

"You killed the witch, then?" Tomas asked.

"No," Tarkin replied. "The girls did. They literally ripped her apart with their bare hands before she realised what they were doing to her."

Both men looked across at the group of women riding together in the middle of the troop.

"Something in those girls gives them an ability to see what lies within others. They seem to know whom to trust," the captain said. "They trust you, Tomas. They trust your men and they trust the girl. And because they do, so do I."

***

Thunderous explosions sounded as waves crashed upon the black rocks far below them. The riders paused at the edge of a steep cliff that overlooked a small inlet with steep edges on all sides. The thin opening to the sea funnelled the tide towards them, concentrating the breakers into one place below.

The whitecaps broke apart so intensely so that the spray shot straight up the cliff face, covering the horses and their riders in a fine mist. The smell of salt in the air wasn't as pleasant an experience for the men of Woodmyst as for the crew of the *Adelandria*.

Tarkin held a spyglass to his eye and directed his attention to a small section of the horizon.

"I can see them," he informed the others. "They have their sails up and are moving slowly. It looks like the current is not in their favour. Some icebergs are heading south, and rather rapidly." He retracted the spyglass into a small cylinder and placed the object into a pocket on the inside of his coat. "We should be able to overtake them if the current continues as it is. And at this time of the year, it will."

The riders turned northward once again.

Large portions of land opened up as the snow-blanketed pines thinned out on the flat ground by the sea. With the flat, liquid horizon on their right and the mountains to their left, they scanned the area ahead more easily now that the thick forest lay to the west of them.

David couldn't help peering in that direction to watch the tree line. The hairs on the back of his neck stood on end, making him feel uneasy as they travelled. It was as if his essence knew someone was watching them.

Parts of the ground gave way to thin causeways where water would usually run before falling over the cliff's edge. For now, snow thickly covered the earth, giving the impression of a smooth curving surface like the rolling meadows of Woodmyst, covered in white instead of green grass and wildflowers. Occasionally, the horses' legs would fall up to the knees in deeper patches of snow, reminding the riders that it hid the true ground from view and that they would need to take care as they steered their beasts.

Before long, they had entered a thick patch of trees through which they had to navigate carefully. Eventually, the wooded area thinned out again to reveal more open land.

And so, they repeated this pattern of entering the forest and exiting to clear ground several times during the day. All the while, the troop kept the sea either within sight or hearing distance.

David dreaded the moments when they entered the tree lines the most. His sense of dread had only grown stronger as the riders pressed onwards. They had stopped momentarily in one such coppice to rest, eat and relieve themselves, but David remained on edge the entire time.

"What are you looking at?" one of Tarkin's men asked him.

He hadn't realised he was staring into the woods, standing to the western edge of the gathered riders who were sitting on the ground at the base of the pine trees. They were talking and laughing as he quietly stared.

"Something is out there," he answered, his hand upon the hilt of his sword.

"Where?" asked the other, placing his hand on his sheath.

"I don't know," David replied. "I just know there is something out there."

The other looked at him, puzzled. "I think you need to eat something," he said before returning to the group.

David kept his eyes to the west and continued to do so when they resumed their journey.

Sometime later, as the sun arched its way towards the mountains, the ground opened up again, exposing the flat horizon to the left and a large sheet of snow as they drew their steeds out of the woods. It was an enormous expanse of land, and it would take them some time to traverse it.

Tomas calculated that by the time they reached the woods on the far side of the area, the sun would set behind the mountain peaks.

"I think we should set up camp in the woods once we reach them," he suggested to Tarkin.

"Agreed," the captain replied. "The trees will give us some protection from the weather."

Suddenly, David was off and running. His horse kicked up snow in all directions as he raced towards the tree line to the west of them.

"Where are you going?" called Oliver, who set off after him.

"I see you, you bastard," David called.

"Here we go," Tomas grunted as he steered his mare after the two men.

Simon and Ivo were on his tail, heading after their friend to find out what the excitement was all about.

The troop all looked to their captain, wanting to go after the others.

"May as well join them," Tarkin called out.

With that, they hastily directed all the remaining horses towards the forest.

David closed the gap rapidly, raising his sword above his head as his steed galloped forward. A vast cloud of snow erupted around the charging horses racing after him.

At the edge of the woods, David leapt from his charger and bolted into the trees, bringing his blade down upon something out of Oliver's view.

"What is it?" he called after his friend.

They heard a sword chopping into wood and snapping twigs over David's angry grunts.

Oliver dropped to the ground, releasing his horse as he ran into the tree line. There, he found David hacking into something resembling a man's body.

Straw and splinters of wood flew in all directions as David kept swinging his blade down upon the figure over and over again.

Tomas bolted to Oliver's side, sword in hand, bringing himself to a sudden stop as his eyes fell upon the fallen shape.

The torn grin silently laughed with its raggedy lips.

The hollow eyes stared back.

David continued to slash and hack as Oliver shook his head.

Tomas dangled his blade by his side as Ivo and Simon joined them.

"Scarecrow," he said.

"Not just one," Simon told him.

He lifted his eyes and peered deeper into the woods about him.

Standing between several of the trees, here and there, were twelve other figures dressed in long coats, wide-brimmed hats, and thin arms stretched out to their sides.

Tarkin's heavy footfalls crunched through the snow as he sidled up to the others. His eyes flickered from the mess of straw and wood upon the ground to the other lifeless figures watching from the woods.

"By the gods."

Fifteen

The flames reached high as black smoke billowed across the sky, blown by the winds sweeping down the mountain's sides, across the plains and out to sea. The troop gathered around the fire, fuelled by straw entrails, wooden bones and hessian skins.

Standing on the open ground, where they had piled the scarecrows before setting them ablaze, David gave thought to his irrational behaviour. He believed he was bewitched.

"I swear it moved," he said. He had been saying this over and over, convinced that the straw man had been taunting him from behind the tree line. "What is wrong with me?"

"Perhaps you saw it move," Tarkin offered from the other side of the fire.

Tomas recalled the story that the captain had shared with him about how a witch tricked him into seeing what she wanted him to see. Perhaps such magic had been used to lure David away from their task.

"But it was straw and timber," David argued. "I think I'm losing my mind, Tomas."

"You're not losing your mind," Tomas replied. "You're meant to believe that you are. She is trying to make you question who you are. Make you doubt yourself."

"What do I do?" the bald giant asked.

"Get a hold of yourself, lad," Jeremy, the scarred crewmember answered. "Press on and don't give that bitch an inch."

David nodded.

"We should try to get to a suitable area to set up camp," Simon put in as he watched the sun slide behind the mountain range. "We have little light left."

"The plan was to set up camp in that coppice closer to the shore," Tarkin stated. "Do we stick with that plan or set up camp here somewhere?"

"I don't want to be near these things," Emily objected.

"Nor do I." Karlena shook her head as she peered into the flames.

"I think we should move," Tomas suggested.

"Agreed." The captain placed his arm around the young Erilian woman and steered her away towards the waiting horses.

The team mounted their steeds and rode to the far side of the clearing, leaving the scarecrows to burn upon the snow behind them. Within moments, the riders reached their designated campsite and started unloading the horses.

Captain Tarkin rode his steed to the cliff's edge so he could scan the horizon with his spyglass as his men set up camp. First, he turned the lens towards the north and slowly panned southwards. He found the marauders' ship far out to sea, almost straight out in front of him, directly to the east.

The vessel was having more difficulty navigating to its destination than he originally thought. At least there was something working in their favour.

He rode back to where he had left his men to find the camp set up and food being prepared over a warm, welcoming hearth. Stumps and logs stood around about the fire for the troop to sit upon.

They tied the horses together in a makeshift pen a little closer to the light than at their previous encampment. There were none more grateful for this than the men of Woodmyst who doted over their horses, patting them and speaking to them as though they were family. Even now, as the captain tied his horse next to theirs, Tomas and the others were spending time with their steeds while the crewmen of the *Adelandria* sat about the fire, ignoring their animals altogether.

His eyes moved to an area where his tent was. Rhydra and Karlena were both teaching Emily more techniques with a blade.

It was becoming a nightly routine. The women would train together before the night's meal. He watched them practise for a moment, noticing that the young apprentice was handling the thin sword more naturally. Her strength was developing, but her movements didn't seem fluid. She swung the blade too far and almost overstepped when trying to counterbalance the sword's weight.

She was improving, though.

He moved towards the fire, where the smell of baking bread and grilled meat enticed his appetite. Jeremy sat on the edge of a log that was else wise unoccupied. Tarkin took position next to him.

"I've taken the liberty of organising a night watch, Captain," he informed his commander.

"Good job," Tarkin replied. "Am I on the list?"

"Of course not." The scarred man smiled.

"Make more rosters for the next few nights," the captain instructed. "Make sure every man takes his turn. Including me."

"What of the Woodmyst men?" Jeremy glanced over his shoulder towards Tomas and the others still spoiling their horses.

"Ask them if they would like to contribute," he answered, removing his leather gloves and stretching his bare hands towards the warm flames. "I'm sure they will, but if not, don't press them."

"Aye, Captain." Jeremy nodded.

Tarkin stared intently into the flames.

"Something wrong, Captain?" the scarred man queried, noticing an odd expression on the other's face.

"I don't know," Tarkin answered. "I've had a strange feeling during this journey, growing inside. Something familiar but..." He looked over to each of the men beside him. "I don't know what it is."

***

Emily clung to Tomas a little tighter than usual as they lay in their tent. He kept his arms wrapped around her as they slept uneasily, occasionally waking up at the sound of rustling wind striking the side of the canvas structure or the coughs of a man on night watch. The constant drifting in and out of slumber caused Tomas to think it would have been better if he had volunteered to simply stay awake and stand with the watchers.

His eyes flung open, and he sat upright.

Something had alarmed him. He looked down at Emily's face. The light of the flickering fire penetrated the tent's wall and softly illuminated her skin.

She stirred, but didn't wake.

"Shh," he heard one man guarding the camp hiss. "It came from there."

Trouble!

Quickly and quietly, Tomas dressed and grabbed his sword before leaving the tent. The sound of crunching snow under his boots seemed louder in the darkness than it did in the light of day.

THUD! CRACK! CRACK!

Not again.

"Did you hear it that time?" the guard asked another standing next to him.

"I heard it," Tomas whispered as he moved around his tent towards them. They both turned instinctively to see who approached them.

"Something is out there," the guard told him.

"I know," he replied. "Probably the same people who put those scarecrows in the woods."

"What do we do?" the other guard asked.

"Nothing yet," Tomas instructed. "The nose is a ruse. Keep looking around to where the noise is not coming from. I'll wake my men."

"Should we get the captain?"

"Let the captain rest," Tomas replied. "We haven't actually seen anyone yet.

THUD! THUD!

The sound seemed distant, echoing through the trees towards them.

Oliver was already striding through the camp towards Tomas.

"They're awake," he informed the other as they met at the fire. "We heard it."

"I need you to watch the western edge of the camp." Tomas lowered his voice to almost a breath. "I think they're across the clearing near to where we set those things on fire."

"That's a long way off." Oliver looked out to the open ground, back towards where they had found the straw men. "They mustn't care if we know they are there or not."

"I think they're trying to make us turn back," David muttered as he joined the others at the hearth.

"Bit of a silly tactic when they are almost literally behind us," Ivo put in. "Besides, why would they kill an entire village just to dissuade us?"

"That village was a territorial concern," Simon stated as he moved past the others and towards the western edge of the encampment. "I think they want the lands to the south. I also think the tree was a warning to those from around here of what is coming."

"Better get out or we will do this to you," Ivo quipped.

"Something like that," Simon replied.

"So," said Tomas as he moved to Simon's side, "what do you make of this?"

"This is their attempt to discourage us." Simon unsheathed his sword. It resonated in a soft chime as it slid from its cover and into the night air. "They tried before and now they're trying again."

CRACK! THUD! CRACK! CRACK!

"They are over there," David pointed. "Watch!"

The men stared intently towards the area that they had been burning scarecrows only hours earlier.

A distant fire, like a small pinprick of light on the far side of the clearing, flickered.

"They have set up camp," Ivo announced. "They are not afraid of us."

"More likely that they are," Oliver suggested. "I think this is a false sense of bravery."

"Keep watch to the east, west and north," Tomas instructed them. "I don't believe they would consider crossing the plain. They will use the cover of the trees."

"So we're not thinking it's a witch then?" David asked.

"There is a witch," Tomas answered. "Either she is out there alone or she has manipulated others to do her bidding."

THUD! CRACK! CRACK! THUD! CRACK!

***

The men kept vigil during the night, watching their flanks with intensity. No one was going to get in or out of the camp without them knowing.

Tomas started another small fire by the edge of the wood and took up position there so he could watch the small light across the plain. He boiled a pot of water on the flames and made tea for the watchmen and himself.

As the night drew on, and the noises continued from far across the way, he wished he had Captain Tarkin's spyglass just to see if he could discover the unseen foe that was making the loud clatter. He realised it was not the work of the men made of straw and wood.

It was then that he decided he and his men needed to keep watch upon the things in the west while Tarkin continued to watch the ship to the east. With danger on all sides of them, the sense of dread had never felt so overwhelming as it did for him at this moment.

Particularly now a woman had come into his life.

A woman he had strong feelings for.

He struggled with the thoughts and affection he had for her. Knowing her for only a few days, he felt a bond with her unlike that he had with any other person. He cared for her earnestly, beyond the love he had for Richard, who was like a father, or Linet, his own sister.

This was different.

This was new.

He had felt nothing like this before.

She was constantly there, in his mind.

In his heart.

He dreamt about her even while he was awake.

Consuming his thoughts and essence of being.

Was this normal?

Was this love?

Finding it hard to fathom, Tomas could only comprehend that, even in the dread of the winter chill and with impending threats on all sides of them, she made him feel warm and complete inside.

He wanted to be near her, beside her, with her.

She was intoxicating.

Purple clouds formed in the darkness above as the dawn approached.

Tomas kept his eyes upon the tiny light far across the plain as he sipped upon his tea. He had lost count of how many cups he had drunk and how many times he had relieved himself.

The trees, ground and sky became more discernible, enabling him and the other watchers to peer about their environment more clearly.

The firelight far away went out.

The noises stopped.

Tomas kept his eyes trained on the area for a while longer.

Had they gone?

Were they manoeuvring to another location, preparing to attack?

Were they simply watching?

One watchman approached him.

"The noise has stopped," he said.

"Keep watching," Tomas ordered. "Stay at your post until the captain dismisses you."

The man quickly turned away.

Tomas continued to watch the horizon.

The light continued to grow, and his view became clearer. Scanning the plain and the tree line on the far side of the clearing, he saw nothing.

No movement.

No enemy.

No scarecrows.

No witch.

The tactic may have been to *dissuade* them, as David and Simon stated during the night, but Tomas was thinking the strategy might have other goals, now successfully dispensed.

He was now tired and had an entire day of travelling ahead.

He had been so concerned with an attack that he had involved his own men, fatiguing them as well.

This was more of a battle involving wits.

In a strange way, the victor of this attack was the witch.

Sixteen

The sun climbed above the horizon as the troop set out on their journey again. The men recalled their adventure from the night before, informing the others of the excitement. Many expressed their disbelief at how they could have slept through it.

Others, like Emily, expressed disappointment the men did not wake them up to be a part of the experience. Tomas gave her a token apology. He wasn't sorry for letting her sleep at all. In fact, he wished he had ignored the sounds and remained in bed with her instead.

The effects of lack of sleep were manifesting.

His eyes were droopy, and his head felt funny. Now and then, he drifted off into a quick slumber. His mare brought him back to reality every time she shifted her pace as she plodded along.

They had passed through another large clearing, making a quick pause so Captain Tarkin could scan the horizon to the east. Icebergs drifting across the sea towards the south informed the riders that the current was still helping them. The ship, however, had made some distance during the night and now appeared as a small blob far to the north.

"We can catch them," Tarkin assured the gathering. "We may need to ride a little harder than usual."

With that, they increased their pace as they moved across the plains, slowing only when they needed to navigate through the thick trees of small patches of woods and overgrown thickets.

At midday, Tomas became concerned for the steeds, as they had not rested. The riders had been working their beasts hard all morning, and it was time for some reprieve, even if it was only to be brief.

"We need to stop," he told the captain.

"We're catching them," Tarkin objected.

"We won't if our horses fail," Tomas argued.

They slowed to a walk. The animals panted heavily.

With the horses walking, the noise of motion subsided, and the captain appreciated Tomas' words. The animals were tired.

"The next group of trees then?" he asked, eyeing a grove not too far away from them.

"That would do," Tomas agreed.

Upon reaching the shelter of the trees, the riders dismounted and took the opportunity to stretch their legs. The horses munched on snow and gratefully took dried oats from any hands that offered them.

"Thank the gods," Jeremy bellowed. "I think calluses are forming on my arse."

"What do you mean, forming?" one crewman called.

The riders chuckled.

"How do *you* know?" another bellowed to the crewman.

Laughter erupted throughout the group.

Tarkin used his spyglass again. This time, the Erilian women joined him. The ship was still far out to sea and to their north. They must have been gaining on the vessel, as some features of the craft were more visible.

No longer did it appear as a mere blob. He could identify the mainsails could and the shape of the hull had become clearer.

"How far?" Rhydra asked from his side as he folded the spyglass and replaced it in his coat pocket.

"We may still have a few days riding ahead," he replied.

"Are you doubting your choice of not bringing the *Adelandria*?"

"The *Adelandria* is too big," he replied. "Much bigger than that thing out there. The current would slow us down even more."

"Do you think we'll find him this time?" Karlena questioned him from his other side. He placed his arm around her and held her tight.

"Don't worry, little one." He kissed her forehead and looked out to the horizon. "We'll find him."

They returned to the others who had gathered in a circle of sorts, some seated and others standing. Tomas and Emily had found a place a little distance away from the others, locked in an embrace and whispering.

Karlena started towards them, but Tarkin quickly placed his hand upon her shoulder. She turned, furrowing her brow.

"Leave them be," the captain told her. "They're still finding each other."

***

The riders set out after an hour of rest. The horses seemed eager to continue the journey, nodding their heads and snorting excitedly as the troop mounted the beasts.

Forming into one long line, they snaked through the thick growth, leaving a trench in the snow as the horses' hooves kicked at the ground. Once in a while, the riders ducked so low to avoid certain branches that they had to embrace their mounts' necks.

The trees thinned out once again, exposing a great plain that seemed to stretch towards the north for almost as far as the eyes could see. This vast expanse of white; adorned with swirling mists of frost as the wind gushed down from the mountainside towards the sea.

The land was lower here, gently sloping towards the shoreline, meeting the water so fluidly that, if not for the breakers crashing violently on the beach, it would have been hard to see where the land ended and the water began.

Some tall trees on the far side of the open ground poked their tips above the mist with significant gaps between them, giving the impression that the forest was thinning. The steep mountain range had crept towards the water's edge, making Tomas wonder if the two would eventually meet.

"Do the mountains ever touch the sea?" he asked Tarkin as the other riders formed up behind them, preparing to cross the bleak vastness.

"I don't know," he replied. "I've never voyaged this far north before."

Pressing onward, they moved down a slight embankment into the plain, leaving the forest behind them. The wind funnelled down the steep slopes to their left, filtering through the forest sitting at the feet of the rocky giants before tearing along the open ground.

As relentless gusts of air hit the riders, they wrapped scarves tightly around faces and necks and pulled hoods over their heads. The horses shifted their weight, leaning to their left as they moved forward.

White sheets of snow and ice moved rapidly across their view, almost obscuring the path ahead. Tarkin could barely see the ocean to the east as he turned his head in that direction. He didn't dare look towards the west out of fear that the gale might tear his face clean off from his bones.

Tomas kept his eyes fixed ahead of them. He could just make out the forms of blurry shadows in the distance, standing in a row. Knowing that having a stable target would keep him from getting lost, he trained the mare to move in that direction.

"Keep your eyes on each other," he called out over the din of the screaming air.

"I can barely see myself," Oliver replied.

"I can't keep my eyes open," Emily cried.

Tomas pulled up beside her and took her reins from her, tying them to his saddle.

"I'll lead you," he told her. "Keep low to your horse."

She pressed herself against the steed's back and wrapped her arms as far as she could around its neck.

"Link your bindings," Tomas instructed the others. "Make a line as we did in the woods."

Tarkin's men formed up and tied their reins to the saddle of the rider in front of them. The link attached to the saddles of the Erilian women before reaching the captain's steed.

Tarkin gave his reins to Ivo, who handed his to Simon. Simon attached his ride to David's saddle, who bound himself to Oliver.

"Emily," Oliver called over the din. "Take my reins and tie them to your saddle."

She reached over and took the cords in her glove. Hastily, she attached them to the ring in the front of her saddle before lowering herself against her mare's neck.

"Go," she called to Tomas.

With a gentle kick, Tomas moved his mare forward. The bindings tightened between each of the other steeds, bringing them in tow one by one.

The dark shadows ahead in the snowstorm grew larger and larger as they approached. He surmised perhaps they were stumps from fallen trees.

That was until he realised, they were too evenly spaced apart. Someone set the stumps in place.

The howling wind, pushing against him with ferocity, reminded him of a screaming woman. The shapes ahead suddenly appeared as the forms of men.

He shook his head and wiped his eyes. Lack of sleep and the mist played tricks on him.

Pressing onwards, using two of the dark figures as landmarks, he aimed for a gap between them. His intention was to pass between them and look for another beacon of sorts beyond them.

Closing the distance, Tomas now saw flapping material around the figures like cloaks waving violently in the wind. His mind returned to creatures with yellow eyes and curved blades that once scaled the walls of his village.

He needed sleep and was struggling.

Other figures became visible as he moved the troop forward. First, he saw five, then eight. Now his eyes counted thirteen.

Their outstretched arms and broad-brimmed hats caused a knot to form in his stomach. He stared intently as the view became clearer and clearer the closer he drew to them.

He wiped his eyes again and shook his head. Surely this must be a trick of the brain.

Opening his eyes, he met the blank stare of hollow eyes. Hessian faces peered towards him, greeting him with raggedy smiles.

He pulled the mare to a halt.

The wind stopped.

White mist fell to the ground and the screaming air erupted with silence.

The plain became suddenly still and calm.

"What magic is this?" Jeremy grunted.

"By the gods," Simon hissed as his eyes fell upon thirteen straw men standing upon the snow.

Emily stared at the figures, wide-eyed and in shock.

Tomas drew his sword and lopped the head off the nearest scarecrow.

"Take back your reins," he called. "We need to get off the open ground."

With the riders taking charge of their own horses, they moved in haste to reach the other side of the plain. Tomas feared that if the weather could pause so abruptly, then perhaps it could restart just as promptly.

The horses needed little encouragement. They sensed the urgency of the situation and seemed to want to be clear of their predicament as much as their handlers did.

They quickly ascended a slight rise towards some trees before the riders took time to regather. They peered back across the plain to where the thirteen scarecrows stood.

"What is going on?" Simon stared into the open ground.

The straw men were gone.

The riders continued heading northward, still shaken from their experience upon the plain. Some questioned if what they saw was real, or if it may have been a trick on the eyes brought about by the weather. Others argued it had to be real after seeing Tomas remove the head from one of the straw men.

Tarkin invited the men of Woodmyst to accompany him closer to the shore. They stayed upon their steeds as the captain used his spyglass to find the marauders' ship again.

The sky was a magnificent blue, and the view was crystal clear. It was as if the snowstorm had not even occurred.

Finding the vessel was easy. Tarkin aimed his lens directly to the east and had them in view almost immediately.

"We've made ground," he announced. "Either that, or the current is forcing them backwards."

"Is that even possible?" Emily asked, seated upon her mare by Tomas' side.

"Oh yes," the captain replied. "I've been caught in such currents many times. The trick is to sail across the flow in order to get out of it. These fools look as if they want to be in that thing forever."

"I guess that's one thing helping us, then." David smiled.

"Why did you come with us?" Tomas asked suddenly.

All eyes fell upon him, silent, puzzled.

"Excuse me?" Tarkin furrowed his brow. "I thought I told you—"

"It's not that I'm ungrateful," he interjected. "I am thankful for your help. And I know you told me you're seeking this *Sovereign* for what he has done to the Erilian women and many of your crew members. But what did he do to you?"

Tarkin eyed the other cautiously. His gaze moved to each of the faces gathered about.

They were all strangers.

His men had continued to ride on and were now out of earshot.

Could he truly trust these people?

Could he call them friends?

"He killed my wife and son," the captain blurted. "And they took my daughter away."

"You know what he looks like?" Simon questioned.

Tarkin nodded, his stare lowered to the ground as tears streaked down his cheeks. The others waited and watched uncomfortably as the captain raised his eyes to meet their looks.

"They broke into my house one night," he began. "Jenya, my wife, heard the noise and woke me. I took my sword and fought as best as I could. I got him, just before his men overwhelmed me and bound me to the rafters. One of them… perhaps him… I can't be sure… My head was spinning from the blows they gave me, but one of them stabbed me with a spike of some sort here," he pointed to his left side, just above his hip.

"So, I was bleeding and hanging by my arms from the rafters while they took turns raping my wife in front of me. They gutted Takmel, my boy, right next to her like he was some fish. Then they brought out my little princess, Sumaiyya."

He looked up at the sky, sobbing.

"Oh, how could they?" he bawled. "She was only nine."

The men didn't need to be told.

Tomas felt a knot tighten in his gut and a lump form in his throat.

"They are not men," Tarkin blubbered. "They are animals and they deserve to die."

He pointed to his forehead above his left eye and ran the finger across his face to the right corner of his mouth.

"I gave him a mark from here to here. So, yes, I know what this man looks like. He is their leader. He is their Sovereign." He spat the word out as if it tasted like filth on his tongue. "And I will be the one to end his life. So now you know why I am here."

Emily's breathing became rapid. Not only was she upset by the captain's story, but also a terrible memory of her own flashed into her mind.

"I've seen this man," she told them.

"Where?" Tarkin wiped his face on his sleeve.

"In my village," Emily told them. She locked eyes with Tomas. "He was the one who took us. He killed my mother."

"Then he is on that ship." The captain turned his face back towards the ocean.

"We need to get ahead of them," Oliver added. "We could surprise them at whatever wharf they moor to and attack as they unload."

"As long as the wharf isn't being manned by his people," Simon put in.

"Too much talk," David snapped as he turned his dapple-grey beast towards the other riders in the distance. "Not enough riding."

The others followed, leaving Tomas, Emily and the captain to follow.

"Thank you," Tomas said to Tarkin.

"No," the other replied. "Thank you, Tomas. I've been holding on to that for far too long."

They rode back to the mass of riders heading north, joining the group near the head of the pack. The captain regained his composure before he was in sight of his men. He gave the Erilian women a wry smile as they eyed him suspiciously, silently asking him, *What happened?*

He nodded his reply. *Everything is fine.*

Jeremy came trotting up alongside him in urgency.

"Captain," he called. "I have some bad news."

"Really?" Tarkin replied. Tomas glanced over to the scarred man, eager to know what the bad news was. Jeremy looked over at him cautiously.

"Perhaps privately, Captain," Jeremy suggested.

"I trust this man, Jeremy," the captain remarked. "The girls trust him. It's about time you did as well."

"Aye, Captain," the other submitted. "I've conducted a count of men. Something in my guts just hasn't been sitting right since the storm on the plain."

"Perhaps you need to find a tree to lower your trousers behind," Karlena chortled. The other women giggled.

"Get on with it," Tarkin said to Jeremy as he silently rebuked the Erilian women with a quick look.

"If I counted correctly before leaving Oakbeach, we had twenty men from the *Adelandria* with us. Twenty-seven all up, not counting our new friends," Jeremy gestured to Tomas and the other men of Woodmyst.

"That sounds correct," the captain acknowledged.

"Well," Jeremy continued. "There are only eighteen men."

"What do you mean?"

"I think we lost two in the snowstorm," he replied.

"Recount," Tarkin ordered. "Make sure."

"I did. I've counted five times. It keeps coming up the same," Jeremy answered. "Two are gone."

Seventeen

Silence fell upon the troop as they made camp for the night.

With heavy hearts, the riders sat by the campfire in a small clearing, with a steep black wall of rock to one side and a sparsely spaced pine forest around them as they considered what had happened to the two missing men. The longest face belonged to the man tethered to them during the snowstorm.

How he could not have noticed their absence was a concept with which he still wrestled. He remembered tying the knot and holding onto the rope as they moved through the plain. His memory, as he told Jeremy, was hazy.

"I remember the scarecrows," he said, sobbing as he tried to recall the event. "I remember when we looked back to the plain and saw that the scarecrows had vanished. I don't know what happened."

"It's a drastic loss," Jeremy told him. "But I think we need to be thankful that you are still with us. It could have been worse. Make sure you have something to eat and get some rest."

Jeremy put his hand on the man's shoulder before moving his eyes over the sombre glares each face wore as they all peered into the flames. He wondered what thoughts plagued them. Clearly, it was a sad time for many of the crew members, but what of the men from Woodmyst and the young lady with them?

Emily stared blankly at the flames as they danced upon the charred logs, embracing and separating, twirling and shimmering in bright orange and red garments. Her mind was with her sister. Trapped on the ship they chased, slowly sailing north against the current.

Tarkin's tale of how the marauders' leader had gained his mark across his face had caused her to fret for her sibling. If only she had stayed with her.

Then they would have raped or killed you, you silly girl.

It was no wonder Captain Tarkin had so eagerly volunteered to join the expedition. After he told them of what happened to his family, particularly his daughter, Emily believed he understood her plight more than any other sitting about the fire.

Tomas rubbed her back with his hand as he nursed a cup in the other. He too, was staring into the flames. His thoughts were with the two men who had disappeared in the white onslaught as they crossed the plain.

Where had they gone?

He considered his fortune that none of his friends came to harm during that experience. Secretly, he was thankful his men were near the front of the line with him. His heart pounded faster as he thought about Emily. What would he have done if she had been one of those taken in the snowstorm?

Guilt overwhelmed him. Being thankful for the disappearance of two of the captain's men just didn't seem right suddenly. He imagined how Tarkin must feel. It would be a hard thing to deal with; losing men you cared for.

On top of his concern, gratitude and guilt, he now felt empathy for the captain of the *Adelandria*.

Perhaps he should have kept his mouth shut that night in the tavern.

Perhaps he should have declined Tarkin's offer to help.

Perhaps if he did so, those two men would still be with the other crew members.

Perhaps the tragedy would affect only the men who had come with him from home.

But he was thankful that none of his men had vanished.

He was glad they were still with him, sitting nearby in the warmth and glow of the fire.

He was glad it was Tarkin's men taken and not his own.

And so, it was. On and on in circles, his thoughts swam around like an endless whirlpool.

***

Sitting directly across the hearth from Tomas and Emily, Tarkin allowed his thoughts to fall upon when those men entered his home. He saw his wife brutally assaulted, his son slaughtered and his daughter...

Tears welled in his eyes. He quickly wiped them away upon his sleeve and drank from the cup in his hand, hoping the men didn't notice.

His daughter's face lingered in his mind. He tried to remember her smile, her laugh, the way she ran and skipped when she played. The way her blonde hair fanned out like golden flames when she spun around, trying to dance. Instead, he kept returning to that dark moment, hearing her scream and watching her suffer, unable to help her. He remembered the *Sovereign* lifting her from the ground and carrying her away over his shoulder, like a sack of oats, never to be seen again.

His eyes moved to Emily, who continued staring into the fire, entertaining her own thoughts. He imagined she felt confused and frightened for her younger sister, especially hearing the story of what happened to his precious Sumaiyya.

Oh Sumaiyya!

Tears streaked over his skin. He wasn't quick enough to go unnoticed.

Karlena, sitting beside him, caressed his face with her gentle hands, stealthily wiping the marks away from his cheeks before kissing him softly.

One by one, the men quietly retired to their tents as the night wore on. Tomas hardly noticed the thinning out of the company as he continued to stare into the flames and held Emily in his arms.

She nestled into him, resting her head against his chest as he wrapped his arms tightly around her. After some time, she kissed his cheek and rose to her feet.

"I'm tired," she whispered.

He stood up and put an arm over her shoulders as she wrapped hers around his waist. Tomas peered around the fire and found that, apart from the three men on sentry duty, they were the only ones left. He hadn't noticed his friends or the captain leave. The look on Emily's face told him she had seen the others disperse. She gave a tiny smile.

I was waiting for you.

A lump grew in his throat, ashamed that he had kept her up with him in the cold of the night. He placed his lips against hers and savoured the moment. She moved into him for a time before pulling him away from the hearth and towards their tent.

Side by side, hand in hand, they strolled to their tent, leaving the fire behind them.

THUD!

Eyes suddenly wide open; Tomas stared into the darkness of the tent. Something had caused him to awaken. He trained his ear to listen for movement. For a long time, there was nothing.

A soft hissing sound, the noise of something sliding across the canvas roof of his shelter filled his ears.

HSSSS! THUD!

Snow.

It was building up on the roof of the tent as it fell gently from above. As it layered, it grew heavy and slid to the edge of the covering before falling to the ground beside the shelter.

HSSSS! THUD!

Emily stirred beside him and buried her face in his chest. He tightened his arm around her and stroked her hair. She gave a soft moan, content. Tomas felt the corners of his mouth lifting into a smile.

HSSSS! THUD!

Closing his eyes, he listened for a while longer. The pattern of sounds continued and eventually became soothing.

The voices of the men on guard duty sounded in the distance as they quietly conversed with one another by the fire.

There was nothing to be concerned with.

HSSSS! THUD!

Tonight, he hoped, might be a night of reprieve. After losing two men, they deserved one night of peace.

Slowly and gradually, his head swam and drift like ebbing waves upon the sea. Before long, he was fast asleep.

***

A shrill scream brought him back to reality.

The first light of dawn, faint and limited, slowly filled the tent.

His eyes took their time to adjust as he turned to the source of the noise.

Emily was sitting up beside him, clawing at him and pointing towards the tent flap.

He sat up and held her as he looked towards where she was gesturing.

There, silhouetted by the open entrance to their dwelling, was the form of a man.

As Tomas' vision became clearer, he could see the figure held its arms straight out at its sides. Its long coat waved gently in the icy breeze flowing in through the entry.

Finally, as his eyes adjusted to the light and his surroundings, he saw the figure was headless.

His stomach tightened, and his heart almost jumped out of his chest.

The hessian-skinned head, still wearing its dark, tattered wide-brimmed hat, sat upon the ground near the feet of the straw man. It grinned menacingly at Tomas with its torn mouth as it stared at him with its hollow eyes.

Emily had stopped screaming and was breathing sharply.

Tomas let her go, jumped to his feet and snatched the head from the ground. He used his other arm to grab the straw man by the torso, tearing the attached pole out of the ground before storming off towards the campfire.

Others, who were awakened by Emily's scream and still wiping the slumber from their eyes, had clambered out of their tents in time to observe Tomas as he quickly walked barefoot across the freezing snow. He dangled the head and hat in one hand as he carried the body of the scarecrow under his other arm.

Without hesitation, he threw the head, body and stake onto the fire, where it immediately ignited on the hot coals, setting new flames to reach into the brightening morning sky.

"What happened?" called David, bolting from his tent. He noticed Tomas standing by the fire without his shirt and boots. "Are you mad? Go get some clothes on, man."

"That was in my tent." Tomas pointed to the burning body of the scarecrow.

David turned to see the hollow eyes and crooked smile of the canvas face staring back at him amid engulfing flames.

"Who?" David spat. "How?"

"I don't know," the other answered as he started back towards his tent.

"Is Emily all right?"

"I don't know," Tomas replied as he ducked under the open tent flap, disappearing inside.

David stared after him for a moment, his eyes remaining on the open entrance of the tent until Tomas reached around and closed the flaps behind him. His gaze then moved to the trees beyond the tent, to something between the trees.

"By the gods!"

He found her hugging her knees, tucking them under her chin as she sat and stared towards the door. Quickly, Tomas dropped to her side and wrapped his arms around her.

"It's all right," he assured her. "I threw it on the fire."

"They won't stop," her voice shook with fear. "Did you see it?"

He nodded. He had seen it. He carried it to the fire. Then he realised her question wasn't referring to what his eyes captured. There was something more to her words.

"What do you mean?"

"It was the same one." She turned her face to him. Her eyes were wide and her skin was pale.

He shook his head. He didn't understand.

"You removed the head from that one on the plain."

He stared at her for a long time, uncertain of what to say.

"Tomas," David called from outside, "you need to come out here."

He looked at her and wanted to stay.

She nodded, giving her approval. *They need you.*

"Coming," he replied as he reached for his boots. He dressed and kissed her forehead before returning outside to where David and Simon waited for him.

"Look around," Simon instructed.

Tomas turned his head to see several of Tarkin's men gathered near the fire. Some were watching the straw man burn in flames. Others were facing outwards, towards the surrounding forest.

Tarkin walked from his tent and towards the campfire, peering this way and that into the nearby woods.

"Has anyone found our sentries?" he called.

There was no reply.

David turned his face towards the trees and tapped Tomas on the shoulder before pointing to a gap between two tall pines. His eyes followed the other's signal and landed upon a figure standing in the snow.

Its arms stretched out to each side, a long coat dangled to just below its knees and the wide-brimmed hat upon its head obscured its canvas face.

Taking a deep breath, Tomas moved his gaze to the right and found another positioned between two trees. Then another, and another.

"There are eighteen," David informed him, "counting your friend on the fire."

Moving his eyes across his surroundings, Tomas found each one of them. They were all in plain sight and all wearing similar clothing.

"How is this possible?" he spoke in a whisper. "Where did they come from?"

"More of my men are missing, Tomas," Tarkin said from his side. "We can't find them anywhere."

"The sentries?" he asked.

"Yes," the captain replied.

"I heard them last night," Tomas told him. "They were speaking near the fire."

"There are no tracks," Tarkin stated. "I'm really concerned."

Tomas sensed the fear in his voice. With five men gone without a trace, how could he not feel afraid?

Tomas felt concerned as well. He just wasn't ready to admit that it was fear yet.

"It snowed last night," Tomas said as he turned to Simon. "Any tracks would have been covered. We'll need to look for other signs. Snapped branches, scrapings on tree trunks."

"I've been looking," Simon told him. "I have found nothing yet. I'll wake Oliver and Ivo. They can help me search."

Tomas nodded as he returned his eyes to one of the straw men standing between the trees.

"It must be the witch." Tarkin peered at the same figure. "How did she do this?"

"She placed one in my tent," Tomas told him.

"No one told me that." The captain glanced at the other for a moment.

Tomas kept his eyes upon the scarecrow.

It stared back at him, grinning darkly, silently.

"I heard Emily screaming," Tarkin said. "Is she all right?"

"She's frightened," Tomas replied, his mind returning to the scared girl with her knees tucked up under her chin.

Tarkin nodded understandingly. "So am I."

Eighteen

Flames stretched into the air almost as high as the treetops surrounding the camp. They had piled all seventeen of the straw men upon the hearth with the one that appeared in Tomas' tent.

Holding Emily in his arms, he watched the figures burn away layer by layer. The clothing and hessian skin vanished as the straw intestines and muscles burst into a blaze of heat and light. Finally, all that remained was the charred, wooden bones.

Placing a hand on the captain's shoulder, Tomas attempted to give a little comfort, reassuring the commander of the *Adelandria* that he had support and friendship from Woodmyst. He then turned and walked back to his tent with Emily, leaving Tarkin to his thoughts by the fire.

The men cleared the camp and loaded the horses, preparing themselves for another day of journeying. The steeds were eager to move on, snorting with excitement as saddles were tightened and cargo was packed.

Sitting upon his horse, surrounded by the Erilian women, Tarkin wore an absent expression. His mind, it appeared to Tomas, was far away. Clearly, he would not be the leader that the crewmen needed for the time being.

Karlena's dark eyes signalled to Tomas that they were waiting for him. With a quick glance around, he saw all the men mounted and ready to move.

The flames still burned as the skeletons of the scarecrows broke apart and turn to ash. Usually, he would put snow upon the hearth to douse it.

But not today.

He let the straw men burn until there was nothing left of them.

"We make for the coast and then north," he called to the troop.

They formed up into two lines and filed through the forest, keeping their eyes peeled for any movement to their sides and rear. There were thick patches of pines that drew the most attention of the riders. Carefully, cautiously, they scanned these areas before passing by, as they would make perfect places to ambush the travellers.

Numbering twenty-eight altogether, the troop kept within proximity to one another, making sure to remain within reach and within sight. None of them wanted to vanish as five of their comrades had done over the past day and night.

The men at the rear of the line talked so loudly to each other that even Tomas could hear their conversation from the front. Usually, he would want silence so he could keep an ear out for intruders that may be hiding nearby.

On this morning, however, he let them boisterously talk. He understood their reasoning for the noisy chatter. They were afraid, and so they were displaying a false sense of bravery. They were also being vigilant and allowing others to know they were still there.

Whenever the volume dropped off, Tomas turned his head around to see that the men were still with the troop. Others along the lines would do the same. Seeing all faces upon them was a signal to the men that they weren't talking loudly enough. Knowing the men were safe, the knot in Tomas' stomach would loosen and he would return his eyes towards the trail.

The conversation at the back of the line moved from a discussion about places they had visited and adventures they had been on before joining the *Adelandria*, to distasteful jokes and songs about women and certain parts of their anatomy.

"I remember one fair lady from Ghardik Cove," one called out, laughing loudly. "She could tie knots in a string with her tongue. She could undo the cords on my trousers with both hands behind her back."

Tomas felt a slight concern and embarrassment for the women in the troop. He thought he might need to bring the conversation to a halt. Peering over to the Erilian women, he found they were smiling at the remark. Remembering they were practically raised on the ship, he knew they were probably used to such tawdry remarks.

Emily, however, was not accustomed to such behaviour. He turned to her to see if she displayed any discomfort or disgust. Instead, she was trying to hide her smile under her hood and behind her hand.

Meeting Tomas' stare, she turned her face away from him. He heard her snort before emitting a soft giggle.

Shaking his head in disbelief, he turned his face to the front, steering his mare towards the wider gaps between the trees.

Ivo, listening to the conversation, smiling at the remarks, kept peering to the east. He watched the spaces among the pines and bare trees carefully. With the rock wall and steeper ground to the west of them, he considered the ground between the sea and themselves to be the more hazardous.

If he was the enemy and wished to attack, then the east was the direction he would come from.

Clear, clean snow spread across the ground like a soft blanket. Dark stumps and trunks poked through the white cover, looking like protruding fingers and hands reaching out of the ground.

Dressed in white flowing clothes, her form silhouetted against the fabric from the sunlight fanning upon the ground as it filtered through the pine leaves; she watched him.

He became transfixed.

Her golden blonde hair flowed softly as a tender breeze enveloped her.

Even from this distance, he could see her deep blue eyes staring at him.

Hungry for him.

Her soft, pink lips silently moved, calling his name.

Ivo.

His heart raced.

His loins burned.

She called to him again.

Ivo.

The softness of her voice reached his ear like a whisper on the wind.

A warm flow ran up and down his spine, down his legs, through his heart.

She wanted him.

He wanted her.

Ivo.

Her call filled him.

Moving past a small group of trees obscured his view of her, and the feeling dissipated.

She was gone.

Ivo looked for her once they passed the tiny thicket. There was no sign of her. Not even marks upon the snow.

He glanced around at the others.

Had they heard?

Had they seen?

Their faces wore smiles as laughter sounded along the line. He found it peculiar that he hadn't heard them only moments ago. Instead, the only sound to enter his ears was that of her soft, enticing voice calling his name.

Who was she?

The men at the back of the line continued to talk about the women they had encountered and their crude adventures.

Ivo questioned the state of his mind. He wondered if he had seen her at all or was it simply a trick of the brain.

Bringing himself back to reality, he tried to focus on the talk from the men behind him. He attempted to keep his face forward but found his eyes drifting to the east, hoping to see her again.

Needing to see her again.

***

Waves crashed upon the steep, black rocks to the south of them. The sound reminded Emily of thunder. She watched as the water moved like a rolling hill before it smashed into the cliff face, sending white spray into the air.

The sea urged the liquid further; the rolling hill folded upon itself and broke apart, creating a foamy wash. It briefly washed upon the dark sand of the shoreline before the endless motion of the tide dragged it away.

The wind blew across the waves, pushing her auburn hair away from her face and trailing over her back. The smell of salt was thick and inviting. She closed her eyes as she turned towards the morning sun and took in a deep breath.

With his spyglass held up to his eye, Tarkin found the ship on the north-eastern horizon. Its sails filled with wind and it was pulling away.

"She's got the wind behind her," the captain informed them, "but the current is still pushing south. She's moving away but slowly." Tarkin folded the spyglass and placed it back into his pocket.

"Then I guess we better keep moving," Tomas said as he pulled his mare to the north and urged her into a trot. Emily immediately followed. David was next to trail his leader with the other men of Woodmyst on his heels. Tarkin nodded to his crewmen, signalling to move on.

The travellers moved away from the beach and rode nearer to the forest that separated the coast from the mountains. Sometimes rocky bluffs prevented them from riding upon the pebbles and sand near to the water's edge.

Snow became their only obstacle as the horses kicked up a flurry of ice and slush. They moved at a quickened pace, maintaining a steady speed as to not wear the horses out.

Tomas drove the band onwards, endeavouring to keep from entering the woods again. He wanted an unobstructed view of what lay in front of him. No one needed any more surprises if they could avoid them.

They stopped now and then so Captain Tarkin could get a bearing on where the marauders' ship was. He kept telling them it was hard to gauge whether they were closing in at this distance.

Onward they drove, maintaining speed and determination to gain distance on the enemy vessel. They utilised effort when the land became steep in places near rocky outcrops, elation felt when they experienced flat or downhill runs.

The sun rose to the highest point in the sky. Tomas steered his brown mare to the top of a rise and heard Tarkin call from behind him.

"We need to take a bearing," he hollered.

The captain's demeanour had improved as the day progressed. He had almost appeared defeated, exhausted and ready to give up in the morning. Now he showed signs of a fighting spirit. Tomas was happy to see the return of the man he had met at the tavern.

As Tarkin drove his steed up the embankment, Tomas peered out to the ocean and scanned the horizon, the sky a light blue; the water beneath just a shade darker. White, delicate clouds fanned across the sky, trailing behind the line where the ocean met the sky.

He stared in wonder as Emily sidled up next to him. It was a beautiful view.

Then he saw it.

A small black blob on the horizon, just visible to the naked eye.

"I can see them," he said to the captain.

Tarkin pulled his horse to a stop and raised his spyglass to his eye.

"It's them," he acknowledged with a grin. "We're gaining on them."

"We take a quick break," Tomas called back to the others. "Only a few minutes. We're gaining on them."

There was no hesitation.

The women grouped together and entered the edge of the woods while the men found their own places to relieve themselves. The riders fed their horses with a handful of oats.

With that done, they mounted their steeds again.

Jeremy conducted a quick count of the group members and announced all accounted for.

No order was given.

No word was spoken.

Tomas moved onwards; the others followed.

***

Riding a small distance ahead of the others, Tomas urged his mare into a canter as he approached the top of another ridge. The waves crashed noisily against jagged rocks to his right.

He rode his beast to the crest and froze.

Below him, a mile or so from his position, was a small seaside village. It had a long wharf with a tall ship moored to it. Five small huts stood in a rough circle and a stable sat on the nearest edge of the settlement.

A tall tower stood on the far side of the village. Its structure was unlike anything he had seen before. It resembled a watchtower made of stone. Its viewing platform was open on three sides, facing the sea. The other side, facing the forest, enclosed and curved, giving the tower a cylindrical appearance.

Dropping to the ground and turning the mare back towards the troop, he smacked her on her rump and dropped to the snow. The mare trotted back to the others, directing herself towards Emily and her mare.

Tarkin, noticing the riderless horse, peered towards the crest of the ridge. He saw Tomas looking back towards him, pointing to him before gesturing for him to approach.

The captain jumped from his steed and jogged up the embankment before dropping to the ground beside the other. He pulled his spyglass from his pocket as soon as he saw what had agitated Tomas. Panning the lens along the dock and halting when he found the ship, the captain took his time to study the vessel.

"It's not our ship," Tarkin told him. "Too much ice has built up around the hull. She's been here for a while."

He moved the glass over the town slowly.

"I count about twenty men in the open," he said. "They've got an actual fire pit in the centre of the dwellings. This was a village for hunters."

"What about the tower?"

"It's a beacon house." Tarkin moved his spyglass to scan the structure. "The back wall on the platform usually has polished metal attached to it. There should be a large lantern up there that's lit at night. The light acts as a sign to guide ships safely to the wharf. It is not intended for ill will. But I can see an armed man on the platform. He has arrows."

Tarkin folded the spyglass and put it away.

"I don't believe these people will be friendly." Tomas frowned.

"Neither do I," the captain replied. "We could go around."

"I don't really want to enter those woods again if we can avoid it," he replied. "There is an evil presence in there that frightens me."

"Me too," Tarkin acknowledged. "Why don't we present ourselves as peaceful travellers and see what happens?"

"That's as good a plan as any."

The men returned to the other riders and mounted their steeds. Tomas told them what waited for them on the other side of the ridge and that they needed to be ready for anything that could happen.

Tomas approached the Erilian women and focused his attention upon Karlena.

"I have a favour to ask," he said. "I need you to stay behind the others. All of you," he directed to the other women by Karlena's side.

"We are warriors," she replied. "We know how to fight."

"But Emily does not," he told her. "And I need to know that she is safe. I trust you, all of you. Please."

Karlena turned to the others, who all nodded, agreeing to keep her safe.

"You have my word that no harm will come to her," Karlena promised him.

"Thank you," he replied before turning his horse back towards the ridge.

"We ride slowly," Tarkin called. "We don't want to appear hostile."

The Erilian women used their horses to surround Emily and her mare as they climbed to the crest of the ridge. There they waited as the men descended the other side towards the village below.

A horn blew from the tower. Several men left the warmth of the fire in the centre of the village and made their way towards the newcomers. Others stopped chores they were doing around the settlement and made their way to the closest edge of the township.

Tomas counted eighteen men in the street plus the one in the tower, making nineteen. Tiny hairs stuck up on the back of his neck as the men on the ground unsheathed their swords.

"Who are you?" called a tall, brawny man at the front of the gathering.

"We are peaceful travellers," Tarkin answered. "We ask for your permission to pass through your beautiful hamlet."

"Do you now?" the man barked. "How about this? Instead of allowing you peaceful travellers through our hamlet, we cut you into pieces. We eat your horses. We rape your women up there. And then we laugh about it until our bellies are sore. How about that?"

"You were right," Tarkin said to Tomas. "They weren't friendly at all."

"We know why you are here, Captain," the brawny man spat.

Tarkin felt his heart stop cold. This man knew he was the commander of a ship. He wondered how much more this fellow and his band of men understood about him.

"Oh, yes?" Tarkin said coolly. "And why is that?"

"We know you seek the Sovereign," he replied. "We know you seek revenge for your family and a missing daughter."

Tarkin felt heat bubbling behind his eyes.

"The Mistress told us you would come." The man smiled. His yellow crooked teeth jutted past dirty, cracked lips. "She told us you wouldn't stop. She also told us of these men with you. The ones from Woodmyst."

Tomas cocked his head as he wiped his eye. A small itch irritated him. He surmised the irritating voice of the fellow had brought it on in the middle of their path.

"She wanted the red-haired girl," the man slurred, "but she has changed her mind. There is another among you that draws her attention now. The Mistress told us that we need to kill all of you and take the red-haired girl to the Sovereign," the man gloated. "She has plans for you."

"Plans?" Tarkin chortled. "You just told us you need to kill us. How could she have plans for us? What is she going to do? Eat us? Boil us in her cauldron?"

The men behind the captain laughed heartily.

Not Tomas. He simply observed the man. Waiting.

"She's the Mistress," the other replied. "She has power. Great power." The man turned towards the forest. "And this is her realm. She's already taken from you. She'll do it again."

Ivo.

Sitting upon his black steed, the young man closed his eyes. Her voice was louder this time. The pull was so strong that he almost turned his horse so he could run to her.

Tomas dropped from the mare and ran at the speaker, sword drawn from its sheath and rising through the air. With one swift motion, the man's head separated from his shoulders. It rolled across the ground before lolling onto its side in the snow, baring its yellow teeth in an unheard scream.

Dumbfounded, the others standing behind the speaker stared at the headless body that seemed to take forever to fall to the ground.

The troop behind Tarkin didn't hesitate. They immediately slid from their horses, brandished their blades and ran towards the villagers.

Nineteen

Several of the townsfolk were on the ground with gushing wounds in their stomachs and chests before they knew what was happening. Swords clashed as the crewmen of the *Adelandria* seized the opportunity to rid the town of the vermin that stood in their way.

Arrows hit the snow harmlessly as the watcher in the tower took aim and let them fly.

Tarkin signalled back towards the Erilian women still in position upon the crest of the ridge.

Sharek pulled her bow from her back and took careful aim. The arrow whistled through the air and many enemies' heads turned towards the sky. The speeding shaft found its target in the tower. The body fell clumsily from the platform. He was dead before he hit the ground.

David hacked into one man on the ground, forcing the heavy blade through the other's shoulder and deep into his ribcage. The blade stuck hard, and he had difficulty retrieving it. Placing his boot against the dead man's chest, he pushed with his leg and pulled with his arms.

The sword slowly slid little by little.

The doors of a nearby hut opened and another five men bolted into the open, directly towards him. They held their own blades high, eager to plunge them into his flesh.

Pulling.

Pulling.

The sword slid a little more. He could feel the steel grinding against the bone inside the other's chest.

"Oh, come on," he yelled.

The enemy drew closer and closer. The sword suddenly stuck hard.

"By the gods," he called.

Swords arched downward towards him.

This was it.

The last moment for David Gyfford.

And just what had he done with his life?

Not bloody much.

"Come out, you bastard," he shouted as he flung and thumped the body against the ground frantically. He rocked the blade back and forth in order to loosen the flesh around the steel.

A sword swung at the legs of the closest attacker, slicing through the shin and separating a portion from the runner. Simon sliced his blade through the air again and connected with a second man across the chest.

"Are you just going to watch me?" he called. "Or are you going to help?"

David heaved on the sword and freed it from the corpse as Simon dropped another of the runners onto the ground. Side by side, the two men fought the last two men that had emerged from the hut. It wasn't long before the two rival soldiers were lying in a pool of blood beside their comrades.

The two men of Woodmyst didn't wait for more of the enemy to come to them. They ran into the fray that was concentrated near the centre of the village. The numbers of their adversaries had increased. David surmised that more men had appeared from behind the closed doors of the shelters.

***

Several of Tarkin's men were engaged in combat to the western edge of the village, pushing the enemy soldiers back towards the centre of the community. They eventually drove the exchange of clashing swords towards the others nearer to the fire pit.

There were more adversaries here, but there were more of their own men as well. The crewmen had learnt how to fight in confined areas from the experience of swordplay on the seas.

Preferring a tighter fighting zone, the men of the *Adelandria* worked together, forcing their foes into small pockets where the crewmen surrounded them. A blade would come from the left, drawing the opponent's attention one way; the killing blow would come from another. Using this form of misdirection proved successful as the number of enemy soldiers thinned while Tarkin's men remained standing.

"Coming from the wharf," Oliver called from among the fighters.

Tomas turned to see more men running alongside the moored ship. He made a quick count of fifteen adversaries heading towards the scuffle.

"Stop playing with them, boys," Jeremy instructed the men. "We've got more coming."

Tomas slid his blade into the guts of his opponent and turned his attention to the men who had come from the anchored vessel. He gave a quick whistle, summoning the other men of Woodmyst to his side.

Ivo was first to join him, having just pulled his blade from the chest of another villager. The other men were still engaged in skirmishes of their own.

"You ready?" Tomas asked him as the fifteen adversaries lined up in front of the two men.

"No," Ivo replied with a wry smile.

TWAK!

An arrow stuck from the eye of the man furthest to the right. With a quick glance over his shoulder, back to the ridge, Tomas could see Sharak taking aim again.

TWAK!

She pierced the next man in line through the chest. The first man fell onto his back as the second raised a hand to the shaft sticking from his heart. His face wore an expression of disbelief as the colour drained from his skin.

He fell onto his stomach, pushing the arrow farther into his flesh.

The others stared at their fallen comrades in wonder.

Tomas and Ivo saw their chance and bolted in, taking out four more of the opponents before they had any idea what had happened to them.

Now there were nine.

They regained their composure and raised their swords in defence against the two warriors.

Oliver came running to their side and wielded his sword as if it were an extension of himself. Natural, fluid, controlled motions executed as he sliced the belly and neck of one man before hacking through the skull of another.

***

Captain Tarkin reorganised his men to encircle the enemy, forcing the opponents towards the centre of the village. The enemy fought hard and marked several crewmen with deep cuts that would certainly leave a scar or two.

Pressing the enemy, the crewmen drove their foes towards the fire pit. It was deep, lined with black, hewn stone, and filled with hot coals. Hot flames danced inside the cavity, reaching high beyond the surface level of the structure.

One of Tarkin's men kicked at an enemy soldier, knocking him into the depths of the flames. A piercing scream filled the air, echoing across the expanse between the village, the mountains to the west.

"Put them all in there, lads," Tarkin ordered.

"You'll never defeat us, Tarkin," one of the enemy soldiers spat. "We are too strong. We have the power of our Lord within us."

The captain thrust his sword deep into the stomach of the man. The soldier dropped his own blade onto the ground by the fire pit.

"Let's see if his power can get you out of this," Tarkin retorted.

The adversary stared at the captain wide-eyed as he slid from the sword, falling backwards into the deep pit of flames behind him.

Parrying and blocking blows, the sound of steel against steel rang throughout the village.

With hacking and slashing, blood and limbs discarded upon the frosty ground, leaving a distasteful mess upon the snow.

On it went until all adversaries were lying on the ground or driven into the pit.

***

The men of Woodmyst, dragging some bodies of their foes behind them, entered the village under the watchful gaze of the *Adelandria's* crewmen. Tomas dropped a body into the fire pit, and his men followed suit before following him back towards the wharf.

"Where are you going?" Jeremy called.

"There are more dead over there," Tomas replied. "We should put them all into the pit."

Tarkin nodded as he peered after the five men.

"Captain?" Jeremy furrowed his brow, confused by the actions of their allies.

"Tomas is right. We can't bury them in this ground. It's too cold. We should burn the bodies." He turned his attention towards the ridge where he saw the women heading towards them. "We will shelter here for the night. Start a new fire near the stable for cooking. I don't feel comfortable eating food cooked over flames fuelled by dead men."

"Aye, Captain," Jeremy replied, before turning his attention to a few men gathered by the fire pit. "Right, you lot. Find some timber and start a fire over there by the stable and get some water on the boil."

"There's a fire right here," one man complained, not wanting to leave the warmth of the flames.

"Captain's orders," Jeremy barked. "Or should I go ask him to explain them to you himself?"

"We're going," another replied. "One fire and boiling water coming up."

Jeremy watched the men leave to fulfil their duty before turning his attention back to his captain. Tarkin had walked to the edge of the village to meet the Erilian women as they approached from the embankment.

Tomas dropped another body into the pit and turned his attention to the women as well. He quickly jogged across the snow to Emily, who was waiting for him on her mare.

He raised his arms to her, and she slid from the saddle and into his embrace. Their lips met and held together for an eternity.

Karlena smiled as she witnessed a rare event, the expression of genuine love. She glanced at the other women and nodded to the two on the ground. The other women followed her gaze and grinned.

Even the battle-weary captain took time to observe the occurrence. He knew the two were fond of one another, but Tomas' actions of running across the village to her could only mean one thing.

The boy was madly in love.

Tarkin had only ever felt that one time in his life. It had vanished when his family was taken from him.

There was no way to regain the feelings he had towards his wife, son, and daughter.

There was no way to replace the emotions and experiences he had with them.

But he could get revenge upon those who stole it all from him.

Tomas and Emily were starting their journey together.

He decided, as he watched the two of them holding one another, that he wouldn't let anyone or anything destroy what they were building.

"I don't think we'll need to worry about Tomas finding a woman anymore," Simon commented as he dropped another dead soldier into the flames.

"Ah..." David smiled. "True love."

"Do you think it might be too late for Richard to give his talk to Tomas?" Oliver chuckled.

The other two snickered.

Ivo, looking on with gladness, suddenly became annoyed at the jesting from the others.

"Come on," he reprimanded. "We should be happy for him."

"We are, Ivo. This has been a long time coming. But you're right." David slapped his large hand on the younger man's back. "No more jokes about Tomas and Emily. Right fellers?"

The others agreed as they all watched with gladness as Tomas and Emily held each other in a deep embrace.

The younger man nodded, the smile quickly returning to his face.

Ivo.

Ivo.

Her voice filled his heart.

He looked for her, but she was nowhere to be seen.

His mind saw the flowing white garments and her striking form beneath them. Her blue eyes pierced his heart and her pink lips slowly formed his name.

Ivo.

Like a distant whisper, she constantly called to him.

Pulling him to her.

Drawing him.

Luring him.

He wanted her.

He needed her.

Ivo.

Ivo.

Twenty

An icy breeze swept down the mountainside and filtered through the forest before rushing across the plain towards the sea. It brought fresh snow and dark clouds full of thunder and flashing lightning.

While the storm wasn't welcome, the men were silently thankful for the wind. The smell of burning flesh emitting from the pit had become unbearable for some who had wandered to the far end of the wharf where the smell of salt awaited them.

Some had offered to cover the pit and extinguish the flames with snow.

"Let the bastards burn," Tarkin replied angrily.

As the flames melted through skin and muscle, the breeze nuzzled the dark smoke rising from the fire pit towards the coast. The captain initially saw this as a blessing, but then returned his thoughts to the ship on the horizon.

Taking his spyglass, he scanned the horizon for the vessel. The diminishing light caused by the sinking sun and thick cloud cover made it hard to find the craft.

Large icebergs moved towards the south and caught his attention momentarily. Their shapes were easily mistaken for ships with full sails raised. The motion was too stable. Ice didn't rise and fall upon the waves the same as a ship because they were solid and weighed so much more. A vessel was hollow, acting as a cork in a barrel where the smallest ripple made it move. Here, a large ship would be pushed and pulled by the kinds of waves he saw.

Then he saw it. It was still there, riding choppy waves with white tops, almost directly east of the wharf.

It rose with its bow smashing through the water's surface, sending a thick spray over the deck at the crest of the wave; crashing back down to the trough. It appeared a moment of foul weather caused them to be stuck in place.

A small smile crept upon his lips.

He thought about what he would do in such a situation.

Drop the sails and anchor for the night.

Not the marauders, however. They continued to push on and gain no ground. Tarkin wished he had a larger spyglass, or telescope, so that he could see the looks upon the crewmen's faces.

Are they struggling with the lines?

Is their commander afraid?

What about the cargo?

What about the captive women?

His demeanour suddenly changed. Now he felt concerned for the prisoners on the vessel.

Ashamed of his selfish ambitions to see his enemy destroyed, he had forgotten that innocent people were on board the ship with the Sovereign.

Lowering the spyglass and furrowing his brow, he no longer felt like watching, just in case the ship foundered out there. While it would be a minor victory for him, he didn't want the little sister of his friend to die.

He dropped to his knees and silently prayed for the safety of the little girl.

Her name is Joanna.

Tears welled in his eyes as he pictured a young girl, caged and alone. Only, because he had never seen her, his image of her was that of his own daughter, Sumaiyya.

Sumaiyya.

***

Seeing Tarkin kneeling upon the snow by the sea, Tomas ordered three men to stand watch upon the tower before ordering another three to relieve them on the fourth hour. He repeated the order to another six men, dividing them into two groups as well. Now, he had four shifts of watch duty that would take them well into the morning.

The sun had gone and a dark, looming sky hung above them. Snow continued to fall gently to the ground as most of the men gathered near a fire set by the stable. A few had dared to venture into the woods nearby and snared a young doe. It now roasted over the flames upon a crude spit forged from one of the enemy soldier's swords resting upon two pitchforks from the stables. The pitchforks were stuck into the ground by their handles so that the prongs stretched towards the sky. The sword rested between the prongs, hilt upon one, and blade tip upon the other.

Jeremy sat amongst them, rubbing his knee; an injury sustained during battle, or an old wound coming back to plague him.

Tomas sat beside him. The smell of venison was alluring; the warmth of the fire was welcoming. As he sat and peered past the flames, he saw Akasati and Rhyodia kneel on either side of Tarkin. They both placed their arms around him and held on to him.

More men came to the fire either for the warmth or drawn by the aroma of fresh meat. Tomas wondered about the wounded or dead. He had noticed none.

"What are our numbers?" he asked Jeremy.

"The same," replied the other, reaching for a cup. A pot of water sat upon the coals nearby, steaming away as the doe roasted above the hearth. "Tea?"

"Thank you." Tomas smiled.

"I could go for a large mug of ale, myself," Jeremy told him as he mixed a quick brew. "I guess that will have to wait until later. It seems the Sovereign, and the Mistress didn't trust the men posted here with many luxuries at all. We found beds, blankets, grain and basic food supplies like dried meat and fish. There weren't even any horses in the stables."

"Perhaps they ate them," Tomas suggested.

"Eat horses?" Jeremy spat with a tone of disgust as he handed the cup over.

"We came close to it one time in Woodmyst." Tomas took the cup gladly and raised it to his lips. "Good."

"Just how the captain likes it." Jeremy smiled. "I thought you loved your horses. Some say, even more than your women. How could you think about eating such a beast?"

"More than our women?" Tomas chuckled. "We train them. We care for them. We treat them well. But they are just tools. My mare pulls a plough in the spring. She also helps to drive sheep and cattle around the pastures.

"I fuss over her because it makes her feel needed. We *do* love our horses in Woodmyst. As far as more than our women, you may need to talk to the women about that.

"One winter, not long after the siege of the Night Demons, we were at the end of our supplies. We were all young, children really, and Richard was practically looking after everyone on his own. There were a few women with young ones of their own and some adolescent girls, but he was alone.

"We weren't starving, but the meat had run out and we had no livestock except for the horses. The decision was made to butcher some horses for meat once the grain had run out.

"We portioned the stock thinly, and our stomachs ached and growled at us for doing so. It was tough. Especially when the supplies ran out entirely. We pleaded with Richard to just hold on a little longer.

"For three days, we didn't eat. We couldn't wait any longer. So, Richard sharpened his axe one night, ready to butcher one of the horses the next morning.

"I still don't know how they knew, to this day, but by some miracle, some people from Oldcastle came to our rescue. They scrounged supplies from around the city at the beginning of the season, but found the road unpassable due to snow and weather.

"Just when we needed it, a band of men braved the weather and brought us more than what we needed to get our village started again. Two cows for milking, some sheep, goats, pigs, grain.

"We made it through the winter and used the warmer months to plant crops, breed the sheep and pigs. Later, we purchased cows for meat, which we now breed ourselves and sell to merchants in Oldcastle.

"But not one horse was eaten." Tomas held up his finger as David approached from the darkness.

"Oh," said the large, bald man, "he's telling the story of the first winter. *Not one horse was eaten.*" David smiled as he held up his finger in a mocking jest. "We all tell that story the same. Especially when we visit Oldcastle. It makes them feel rather good about themselves. It also makes the ladies act a little less prudishly. Did Richard ever tell you that your brown mare was the one he sharpened his axe for that night?"

Tomas shook his head as a wry smile crept over his face.

"I'm joking," David laughed. "I honestly believe he would have gone through every other beast we had, even Simon, before the thought of eating that horse of yours would have even crossed his mind."

"You would have gone first," Simon retorted as he found a place to sit by the fire. "You were always bigger than the rest of us. I remember you as a boy. Wide and tall. The horses ran from you out of fear that you would try to mount them."

"That's why we had to go all the way to Kailibard to purchase that monster you ride now," Oliver put in as he joined the men.

"I thought you went to Kailibard because there was a prostitute there who could make knots with her legs and arms," Ivo remarked. The men around the hearth burst into laughter.

"That's what you told me, Simon."

"I did no such thing," the other barked.

"She could tie herself in knots?" Emily asked whimsically as she sat beside Tomas.

The men laughed harder and louder.

"Don't you believe a single word he is saying, my lady," Simon chuckled. "We went there to buy a horse. Help me out, Oliver. You were there."

"I didn't visit that certain establishment you harped on about all the way home," the other chided.

"What kind of knots did she show you?" Tomas asked.

"You're a dead man, Ivo," Simon roared before he burst into loud laughter.

***

After they'd eaten the doe and the flames had faded, the travellers showed signs of weariness. Some drifted off at the side of the hearth as the talk continued into the night.

Eventually, Tarkin gave the order for all men to retire to the huts. The tents would remain bundled upon the stable's floor.

Because there were only five small huts for them to reside in, the captain designated one hut for the women, one for the Woodmyst men, and the rest for his own. He and Jeremy joined Tomas and his party in a hut beside the stable.

"My first night without my ladies," Tarkin commented as he pulled the covers over his head.

"My fourteenth without one of mine," Jeremy quipped.

"You poor man," David replied, sounding earnest. "Perhaps Ivo can pretend to be one of them and cuddle you during the night."

"Bastard," Ivo retorted.

"All right," Tomas chided. "We had a long day and we've another ahead."

"Sorry, Tomas," David replied. "It must be difficult trying to sleep when you're used to having a woman by your side as you sleep. Perhaps Ivo can pretend to be…"

"Quiet," Tomas barked.

An immediate silence fell upon the hut. For an eternity, the men stared into the darkness, as they believed David might have gone a little too far with his humour. It was unlike their leader to react so angrily. The quest may have taken its toll on him, weighing heavily upon his mind and heart. David was about to apologise, opening his mouth to speak, when Tomas' voice broke the silence.

"Although," he mused, "Ivo still hasn't grown his man-hair yet. There is a chance that he has smooth skin like a woman."

The men had laughed before Tomas had finished.

"Come on," Ivo whined.

The laughter echoed across the expanse of land between the shore and the forest. The sound wafted through the trees and deep into the shadows of the woods.

***

The first shift upon the tower began. From their vantage point, they could make out the silhouette of the tall mountain range and the silver haze of the moon trying to break through the thick clouds above. The flickering orange glow from the lanterns on board the marauders' ship on the horizon was the only visible light.

"Should be an easy shift, lads," said one watcher.

"Let's hope so," another replied. "Do we keep our eyes on the ship or the forest?"

"Both," said the third. He was looking over the northern edge; his arms leaning against the waist-high stone wall.

The clouds broke apart momentarily and sent a shaft of silver moonlight into the woods. The ground, not far beyond the tree line, glowed softly. A gentle white light.

She was there.

Standing in the centre of the pale glow, a woman adorned in white garments faced them.

"Look," the third man managed. His voice was raspy and barely audible.

The light faded back to complete darkness as the others turned their faces to where he was looking.

Nothing.

"What did you see?" asked another.

"A woman in white," he replied, shaking his head in disbelief.

"You're just tired," the other suggested.

"She was there," he pointed. "Right there."

The others looked at him in disbelief, tiny smiles forming.

THUD!

The noise resonated from the dark shadows beneath the trees. The watchmen felt cold shivers run up and down their spines as they stared with wide eyes towards the very place that their comrade had gestured to just moments before.

CRACK!

Suddenly, they weren't smiling anymore.

Twenty-One

Noisy clattering, thumping and scraping sounds emitted from the huts as all the men scrambled to get dressed and outside as hastily as they could. Several spat foul words as they fumbled with buttons and chords, buckles, and straps.

The Woodmyst men were first to stand upon the snow, facing northwest towards the area from where the sounds came. Oliver crouched, resting his elbows upon his knees as he squinted and attempted to see beneath the low limbs of the pines that lined the border of the forest. He saw nothing, but the sounds demonstrated someone or something was busying itself beyond his vision.

THUD!
CRACK! CRACK!

The sound echoed, coming from the south. The men turned their faces towards the unfamiliar noises. As if communicating, the noises cut across the cold air from the northwest again.

THUD!
CRACK!

The pattern repeated from an additional source directly to the west.
"They're talking," Tomas said. "Signalling positions."
"How do you know?" David asked.
"Listen," Tomas held a finger up.

THUD!
CRACK! CRACK!

The sound rang from the northwest.

"South," Tomas pointed.

Sure enough, the pattern repeated from that direction, and a little closer than before.

THUD!

CRACK!

The call came from the northwest again.

"West," Tomas pointed.

As predicted, the answer came from the west.

Rising to his feet, Oliver turned his attention to the tower.

"Where are the watchers?" he asked as other men gathered behind them. Tarkin made his way to Tomas' side.

"What's out there?" the captain asked.

"We don't know," the other answered, keeping his eyes fixed on the tree line to the west. "It would seem your men are missing from their post."

Tarkin turned his attention to the tower. His eyes found an empty platform where three of his men no longer stood.

"I want the next watch upon that tower," he ordered. "Jeremy, go with them. See if you can spot our missing men from up there."

"Aye, captain," the other replied before racing off across the snow with the other three men.

THUD!

CRACK! CRACK!

The crew of the *Adelandria* faced the northwest.

The men of Woodmyst kept their eyes upon the west and the south.

The southern reply was louder and closer.

The northwest called again. The noise emitting from that direction, Tomas noticed, didn't seem to change position. It was always coming from the same place. Only the southern and western noises appeared to be changing pitch as they drew closer and closer.

THUD!
CRACK!

The western answer was louder than the southern.

Tomas drew his sword. His men did the same.

"They're going to attack," Tomas informed the others gathered about.

"Who?" Tarkin asked as he pulled his blade from its sheath. "Who is going to attack?"

"I don't know," he replied. "But I believe their commander is over there." Tomas pointed to the northwest with his sword.

The crewmen gripped the hilts of their weapons tightly, ready for battle.

THUD!
CRACK! CRACK!

Jeremy took the stairs inside the tower two at a time, his sword held at the ready. The three men behind him struggled to keep up as he climbed higher and higher.

The stairs were narrow and wound upwards in a spiral with thick stone walls on either side. There were no doors or alcoves, no windows or portholes, leaving the men to use their hands to feel their way through the ascending passage in pitch darkness.

Feeling confident that there was no place for enemy soldiers to hide, Jeremy angled his blade high and swung it from side to side with each step he took. In his mind, someone standing in his way would feel the tip of his blade before they could surprise him with a weapon of their own.

"Come on," he called to the men behind him.

"We're on your heels," one of them answered, breathing heavily and sounding a little farther away than he would have liked him to be.

Gradually, the stairs became visible as Jeremy grew nearer to the open platform. The moonlight that seeped through the clouds allowed a dull silver glow to spill down the stone steps.

He ran onto the viewing platform with his sword held high, ready to fight.

A stone floor and walls, night air and emptiness awaited him. The men were gone and there was no sign that they had ever been here.

The other three men behind Jeremy filed onto the platform as the other sheathed his sword disappointedly. They breathed heavily and panned their eyes across the space at the top of the stairs.

"What?" one man said, wheezing with each breath. "No one to fight?"

"Luckily for you," Jeremy quipped, turning to face the three men. "After all, you're the very image of a battle-ready warrior." He mocked the three men by wheezing.

THUD!
CRACK!

The three peered over the tower's stony guardrail to view around the wall covered with polished steel plates towards the woods to the west.

Jeremy turned his attention towards the ocean, smelling the salt in the air, and spotted a tiny orange dot on the horizon towards the north-east. The marauders still seemed to struggle with their voyage.

"You." Jeremy pointed to a man before directing his attention to the light upon the sea. "Keep your eyes on that."

The man moved into position on the eastern edge of the tower.

"You two," said Jeremy, as he turned to the others. "Watch the ground to the north and south. See if you can spot our missing men. Call or whistle if you find anything. Do not poke your heads around that wall to see what lies to the west again. You might find an arrow in your forehead from some skilled marksman. Keep your eyes upon what you can actually see."

"You're not staying?"

"My place is by my captain's side," he answered before returning to the dark stairwell.

THUD!
CRACK! CRACK!

From the northwest.

THUD!
CRACK! CRACK!

From the south.

THUD!
CRACK!

From the northwest.

THUD!
CRACK!

From the west.

The responding echoes were edging closer and closer to the small village. Tomas could sense that the enemy was very close. So close if it were lighter, they could see them in the woods.

Heavy cloud cover over the moon, and deep shadows among the trees hid their opponents from their eyes. It was a mystery to the men in the open who or what they were up against.

The sounds of call and response grew louder and louder, brewing fears into some men in the snow. Not knowing their adversaries caused them to picture hordes of creatures they had heard of only in stories gathering to bring destruction.

"Gather your strength," Tarkin called to his men, sensing their apprehensions. He imagined the enemy were more of the kinds of men that they had encountered earlier in the day. To him, the adversaries were simply returning to reclaim territory that the riders had taken.

For Tomas, their foes had been taunting them since the beginning of their quest. He believed they were about to face a band of men that had been making these strange noises near their campsites. They were responsible for placing the scarecrows and the vanishing of their men. Their commander, he had no doubt, was a manipulative woman known to be a witch.

He didn't know if magic existed as it did in the tales he had heard about such creatures, but he knew he needed to keep an open mind. After all, he had seen dragons and other strange creatures in his youth.

But a witch?

Was it possible that a woman could harness the power to control, enslave, and compel others to yield to their will?

Perhaps with promises of delivering kingdoms into another's hands, a woman could ensnare a man to do her bidding.

Perhaps with sensual, alluring temptations and manipulating lusts, she could bend one's mind to her own.

Perhaps with noisy repetitions that induced an increasing sense of fear, such a creature could cause armies to fall.

Tomas gripped his sword tightly.

If she is there, he thought, *she needs to die.*

THUD!
CRACK! CRACK!

The din grew intolerably louder and louder.

THUD!
CRACK!

It drew nearer and nearer.

Resting on the boundary of forest and open ground, the sounds from the west and south found their positions. There were calls from the northwest, west, and southwest.

THUD!
CRACK! CRACK! CRACK!
THUD! THUD!
CRACK!

The woods erupted with a mangled sound.

It was noisy, raucous, and had no pattern.

"Get ready," Tomas called, understanding that the pandemonium was a last-ditch attempt to instil distress into the men on open ground.

Some men steadied themselves while others jumped up and down on the spot, getting their hearts pumping.

Tomas turned to see the Erilian women surrounding Emily by the fire pit. All were armed and ready, including his beloved. They held thin blades at the ready.

"My ears are stinging," Simon called over the clatter.

Jeremy ran across the village from the tower to his captain's side.

"The men are gone," he called. "The tower was empty. The ship is still on the horizon and I've left the men up there to keep watch."

"Good," Tarkin called back. "Get ready for battle."

Louder and louder, the sound grew, filling the night so strongly that the men believed they could feel it.

The men of Woodmyst thrived on the experience, allowing the tangible sense of sound to build their adrenaline.

They wanted to fight so much that they were almost willing to run headfirst into the dark woods to slay the enemy where they stood.

Then suddenly, the sound stopped.

A thick silence hung in the air, resonating loudly in their ears.

The dark shadows beneath the trees stared blankly across the expanse of snow towards the village. It was as if nothing had happened at all.

Confused looks and furrowed brows crept upon the faces of the men gathered at the edge of the village.

"There," one called, pointing to a place between some trees. By the time the others had moved their eyes to where the other gestured, they only saw darkness.

"Over there," another called, directing his finger to another place on the tree line. Again, after the men turned their faces, nothing.

"There," called another.

"There's one," called another, pointing elsewhere.

Tomas kept his eyes directly forwards, ignoring the calls. He fixed his vision upon a tunnel formed by overhanging limbs and stretched branches of pines and leafless trees.

Standing deep in the arch was the silhouette of a lone figure. Its arms stretched out to its sides and the distinct shape of the wide-brimmed hat told him it had to be one of the straw men that kept appearing along their path.

"I see you," he said as he watched the figure slowly lower its arms to its side.

The long coat flapped behind it like a cape as it started running towards him.

With a grunt, Tomas ran forward, sword high and heart pumping loudly as he raced across the snow.

"What's he doing?" Jeremy called to the other men of Woodmyst.

His answer came in a flurry of snow as the four men blindly chased after their commander.

"Go on," Tarkin called as he too started running across the expanse of ground between the village and the trees.

Not hesitating, the crew of the *Adelandria* followed their captain, keeping their eyes fixed upon Tomas, hoping he wasn't losing his mind and that he had seen something.

Anything.

It burst from the tree line; claw-like hands stretched out to attack.

Some men slowed their advance, not believing what they saw.

A straw man raced swiftly towards Tomas.

Its ragged mouth opened in a silent scream.

Its hollow eyes glaring at its prey.

Nearer and nearer, the two opponents drew.

Tomas slid his blade in an upward arc, connecting with the scarecrow at the crotch, slicing it open up to the chest. The straw man stumbled and tripped, spilling chaff from its wound as it tumbled across the snow.

Turning, sword at the ready, Tomas saw the men still running across the snow towards him. Between them and him lay the wounded scarecrow.

It bore a wound that would have killed any living creature.

But this was a man made of wood and straw.

Slowly, it raised itself to its feet, more straw falling from the gash in its torso.

Believing it may simply be a man in costume, Tomas plunged his sword deeper into the fiend's chest.

Dark, hollow eyes stared at him, unmoved by the experience of being stabbed through. Tomas withdrew the blade and lopped the creature's head off with one swift blow.

The canvas head bounced across the ground, leaving its hat at the straw man's feet. The body remained upright.

Tomas took a step backwards, not believing what he was seeing.

This is true magic.

The straw man's body stretched its wooden claws forward and lunged towards Tomas. The blade hacked downwards, lopping off one of the figure's arms at the shoulder.

It stopped in its tracks and bent down to retrieve the dismembered body part.

The other men caught up with Tomas and gathered around the spectacle.

"What's it doing?" Oliver asked as the straw man lifted the arm to its shoulder. Stiff tendrils of straw stretched from the shoulder socket and appeared to grip the separated arm, re-joining it to the body.

Tarkin started hacking at the scarecrow over and over and over until it fell into a pile of straw and broken wood upon the ground. He then stomped upon the timber ribs and limb bones, cracking them beneath his weight.

"Let's see you put yourself back together now," he said before spitting upon the mess upon the ground.

"Look," called one man.

All eyes turned towards the tree line.

Emerging slowly from the dark shadows along the tree line were more straw men.

Dozens of them.

Twenty-Two

Like a torrential wave, the straw men raced from the shadows and onto the open ground. They fixed their eyeless faces upon the men standing together.

"Any ideas?" Tarkin questioned.

"I was going to ask you the same," Tomas replied.

Long coats flapped behind the scarecrows, revealing their lean bodies as they bolted towards their targets. Their long, twisted wooden claws stretched out towards the travellers as they drew nearer.

One crewman was the first to confront the enemy. A straw man lunged towards him with its claws aiming for the man's throat.

Swinging his blade wildly, he lopped one hand from an outstretched limb. He tried to bring his sword back towards his adversary, but was too slow.

As the dismembered claw rolled across the snow, the other found its target and pierced the crewman's throat.

"By the gods," called another of Tarkin's men as the straw man dug his claw in deeper and deeper until the twisted fingers burst through the back of the neck.

It closed its grip before yanking its arm back quickly.

CRUNCH!

The man fell to the snow, his head lolling from side to side as dark blood gushed from the gaping wound in his neck.

The creature continued to hold a mess of wet flesh and several segments of vertebrae in its grasp. It slowly turned its head, as if looking at each of the men before it, gloating.

"You bastard," called another man as he brought his sword down in a long arc. The blade smashed through the wooden rib cage, separating the creature's arm and a section of its torso.

Another crewman swiped at the straw man's legs with his own weapon, breaking through the thighs and forcing the figure onto the ground.

With no claws to grab with and no feet to stand upon, it simply turned its hollow sockets towards each of the men nearby.

It wasn't over.

The men formed a line of sorts as the other scarecrows reached their position. They hacked and chopped madly, with little effect. The creatures didn't feel pain and could mend themselves quickly.

With their attention upon the many straw men surrounding them, they didn't notice the first one that Tomas encountered repairing itself upon the snow. With its broken bones back in position and its limbs reattached, it retrieved its canvas head from the snow with its gnarled claws.

It placed the hessian back onto its neck. Straw stems reached out to the head, finding the open gash and linking with the dry stubble inside the canvas sack. And like that, its head reconnected.

It moved its eyeless gaze across the expanse, seeking the one who had broken it. Within moments, it found the one it wanted.

Captain Tarkin.

Swiftly, it moved across the snow towards its intended target. It would have gone unnoticed if not for Oliver.

He had taken the head from another straw man and used a moment between blows to look back towards the village. He intended to check that the women were still safe, particularly Emily. Instead, his eyes fell upon the scarecrow running directly towards the captain.

"Tarkin," Oliver barked. "Behind you."

The captain turned in time to see the straw man within an arm's distance away. He instinctively raised his sword and piked the creature through the face. It stuck fast and dangled from the long blade.

There was no weight in the straw man.

Tarkin raised his blade as the figure flailed violently, attempting to strike the captain with a claw or boot. With one swift motion, the captain hurled the straw man from off the tip of his sword, over the heads of the men in battle and upon the snow behind the other scarecrows.

"I've got an idea," Oliver called as he started running back towards the village.

"Where are you going?" David bellowed. "The battle is here."

"I'll be back," he assured the other as he hastily made his way across the snow.

Several of the straw men made it through the line and raced after Oliver. David was about to go after them.

"No," Tomas commanded. "You are needed here."

"But Oliver," David replied. "What about the women?"

"Those women fight better than you," he answered as he dropped a straw man to the ground before stomping upon its chest with his heel. The wooden ribcage snapped loudly with each impact. Tomas then kicked the creature hard, sending it flying across the snow towards the tree line.

Turning his attention to another straw man, he knew he would see his previous opponent again. It would simply repair itself and attack.

He hoped Oliver really had a plan that would stop these fiends.

***

Pointing frantically, the Erilian women called to Oliver as he ran towards them. His heart pounded in his ears, causing every word they yelled to go unheard.

He saw they were pointing to something behind him.

The battle, perhaps? I'm about to fix that, I hope.

He risked a look.

Quickly turning his head towards the fray behind him, he saw the gaping, torn mouths and hollow eyes of five straw men pursuing him. They were closing on him.

He almost stumbled, arms flailing in wide circles and legs kicking out, sending puffs of snow into the air. He returned his attention to where he was going and saw three of the Erilian women racing forward with swords at the ready.

"Fire," Oliver called. "Fire. Fire."

They looked at him quizzically.

"Fire," he repeated, feeling his breath leaving him. "Fire."

Karlena seemed to understand. Racing back to the campfire near the barn, she grabbed an arrow from her quiver. As she ran, she tore a fragment of cloth from her sleeve and wrapped it around the tip of the arrow.

Oliver ran past the women and directly towards the fire pit just beyond them. The Erilian warriors engaged with the five straw men as Emily followed Oliver into the centre of the village.

He slowed his approach, pulling to a complete stop before turning on his heels. Emily ran to his side as he saw what the others were doing.

"No," he called to them. "Over here. Get them to the fire!"

Emily understood his intentions and started shouting at the others.

"Draw them over here," she called. "We'll put them in the pit."

Karlena made her way back to Oliver's position. She held a thick lump of wood that was alight with flames at one end and a five of arrows with cloth wrapped around their tips.

"Hold this," she instructed Emily, holding the lump of wood out to her. Emily took it carefully, keeping the flames away from her.

The other Erilian women moved away from the straw men and retreated to the fire pit with the others. The creatures gave chase and continued to battle near the flames.

Karlena placed an arrow onto her bowstring and dipped the cloth tip into the flame that danced upon the edge of the lump of wood in Emily's hands. She took aim and flung the flaming arrow into the chest of one straw man.

Almost instantly, the torso of the straw man erupted in flame. The dry intestines of the scarecrow provided the perfect fuel for the arrow tip, setting the creature ablaze in mere moments.

Rhydra, who was battling this figure, kicked the flaming straw man into the fire pit, where it continued to writhe and struggle in the intense heat within.

"Hurry Karlena," she called.

Karlena let loose a second flaming arrow, and a third, hitting two targets. The women forced those two scarecrows into the pit also, where they violently flailed as flames engulfed them.

"Save your arrows," Oliver instructed as he assisted the Erilians in forcing the remaining two straw men into the pit.

"We need to get to the battle," Sharek stated.

"We need arrows and fire," Akasati put in. "How do we carry fire?"

"I have an idea," Oliver replied.

He turned to the tower and gave a loud whistle. Three heads poked over the side.

"Can you hear me up there?" he called.

"Yes," came a reply.

"Is the tower lantern still in place?"

One head disappeared momentarily.

"Would it be a glass cylinder?" one man called back down.

"How would I know?" Oliver called back up. "Bring it down."

"They call themselves crewmen," Karlena quipped. "Surely they must know what a lantern looks like."

"Wrap some cloth around the tips of your arrows," Akasati instructed the others. "Just as Karlena did."

"Shouldn't we use oil?" Rhyodia asked.

"Do you see any oil?" Akasati responded.

The men exited the tower, one of them carrying a glass cylinder roughly the size of his head and encased in a steel cage. He dangled it by a chain handle in front of him as he approached.

"Is this what you want?" he called.

"You idiot," Rhydra shouted. "That is a lantern. We have the same thing on the *Adelandria.*"

"See," another snapped, hitting the lantern-bearer on the arm. "I told you."

"Is there any oil in it?" Oliver asked.

The man gave it a shake with both hands. The sound of sloshing liquid resonated from within.

"I think so," he replied.

"Either that or water," another remarked.

"Only one way to find out," Karlena said as she took the lantern, placed it on the ground, and opened the casing. She lifted the glass cylinder, removed her gloves, and felt the wick with her fingers. It was damp. She lifted her fingertips to her nose and smelt the familiar aroma of oil. "Light it."

Oliver took the lump of wood from Emily and held the flame near the wick. It lit instantly.

Placing the glass and the casing back in place, Karlena lifted the lantern and turned towards the battle on the open ground.

"You three stay with Emily," she instructed the three watchmen before turning her attention to Oliver. "What about you?"

"I told them I would be back," he replied. "I must go."

"Then let's go," she replied as she turned towards the west.

***

Flinging another straw man toward the trees, Simon directed his attention to another approaching from his left. The fight was taking its toll. He was weary, and his legs felt more like water than muscle.

Several pools and smears of blood adorned the surrounding snow, spilling from five of Tarkin's crewmen who had fallen during the exchange. Even before their demise, the men were outnumbered and had little hope of defeating an enemy such as this.

Still, they continued to tear the straw men apart, fling them away, only to face them again and again. Simon surmised he had faced the same one over three times already.

What was worse, the scarecrows seemed bent upon the destruction of those who had defeated them in the previous skirmish. Simon had noticed several of the creatures rising from the snow, scanning the line of men until they found their foe.

It seemed ridiculous.

He imagined that if he survived this, no one would believe the tale if he told it.

Who would?

With the numbers of men thinning and the enemy maintaining forces, Simon speculated their end was near. His mind wandered to the ship upon the sea and the prisoners on board. If they were to fall here, they would have failed those poor souls.

No!

He would not give up that easily.

He had to win.

He had to save those people.

With a quick swish of his blade, he separated the head from another straw man. He then swung the blade back and hacked the creature into two pieces across the torso. The arms and legs kicked and reached for him as he stuck the point of his blade into the upper body.

He tossed the section into the southwest before hurling the lower half of the body towards the northwest.

"Let's see how quickly you get back together now," he shouted as he kicked the head directly towards the west.

Another raced towards him from his right, starting the process over again. He raised his sword, ready to make contact when, suddenly, a flaming arrow shot past him, planting itself into the stomach of the attacker.

The creature burst into flames as it ran forward. The chaff inside the hessian skin was ablaze in moments.

It fell to the ground, writhing and twisting, as if in pain.

Simon turned to see a line of Erilian women brandishing bows and flaming arrows. They started picking their targets carefully before letting the arrows loose.

They hit more straw men, causing flames to burst from their forms. It reminded Simon of the dragon fire that engulfed Woodmyst during his childhood.

During that time, the sight of the flames had caused deep sorrow and anger in him. This time, he felt elation as he watched the straw men fall, one after the other.

The creatures were flung onto the open ground, away from the men, so the band of archers could get a clear shot at the enemy.

The men gave a raucous cheer as the last of the scarecrows fell in a pile of flame.

It was over.

"Good work, ladies." Tarkin smiled as he sauntered over to the Erilian warriors.

David slapped Oliver on the shoulder as he strode past his friend, making his way back towards the village.

"We need to collect the bodies and throw them in the pit," Oliver said to the others. "All of them."

Tomas stopped in his tracks, eager to get back to Emily.

"You're not just talking about these things, are you?"

"No," Oliver replied, shaking his head. "There is dark magic here, Tomas. We need to burn our own as well. I've heard tales of mystics using their powers to raise the dead. We shouldn't allow the possibility of that to occur."

"Burn my men in that pit?" Tarkin seemed offended. "Treat them just like the enemy?"

"We could make a pyre," Oliver suggested, trying to apologise.

"No," Jeremy interjected. "We don't have the time. The pit will suffice, Captain."

"They were good men, Jeremy," Tarkin argued.

"I know," the other replied. "But what if Oliver is right? We need to catch that ship, Captain. We need to catch the Sovereign. We don't have time for fancy burials."

Tarkin looked to the ground and saw the many smears and streaks of blood upon the snow. Blood that belonged to his men.

Jeremy and Oliver were right. Time was their worst enemy now and skirmishes like this were simply slowing them down or wearing them out.

He nodded reluctantly. "The pit will do."

Twenty-Three

They had fashioned a crude sled from supplies discovered in the stable. Made of several timber slats coarsely nailed to two long beams of wood, acting as runners, then tethered to David's gigantic horse to bear cargo from the battleground to the fire pit.

With care, they took the fallen men back to the village to be prepared for their burial. Wrapping the bodies in cloth found in the huts, the Erilian women carefully covered the men from head to toe.

Others returned to the open ground in front of the tree line, on Captain Tarkin's orders, to collect every piece of the straw men that they could find. They searched and gathered discarded body parts and scattered straw that lay upon the snow.

"The burnt pieces and ash also," Tarkin called. "I don't want to chance these things putting themselves together and coming back for us again."

The men loaded what they could find and pick up with their hands onto the sled. Some of the dismembered claws continued to flex and move as they fell onto the pile of chaff and wood heaped onto the timber slats.

Surrounding the sled as they made their way back to the village, the men picked up any fragments that fell from the load as it moved and tossed it back upon the cargo. They didn't want to leave anything behind.

At the edge of the settlement, they unharnessed the horse and four men towed the sled to the side of the deep fire pit. Using spades and pitchforks, a few of the crewmen pushed the remains of the straw men into the flames.

"The sled too," Tarkin ordered. "I intend to burn this village to the ground before we leave. We may as well start with that."

The four men took the sled by the shafts and turned it so its rear was sitting on the edge of the pit. With a great shove, they pushed the timber vehicle into the flames where it crashed down to the bottom, shafts sticking into the air above the fire pit.

The intense heat enveloped the crude device and bit into it almost immediately. Flames danced up and along the wooden beams before reaching towards the sky.

The gathering watched the fire in silence for a moment as the men of Woodmyst carried one of the fallen on a canvas sheet, Ivo and David on one side, with Simon and Oliver holding the other. Tomas followed closely with Emily on his arm. They carefully lowered the body to the ground by the edge of the pit.

The women had wrapped the man tightly in a white sheet, obscuring the wounds he had sustained in battle. They followed a ritual carried out onboard many ships. They would swathe the body of a crewman in his bedding before being weighted with iron and lowered into the sea.

They've done well, Tarkin thought as he reflected upon the job the Erilian women had done in preparing the man for his farewell.

"The others are ready also," Tomas informed the captain. "We need some men to help us."

Tarkin nodded as he stared at the wrapped body lying on the ground. Jeremy responded to the signal by tapping several men on the shoulders as he walked through the gathering towards the hut where the fallen men lay.

"Give us a hand, lads," he whispered as he passed by.

Moments later, five bodies swaddled in linen rested side by side in the snow. Rope around the torso and legs of each fallen man left four long stretches of cord exposed to aid with lowering the bodies into the fire.

Tarkin, taking the length of one rope himself, insisted that the men of the *Adelandria* be the ones to send the departed crewmen into oblivion. The men of Woodmyst understood, knowing they would have requested the same if they wrapped one of their own in cloth and awaiting the pyre.

With three other men assisting, taking up positions on four sides of the fire pit, Tarkin lowered the first into the flames. Orange and yellow flares wrapped around the linen-covered body as it descended deeper and deeper.

The rope slackened as the body rested upon the bottom of the pit. Tarkin threw the remaining length of rope into the fire after the body and returned to take another of the fallen to the flames.

Jeremy and three others had retrieved the next man on the ground and repeated the process. The gathered looked on in silence, sorrowful for losing good friends, angry for the manner of their demise, thankful that it wasn't them being lowered into the pit.

Emily found tears welling in her eyes. She didn't know these men at all. Yet, she felt remorse and deep sorrow as she watched the flames reach higher and higher as they lowered each man into the fire.

The Erilian women looked on stone-faced and heads high. They had spent so much time delicately preparing the bodies for this moment. Emily wasn't sure if it was respect or pride for the lost men that the female warriors were showing, but she allowed herself to cry for them.

Tomas misinterpreted the emotion and hugged her tighter. It was a sentiment she welcomed as she snuggled against him, peering into the warm glow with tears streaking down her cheeks.

***

Sleep was uneventful and not worth the effort. None of the men had ever encountered such an enemy before; fiends made of straw and wood that were neither living nor dead, as far as Tomas was concerned.

The terror, confusion and sadness upon everyone's faces told him they wrestled with the same internal struggle as he. His fight, and theirs, was now with uncertainty.

He wondered how they could defeat such creatures that didn't require air and water to survive. All they needed was their substance, the materials from which they were made of.

Chaff and timber.

Even the threat of fire didn't seem to stop them. They had burnt the scarecrows before, only to have them appear on their trail again and again.

This time was different, however. This time they moved with such fluid motion that they were firstly mistaken for men.

Tomas considered the power behind these creatures. He assumed it belonged to the witch targeting them. Following them.

It was too coincidental to be otherwise.

Was she really in league with the Sovereign? Or was that just some idle speech by the townsman when they first arrived in the village?

He could not be certain, but they have made some arrangement. The townsman mentioned instructions for them to take Emily to the Sovereign. This made his resolve to protect her even more absolute.

Even so, a part of him wondered how this would help defeat an enemy that was not alive, nor were they dead. They just simply *were*.

Uncertainty continued to flood him within, churning and bubbling like a tempestuous storm.

How were they going to survive?

They were all tired after battling men in the afternoon. Their weariness had only increased after combatting straw demons at night. What was worse was the knowledge that the scarecrows needed no rest. They could keep going until the men failed and then continue.

Tomas didn't like their chances.

Emily held him tightly around the waist as they peered at the flames of the deep fire pit.

The crude sled and remains of the men who had died in the conflict earlier in the night had disappeared into the orange glow.

Wrapping his arms around her shoulders, placing a hand gently on the back of her head, he kissed her on her forehead as he considered their quest.

She had full hope they would find her people, save her sister, and return to her father. He had hoped for the same until this moment.

Daring not to tell her how he felt, he just held her, allowing her to believe they had a chance.

Perhaps that would be enough.

***

The faint glow of morning light appeared on the horizon. Clouds swirled high above the village as they made their way out over the sea. A flock of seabirds collected upon the yard beams attached to the masts of the moored ship and decorated it with thick white excrement.

Standing upon the end of the wharf, Tarkin noticed that the pale adornment was thick and appeared in long, wide lines that ran up and down the masts.

"Well," he said, raising his brow. "This girl's been here a while."

The captain also observed the breeze was gentler nearer to the ground than it was among the clouds. This should make travelling somewhat easier for them as they rode onwards. He just hoped the marauders' ship wasn't benefiting from the wind higher above him.

He pulled his spyglass from his pocket and scanned the horizon. Finding the faint orange glow of lantern light, he could see that the ship had made some distance overnight.

Although he could not determine the finer features of the vessel, he knew the sails were full, and the wind was in their enemies' favour. Perhaps the current was aiding them as well.

They needed to leave.

He hurried back to the village, where the others crowded around the fire pit, staring into the flames. He gave a whistle, causing the gathering to snap out of their trances.

"Prepare the horses to leave," he ordered. "Take what supplies we can. Especially food and linen. Then we torch the town."

The men scurried off to prepare for their journey as Tomas approached the captain with Emily and the Erilian women in tow. All wore looks of concern.

"Are you sure that you want to burn the village?" he asked. "That ship out there will see the flames. They may figure that someone pursues them."

"I no longer care, Tomas," Tarkin replied. "He probably knows already. And if not, perhaps he should."

"You haven't rested," Rhydra said. "You need to think this through."

"Why?"

"You might put the prisoners at risk," she replied.

"I don't think so." He started walking towards the stable. "He needs them alive for whatever reason. Otherwise, and forgive me Emily, he would have killed them all at their village. The cargo is too important to him."

Slightly offended at the word *cargo* being associated with her people, Emily internally agreed with Tarkin's words. They need the women for something. She didn't really want to discover the true reason for their abduction. She just wanted Joanne, her sister, back in her arms.

She stopped dead in her tracks and sobbed.

"Look what you did," Karlena barked at Tarkin.

"No," Emily said to her as Tomas came to her side.

"I apologise, my lady," the captain said earnestly.

"No," she said again. "I agree with you. I just want my sister back."

Tarkin approached her and took her hands in his.

"We'll get her back," he promised. "We'll get all of them back."

He turned his attention back to the stable and moved off.

"So, you'll reconsider burning the village?" Rhydra called after him.

"No," he replied. "We still burn this shithole into the ground."

***

As the horses gathered at the northern edge of the village, Tomas and the other men of Woodmyst strode through the small town with flaming torches in their hands.

They started with the ship that was moored on the wharf.

Oliver ventured below deck and found the sails folded and stowed away towards the bow of the vessel. He ran his torch along several pieces of the folded canvas sheets before hastily climbing back to the top deck and then clambering down a rope ladder to the surface of the dock.

They stayed beside the ship, making sure it caught alight before moving back into the village. Orange glows emitted from portholes along the side of the hull before tongues of fire poked through them to lap at the flanks of the ship.

The birds resting upon the yard beams took to the air as the deck burst alight with dancing flames.

"Oliver and Ivo, take the tower," Tomas commanded as they walked along the pier. "The rest of us will burn the town. We'll meet back at the horses."

With that, they fanned in different directions. Tomas headed directly for the stable as David and Simon directed their attention to the huts encircling the fire pit.

Pushing the stable doors open, Tomas glared into the dark interior of the building. The sun had not yet breached the horizon and the swirling clouds in the sky above dulled the morning light. This made it difficult to view the interior structuring of the stable.

Dark silhouettes of wooden beams and partitions between the stalls lined each side of the building. Tomas held his torch in front of him as he moved towards the rear of the building. Once there, he doused a pile of straw with flame before turning towards the open doors. As he returned to the entrance, he lit more piles of hay that lay within the stalls.

He exited the stable and entered the cool of the morning air to see three huts burning and a fourth showing the glare of fire through the windows. He moved around the village, keeping closer to the water's edge as he passed by.

The tall stone beacon tower stood before him. The door at the base was open, with no sign of Oliver or Ivo nearby. His eyes climbed the structure to see large flames forming on the platform.

He wondered how the men could achieve flames of such size and what the fuel source could possibly be. As he contemplated this, Ivo and Oliver burst through the door at the tower's base at great velocity.

Oliver held a lantern, not unlike the one that was discovered upon the beacon's platform earlier by the watchmen. He stopped a few feet from the door and tossed the lamp back through the door. Ivo kept running towards where the others waited for them with the horses. Oliver quickly resumed running, heading for Tomas.

"We found the oil stockpile," he called.

A great yellow and orange ball of fire exploded through the narrow entrance to the tower. The force threw Oliver into the air. Tomas felt the heat ripple across his face. He dropped to his knees as Oliver came crashing down into the snow.

Tomas observed a pillar of fire engulf the top of the tower. Intense light filled the village, exchanging the dark morning light for radiance brighter than the noon sun.

If the marauders' ship missed the glare of the stable fire, they certainly would have seen this.

"What the blazes?" bellowed David as he stood outside the hut with his flaming torch in his hand.

Oliver laughed loudly as he rolled onto his back so that he could observe his work.

"I think the known world just saw and heard that," Simon called, a wide smile across his face. "That was brilliant!"

A loud cracking and crunching sound started bellowing from the construction. Tomas couldn't believe his eyes as he watched portions of rock breaking apart near the base of the tower.

"We need to move," he called as he quickly got to his feet.

The others didn't question his words. They simply turned towards the awaiting riders and ran as fast as they could.

Large chunks of stone ruptured, sending shards of rock across the snow in all directions. The greatest portion flew into the water, kicking up a spray of white foam as it fell beneath the waves.

The men of Woodmyst slowed their pace once they reached the far side of the village. Ivo was waiting for them there, watching the whole thing unfold from a safe distance.

They turned to watch the tower, draped in a giant flaming cape, slowly topple towards the shore. It smashed into ruin upon the snow-covered ground, flames caressing the oil-smothered stone and wood.

"Bloody brilliant!" Simon breathed.

Tarkin gave the order to move out when all had mounted their steeds. The men of Woodmyst let the others ride ahead as they formed up at the rear of the group, looking over their shoulders as thick, black smoke from the burning village billowed into the sky.

Twenty-Four

Although others surrounded her, Emily felt lonely. The captain's words had reminded her she was the only member of her small community amongst her current companions. Her father, Tomas had told her, was safe in Woodmyst. She pictured him sitting in a quaint room that Tomas called home.

Her memory returned to a time before they moved to the mountains within the Forest of Khun. Back to a time when her sister was a newborn, and she was still a child.

Emily fondly recalled sitting on her father's knee as he read to her from a thick leather-bound book. Echoing tales of knights in armour battling dragons and other beasts that she believed existed only in the minds of storytellers called through her thoughts as she pictured his kind face.

She remembered the deep lines that scarred his cheeks from laughing and smiling. His enormous hands would clap in time as she danced in their sitting room. Her memory of dancing made her smile as the young Emily's idea of dancing was to simply spin around until she became giddy, ending up on the ground in a giggling heap. Then he would reach out to her with his enormous hands and lift her to his lap again, where he would hold her against his chest until she became steady again.

She missed him.

It was because of him she was on this quest to get her sister back. She had no choice. If she hadn't stumbled into the men of Woodmyst after escaping the marauders, she would have found the courage to pursue them herself and on her own.

Joanne needed to be brought home to her father.

Even though she had fond memories of her father and the manner in which he treated her as she grew, she recalled that Antony Grenefeld loved his younger daughter more. He doted over her more and spent more time with her than he did with his elder daughter.

Her father did not completely ignore her, and as she grew older, she spent more time with her mother than with him. He still showed her affection and talked with her more about adult things, such as marriage and meeting the right man, before delving into making lifelong promises. But his relationship with Joanne was more binding than she had ever had with him.

It would break his heart if Joanne was lost forever. Emily knew she simply could not return to her father without her sister.

She turned to look towards the rear of the pack, past the ten crewmen of the *Adelandria* and to the men of Woodmyst behind them. Riding in the middle of them was her beloved.

Emily had to return to her father so he could know she had found him. This man was the one with whom to share those lifelong promises. She wanted to be with this man for her remaining days, and she hoped there would be many.

Even now, she longed to be with him, wondering why he was riding behind and not by her side. She was sure he had his reasons, and that they were justified, but that didn't prevent her from still feeling alone.

Tomas smiled at her.

She believed he wanted to be with her, too. Returning his smile, she turned her head towards the front of the group.

Tarkin sat tall in his saddle as Jeremy rode by his side. They were discussing something she couldn't quite hear. She had heard the Sovereign mentioned many times and believed the captain was simply venting his frustrations about his enemy to his first mate. Jeremy sat in silence for most of the way, contributing to the conversation now and then when he could fit a word in. Usually, that set the captain off on another tangent, where he mentioned the Sovereign several times again.

Akasati, riding to the side, rolled her eyes as Tarkin started up his ranting again. She moved her attention elsewhere, trying to block out the discussion by concentrating on the view as they climbed to higher ground.

The forest had crept towards them, closing the open ground between the tree line and the coast. The sloping grounds that swept towards the shore became less frequent as more and more black rock exposed itself through the ground to their right.

Waves crashed noisily upon the stony drops where the water met the land, reminding Emily of distant thunder. She enjoyed the sound and relished the smell of salt in the air, but would choose to be on a meadow by a river or bubbling brook in a heartbeat if the opportunity presented itself.

"I think we're going to have to enter the forest again," Karlena said from her side.

Emily looked past the captain to the open ground in the distance. It rose and fell a few times, exposing ridges and hills, but no sign of trees blocking their path.

"What makes you say that?" Emily asked. "I don't see where the forest crosses our path."

"See the mountains in the distance?" Karlena pointed.

Emily followed her motion and saw faint, giant shapes covered in mist. They were far away to the north and seemed to jut out from the coast and into the sea. The cloud cover and early morning light hidden behind them obscured many things from her vision. The Erilian women, however, seemed to be attuned to many things that others were not.

"How can you see that?" Emily asked as she squinted to focus her sight.

"I just can," she answered. "It's covered with trees and, from what I can see; they reach all the way down to the water's edge."

"You're making that up." Emily looked at the other disbelievingly.

"We could look through Dakmel's spyglass if you like." Karlena smiled.

Emily set her eyes upon Tarkin, who was deeply engaged in discussion. "I don't think he really wants to be bothered right now," she replied.

"I wish you would!" Karlena shook her head. "Anything to shut him up. Sovereign this and Sovereign that."

"His family—" Emily started, pausing when she realised that discussing the captain's past might be painful to the Erilian women who truly loved him. "I'm sorry."

"Don't apologise." Karlena smiled. "He seeks revenge for what happened to them. We also seek revenge for what that bastard did to us. So do you. What happened to his family, your family and ours is what keeps driving us onwards. I just wish he wouldn't harp on and on about it. It's as if he's feeding his hatred on purpose."

Emily suddenly felt pity for the Erilian woman riding at her side. There was pain in her voice. She cared deeply for the man she followed and displayed concern for him and his frame of mind.

"I don't know," Karlena said as tears welled in her eyes. "Men. What do we do with them?"

Emily smiled sentimentally as she gave a quick shrug.

She peered towards the ocean where seagulls swooped into white tips, bringing back tiny fish that swam beneath the surface. Monstrous white walls of foam erupted upon the jagged black rocks at the water's edge.

As the distant sound that reminded her of thunder reached her ears, she thought again about her family. How much she wanted to be that little girl at home, spinning until she fell down!

Even with all these new friends surrounding her, she felt so desperately alone.

***

A soft breeze swam between the steeds' legs, sending small ribbons of frost and snow into a spiralling dance before they separated and dissipated as the wind subsided. Before it vanished completely, the draught would pick up again, gather the loose particles of snow from the surface and force them into spinning wisps.

"It wasn't enough that he should just take my family," Tarkin said. "He has attacked and slaughtered people from all lands. He's not right in the head."

"Not right," Jeremy agreed. He had learnt long ago to just agree with his captain when he was in this kind of mood.

"He has to die, Jeremy."

"Of course." The other nodded.

"He rapes and butchers women and children," Tarkin said, justifying his reasons for wanting to end another man's life. "He slays all the males. Have you noticed that?"

"I did."

"All of them," the captain shook his head. "Even the newborns. I've seen the bodies. They didn't just run them through with a blade. They grabbed them by their little ankles and smashed them against trees and walls."

Tarkin wiped his eyes.

"Sovereign," he spat. "I would love to grab him by his ankles and smash his skull open upon a rock or two."

"I know," Jeremy said as he gave thought to the many innocent victims of the Sovereign.

"What is his purpose?" Tarkin asked. "Have you ever wondered?"

The other nodded as he contemplated what he would like to do to the Sovereign. His mind wandered into a memory where he saw a young woman who once lived in a villa next to his own.

To him, she was strikingly beautiful, with dark hair and hazel eyes. He remembered spending many nights talking with her, just talking. They would converse about deep, meaningful matters that they were both passionate about. Time was always their worst enemy with the morning sunlight constantly intruding in their affairs, causing them to realise that they had been in each other's company the whole night through.

Art, literature, poetry and philosophy dominated the subject of their discussions. There were many moments of lifelong ambitions and the discussion of marriage came up once or twice, but the natural progress of their relationship would have seen them become husband and wife, if not for the Sovereign.

Jeremy missed her and still reserved a space for her in his heart. Only, the space had become a chasm and his heart had become colder as age drew him onward.

Unlike the captain, Jeremy did not wed his beloved or to have children with her. But he loved her, still loved her as much as was humanly possible.

Many years had passed since he had last felt her embrace, her kiss. He tried to envision her smooth skin, naked by the fire when they first came together as one.

His memory had become like a mist, allowing only a hazy recollection of what once was. He felt a tickling sensation upon his scarred cheek as a tear ran from the corner of his eye towards his jaw.

"Meaghan."

"What was that?" Tarkin asked.

"Sorry?" Jeremy furrowed his brow. Had he said her name aloud?

Tarkin looked at the other and frowned.

"I'm the one who should apologise, old friend," the captain replied. "I've brought some terrible memory back to you with all of my ravings."

"It's all fine," Jeremy said. "I was trying to remember what she looked like."

"I understand." Tarkin nodded as he gave thought to his own family.

Jeremy's eyes were red and filled with tears. "I can't remember her anymore," he blubbered.

The captain pursed his lips as he considered the words to say.

"I remember the night when that bastard came into my house," he began. "I remember the looks upon the faces of my family. The horror, the fear, the shame. I'll never forget that. But, like you, it's the fond moments that I struggle with.

"I've allowed my hatred to cloud my thoughts for far too long. But I can still remember times of laughing and love.

"Sometimes, I can use these to recall images of my son and daughter at play, or my wife and I making love or just simply sharing a quiet moment. The gaps need to be filled with my imagination, but I try to reflect upon the pleasant moments from time to time.

"Perhaps I should have been doing this more often," he said, hoping his words were of some comfort to his friend.

"Thank you, Captain." Jeremy wiped the tears away with the back of his sleeve.

Tarkin retrieved his spyglass from his pocket as he pulled his steed to a halt. Jeremy signalled for the riders to stop as Tarkin scanned the horizon and found the dark vessel far to the north.

"The current and the wind are working for them," he said, deliberately changing the focus of their conversation. "We won't catch them now."

"What will we do if we lose sight of them?" Jeremy asked, moving back into his role as the first mate.

"Keep moving north until we find the port that shelters that ship," Tarkin replied. "They can't sail forever."

Putting the glass back in his pocket, Tarkin urged his horse onward. Jeremy signalled the others to move out with a whistle and a hand gesture.

Pressing on, the steeds trudged through the thick snow as jagged, black rocks appeared along the shoreline more frequently and the mountain range gradually snaked towards the sea. The passage of land upon which they travelled was becoming narrow. The forest that hemmed the feet of the mountains drew nearer and nearer.

***

With his eyes peeled to the west, Tomas watched the trees. He wanted no more surprises coming for them from the trees. Occasionally, he slowed enough to spin his brown mare in a tight circle to see if they had anything tailing them. Fortunately, only the ploughed snow from horse hooves disturbed the ground and a pillar of dark smoke in the ever-increasing distance signalling where they once were.

He would rather travel closer to the water's edge, but the black, uneven rocks to the east would prove too treacherous for the steeds to manage. The feeling of unease overcame him frequently as the forest gradually gained ground on them.

They were still riding at what Tomas regarded as a safe distance from the tree line, but it was getting closer and closer with every step their horses took. They would be in the thick of the woods before they knew it.

The worst feeling hit him when he surmised that by the time the sun passed behind the mountain peaks, they must make camp among the trees. He suddenly wished for another hamlet, a fishing village or farmhouse they could commandeer for the night.

It was still morning. The sun's orb of light showed through the veil of grey swirling cloud cover as it climbed into the sky.

Not even mid-morning yet, and he was already thinking about camp.

The mountains drew closer and closer to the shore, pushing the trees towards them. There were more pines here, covered in clear snow.

Tomas found the scenery exceptionally beautiful. He imagined it was just as much a sight to behold during the warmer seasons, with the snow melted and the grass covering the slopes.

The ominous sense of terror from within the forest overshadowed the splendour of the environment, putting Tomas at a constant unease as they progressed towards the north. He felt the hairs on the back of his neck standing on end. A deep chill ran up and along his spine as he continued to watch the trees.

Always watching the trees.

He thought he was allowing paranoia to gain a level of control over the state of his mind. That was until Simon suggested that two of them should watch the forest at all times.

"That's where they will come from if they choose to attack," he said. "The sea is easy enough to keep an eye on. Besides, Captain Tarkin keeps pulling up to take a view through his glass. All his men are looking towards the horizon as well. I think we're the only ones to be watching the west at the moment."

"My thoughts exactly," Tomas replied. "I thought I was the only one watching the trees. It's good to know someone is of the same mind."

"I've been watching too," Oliver admitted. "I want no more of those straw bastards creeping upon us."

Ivo's eyes were also scanning the trees. He wasn't searching for the straw men or spying on a sign of an attack. His eyes were looking for her.

His mind was transfixed with the image of the woman; draped in sheer, white garments.

He saw her long, flowing, blonde hair softly dancing in the breeze. He heard her sweet, enticing voice calling, calling, calling.

Ivo.

Ivo.

He shook his head, attempting to rid his mind of the thought.

"Are you all right?" David asked, noticing the movement.

"Just tired," he lied. "No sleep last night."

"You and me both, little brother," the large man chuckled. "Jump down and rub some snow on your face."

"What?" the younger man asked.

"Rub some snow on your face," David repeated. "The cold shock will wake you up for a time."

Ivo looked at the other questioningly.

"I guarantee it." David nodded.

"I'm not jumping down to rub snow on my face," said Ivo with a wry smile.

"Why not?" David waved a hand at the travellers in front of them. "No one cares what we do back here. They're too busy watching the horizon for the ship and trying not to fall asleep as they ride. It might be worthwhile if we all jump down off the horses and have a decent snow rub."

"A snow rub?" Ivo quizzed.

"When you think of a better name for it," David pointed to him, "let me know."

"All right." Ivo frowned. "Why don't you get off your horse and show me how to perform this famous *snow rub* that you just created?"

"No need," the other replied.

"Why?"

"I'm not tired," the bald giant informed the younger man. "I can go for days without sleep."

"Rubbish," Oliver put in after listening to the whole exchange. "I spotted you sleeping on your horse not more than a mile back. The others were just too tired to notice."

"I was just resting my eyes," David argued as a smirk crossed his face.

"And snoring?" Oliver added.

"I was clearing my throat," he managed, before erupting in laughter.

The others, listening to the exchange, laughed with him. Tomas felt better after experiencing the moment of light-heartedness.

Ivo, however, was lost in thought again. Feigning a laugh, he wiped his eyes and peered off towards the woods. She entered his mind once more, calling him over and over.

Ivo.

Ivo.

Ivo.

He wanted her.

He needed her.

He loved her.

Twenty-Five

Tomas sat on his brown mare at the crest of a gentle slope. The others had continued as he took time to stop and look back the way they had come. The pillar of black smoke rising from the village was far in the distance, almost upon the horizon.

They had made a lot of ground in the time they had been travelling. The sun, still veiled by swirling grey clouds, was directly above the riders. He gauged they had been on horseback for nearly six hours without rest, not counting small stops for necessary reasons.

Turning his horse back towards the group, now ascending the next embankment some distance away, Tomas urged the mare onwards at a trot. He still felt uneasy about the encroaching forest to the west, and was sure that someone or something was watching him from amongst the trees.

He had initially stopped atop the hill to see if they were being followed. The sense of a constant threat nearby kept tugging at him from within. His eyes had been scanning the trees for the entire journey.

Something urged him to look back.

All he saw was snow and smoke. Nothing more.

With lack of sleep, muscle fatigue and a wandering mind, Tomas was sure paranoia was getting the better of him. Something terrible was definitely out there, somewhere. He was certain that it was travelling with them, keeping at a distance where it remained unheard and unseen.

As he crossed the vale between the two sloping hills, he saw Tarkin upon his steed to the far right of the troop. His spyglass was up to his eye again, pointed to the north. Before Tomas reached the top of the rise, the riders continued. Only the men of Woodmyst and Emily waited for him.

"What did you see?" Simon asked.

"Nothing," he answered. "I feel eyes on us still."

"As do I," David acknowledged. "My concern is whether we outnumber them or they outnumber us."

"The captain presses on," Oliver said.

"We need to rest the horses," Tomas told them. "We've made many miles today already. No matter how hard we try, we won't catch that ship today."

He looked to Emily, who wore a sullen expression.

"I'm sorry," he said to her.

"I know," she said. "It's nobody's fault. We need to rest."

Tomas sidled over to her and placed his hand on her thigh. She responded by placing her hand on his.

"Ride ahead," he instructed Oliver, "and inform the captain that we need to rest the horses. Six hours is far too long without a decent break."

With that, Oliver kicked hard and sprinted his steed across the snow.

The others watched him kicking up white powder in all directions as he galloped his horse down the side of the hill towards the group of riders crossing the plain. Tomas directed the mare forwards. She followed Oliver's tracks at a slow pace as the other horses around her fell in line.

Riding in silence, they watched as Oliver made his way past the bulk of the group, slowing up to come alongside Tarkin at the lead of the pack. The captain pulled to a stop as he and Oliver exchanged words.

Tarkin pointed towards the trees.

What are you doing?

Tomas watched with unsettling curiosity.

Oliver now pointed towards the forest, motioning with his hand in a sweeping gesture towards the next rise along their path.

Tarkin gave a signal to his men and turned the pack towards the tree line.

No. Not the forest.

Tomas dug his heels into his charger's flanks. She leapt into a full sprint down the hill towards the troop, aiming to cut them off before they made it any closer to the woods.

He was nearly at the bottom of the rise before the others with him realised what was happening. They gave chase, but knew there was no chance of catching up with their leader. He and his brown mare were simply too fast.

They could hear him shouting as he raced forward, but his words were lost in the air as it rushed by their ears.

"Not near the forest," he called. "Not near the forest."

A few of the riders heard his voice, but like the men of Woodmyst riding down the hillside, they didn't understand. They gave him confused looks as he drew nearer, still calling the same thing over and over.

"Captain," one man shouted.

Tarkin pulled to a stop and turned towards his crewman. His gaze locked onto Tomas, who was racing towards him at high speed. He could see the other saying something and could just make out his voice.

"What's he saying?"

"Something about the forest," Sharek replied.

"Not near the forest," Rhyodia said. "We should not go near the forest."

She turned her eyes towards the trees and saw her. The woman in white was standing at the tree line, watching them.

"Look." Rhyodia pointed.

The riders stared, transfixed. She was a vision of beauty.

Some tussled with the concept that she may just be a trick of the brain brought on by lack of sleep and exposure to the winter conditions. Others wanted to be with her and felt a craving to please her, however she willed.

Tomas pulled his horse to a halt as he spotted the woman in the forest. She turned her piercing blue eyes towards him and smiled.

He lowered his brow angrily and clenched his teeth tightly.

You won't have me, bitch.

Seeming to lose interest, she turned her gaze from him and locked onto another that approached from the hill.

Ivo.

Ivo.

He wasn't sure if he was dreaming, awake, alive or dead. She was here. Right here and they all saw her.

His heart was beating faster. His head swam with the sensation of spinning ecstasy. He steered his horse towards her and made his way towards the forest where she waited for him.

Tomas followed her eyes and saw the pull that she had on Ivo.

His anger deepened as his body tensed. He pulled his sword from his sheath and held it high.

"You will not have him, witch," he called across the snow as he lowered the tip of his blade towards her. "But I will have your head on a pike for what you have done."

He kicked hard.

The mare lifted her forelimbs into the air, kicking wildly.

She raced across the plain as fast as she could. Tomas saw red as he sped past the crew of the *Adelandria* and their captain.

The woman in white moved her eyes from Ivo and locked onto Tomas. They grew wide with fear as he drew nearer and nearer to her.

Ivo suddenly stopped in his tracks, a little confused. David rode to his side.

"Are you all right?" he asked. "She must have had you in a trance or something."

Ivo stared at her. She still stood at the edge of the woods, lovely, elegant and alluring.

Why did she stop calling?

He was aching to be with her. Seeing her so near was beyond torture.

Tomas swung his sword downward, aiming to lop her head off in one swift blow.

She swept her hand towards the ground as if brushing something away.

A sudden wall of snow, frost and white powder sprung up from the ground, obscuring Tomas' view of the woman.

It spooked the mare, pulling to a stop so quickly that she almost sent her rider flying from the saddle.

Several horses on the plain threw their forelimbs into the air, sending their riders to the ground. Others turned to run, but their quick-thinking handlers manoeuvred them back in place.

Clinging to her back with his legs, Tomas corrected his posture and grunted his disapproval of his steed's behaviour as the bulk of the wall crashed back to the ground. A thick mist of frost hung in the air, slowly descending to the surface.

"What was that?" he barked at his horse. "We almost had her. Scared by a little snow? You've been through worse."

She snorted an unapologetic reply as the cloud of frost settled back to the ground.

The woman vanished.

Tomas stared into the forest for a long time.

He knew she was still in there somewhere. Feeling her gaze upon him, he knew she was still watching and waiting for an opportunity.

"We stay on open ground," he called to the men behind him. "Not near the forest."

***

Gathered in a tight circular formation, the men stood on the open ground with their eyes fixed towards the forest. The horses roamed a little distance away from them, between their position and the black rocks by the waves. Some steeds kicked at the snow, finding frozen roots to grate their teeth against. Others waited for the men of Woodmyst to approach with the small sacks of oats they carried, offering the animals a handful of feed as they passed by.

Tarkin stood by his men on the snow, watching for the witch to return. He couldn't believe he had almost led all of his remaining crew members straight to her. Upon reflection, he knew moving towards the trees was a tactical error, but something had blocked his judgement, allowing him to see only the possibility of shelter from the elements.

Was he bewitched?

Was the woman in white manipulating him?

Was it merely that he was tired and not thinking correctly?

Was it that his obsession to take revenge upon the Sovereign was blinding him to the blatantly obvious?

Karlena snuggled against him and rubbed his back.

"We should travel a little farther," she said to him. "But we should stop again before the sun reaches the mountains' peaks. We need to sleep. All of us."

"The witch will come when our eyes are closed," he said to her softly, hoping his men didn't hear him.

"She might," Karlena agreed. "She might not. Perhaps she'll keep her distance. I saw fear in her eyes."

Tarkin looked at the woman by his side.

"What do you mean?"

"All the men," she explained, "this woman transfixed even you. I saw lust and yearning on some faces. Others looked like slaves ready to obey. You wore the face of a very confused man. It was as if you saw something... I don't know how to explain it. It was as if you recognised something in the landscape, even though you have never been here before. You simply could not take your eyes away from her. Not one of you could. Except for Tomas."

Tarkin lowered his brow and shook his head slightly. He had no recollection of the event playing out, as Karlena explained. He remembered seeing the woman in white, the sudden appearance of the wall of snow and frost, and Tomas upon his mare. There were no other reference images in his mind. For him, the experience was quick and over within mere moments.

"She was afraid of him," Karlena continued. "Maybe she will hide in the shadows tonight."

"Maybe," Tarkin replied as he recalled the vision of Tomas upon his steed, sword drawn and standing in front of the forest defiantly as the wall of snow crashed back to the surface. "He frightened her away?"

"I think so," she replied. "Yes."

"What about the other men with him?"

"They were too far for me to see clearly," Karlena answered. "But she seemed very interested in them."

"I think I know why." The captain frowned as he scanned the trees for movement. "She wanted the girl. Emily. One man in the village said as much before Tomas silenced him. I think the witch is angry at him."

"Now she is also afraid of him," she said, turning to see Tomas holding the bag of oats open so Emily could reach inside to retrieve a handful of the contents. The auburn-haired girl smiled as she held her palm flat so that one horse could take the oats from her.

Tarkin watched the man from Woodmyst with interest. There was more to this man than he had first believed. He had a sense that there was something different, something special about this man.

Others had sensed it, too.

The men from his homeland had noticed it, but perhaps they didn't understand. Perhaps they had grown up with it and whatever it was about Tomas was simply part of their everyday life.

Those that hadn't known him before joining him on this quest felt there was something admirable, something tangible that lived just beneath the surface. The crewmen of the *Adelandria* had felt it, recognising true headship and displaying a willingness to follow him.

A small portion of jealousy swept over Captain Tarkin as he gave thought to this. His men had shown no sign of wanting to change allegiance, but that this one man could influence others in such a way made him envious.

The Erilian women had noticed it too. They would usually scrutinise and measure a person for a long time before showing trust towards any man. But they had an instant liking for him. Tarkin had never seen that before.

The auburn-haired girl had also felt an attraction to him quickly, having only met him a few nights before, and then to share his bed.

A quick jab from envy hit the captain again.

Tarkin smiled as he shrugged off the feeling.

Tomas was a leader, a reluctant one. He saw himself as an equal to all, but they saw him as so much more. Some unseen power shielded him, protected him, even if he didn't recognise it. Everyone else could feel it. They were all drawn to it.

And now the witch had noticed it, too.

She was afraid of him, and this made him a target for the enemy.

"We set a watch over Tomas," Tarkin ordered the men around him. "He needs to be protected at any cost."

Twenty-Six

Far on the northern horizon, the marauders' vessel had become nothing more than a blurry spot in the spyglass. If there was any consolation, it was that the ship appeared to be drifting back towards the shoreline.

Tarkin admitted to himself that it could be merely wishful thinking. He knew little of the world ahead of him and, for all he knew, the coast could suddenly turn towards the west. This would mean the marauders could cross a wide expanse of water, getting away from them for good.

He focused his hopes on positive thoughts.

They are steering towards the shore.

A large, towering mountain in the distance stretched a snow-specked rocky limb over the smooth landscape and into the sea. He perceived there might be some climbing to do once they reached the location.

The monstrosity obscured his view of the shore beyond it. As far as his spyglass would reveal, the mountain was the end of the world. Yet the ship had sailed beyond it, informing Tarkin that the water continued onwards. He could only surmise that the land did, too.

More and more icebergs crowded the ocean. The farther north the travellers rode, the more he noticed these natural vessels upon the sea.

How the ship could manoeuvre through them so easily was something at which he marvelled. Yes, it was a smaller transport than his, and therefore was easier to steer. There were so many icebergs, and giants by his reckoning, that striking at least one wasn't just probable, it was certain.

The riders moved on, keeping their distance from the tree line. Their eyes were constantly scanning the shadows beneath the pines for a sign of the woman in white. If she was there, she was keeping well out of sight.

Tomas couldn't help feeling that the witch was still watching them. He placed himself between Emily and the trees, more for his comfort than hers.

He noticed the crewmen of the *Adelandria* moving positions as they rode, setting themselves around him. He looked to Tarkin, riding at the front with Jeremy and the Erilian women by his side, and wondered if the actions of the men were by his design.

As he aimed to protect Emily, they appeared to be attempting to protect him.

He didn't like it. Special treatment was not something he had asked for and being hemming in made him feel caged.

"Captain," he called.

Tarkin turned in his saddle to face the other.

"Thank you for the sentiment," Tomas began. "But please instruct your men to either fan out, follow me or ride in front of me. I do not need such a close escort."

"I apologise, Tomas," the captain replied. "It's just that I believe this witch has you on her mind now. Karlena informed me you frightened her. She may come for you."

"Let her come," David called back. "Use him as bait and bring her into the open where we can welcome her with swords and daggers."

"I don't think it would be that simple, Master Gyfford," Tarkin answered. "Apparently, she has the power to manipulate men. The only one to not succumb to her power was Tomas."

"What of the women from Erilian?" Simon called. "Were they under her spell also?"

"No, we were not," Rhydra replied.

"Good," Simon smiled. "Then if the bitch has us under her spell, you can attack her instead. I see a good outcome here."

"She won't attack on open ground," Tomas said. "She'll send more of those straw men to do that. She wants to draw us into the woods, like a spider luring insects into her web."

The riders turned their faces to the woods, seeing the trees as more of a trap than just some forest that lined the feet of the mountains.

"Fan out," Tarkin finally ordered his men. He didn't enjoy exposing Tomas, but he understood the man's wish to be left to his own discernment.

Besides, David and Simon were right. They would have a better chance of defeating the witch if they could draw her onto the open ground.

Tomas was correct as well. It was more likely that they wouldn't see her unless they entered the forest. Her only way to get to them would be to send her raggedy slaves.

Weighing both possibilities, Tarkin came to a third possibility that she would simply leave them alone until the opportunity to strike presented itself. Their task, as they rode towards the north, was to make sure no opportunities arose.

Sticking to the open ground, checking their distance to the trees, Tarkin kept the group at what he regarded as a safe distance. His additional concern was how to maintain their safety once they reached the encroaching mountain that crossed their path in the distance.

There, they would need to enter the woods.

There, they would be in danger.

There, they would be insects to the web.

***

Arriving under the ominous presence of the towering mountain, Tarkin ordered the riders to stop. He scanned the expanse between their position and the forest that stretched from the base of the giant, high up its sides.

Dark patches of rock peppered the flanks of the mountain where the trees thinned out and the ground was too steep to keep them. Swirling clouds that had hovered overhead for the entire day obscured the peak from view.

He traced the ridge of the mountain towards the sea where a sharp crest with jagged rocks that poked through the snow like blackened teeth trailed off into the savage water. White spray met the land there as waves crashed upon the elevation before tumbling back to the surface.

There must be a safe place to cross the obstruction. For the moment, he could not see it.

He would look for a way to pass later.

Setting up camp must take priority.

Heeding to Tomas' words of warning, Tarkin instructed the troop to set up tents upon the open ground. There were no arguments. After the experience with the witch earlier in the day, no one wanted to risk the possibility of a surprise attack from an intruder in the woods again.

With the tents pitched, the men tied the horses together in a makeshift pen using ropes and tent poles from one of the unused shelters. With several men missing from their party, Captain Tarkin didn't see the point of erecting all the tents just for the sake of it.

"I think we may discard one or two after tonight," he told Jeremy. "There's no use carrying extra weight when we don't need to. We've ten men missing. That means we're carrying two tents that are not being used."

"Aye, Captain," Jeremy replied. "Perhaps we should burn the canvas, just so our enemies don't privilege too much from our loss."

"Good idea," the captain replied. "We need to get firewood first."

"We go together," Tomas suggested as he approached. "All of us. I would ask the women to stay behind to protect Emily while all men enter the woods together, collect what kindling we can and leave as one."

"We need firewood," Tarkin said again, attempting to build up the courage needed to enter the woods again.

"Best to do so now while there's still light in the sky," Oliver said. "It'll be dark soon after the sun passes the mountain range."

***

Forming a circle around Emily, the Erilian warriors armed themselves with discarded tent poles they cut in half to shorten their lengths. The rods now resembled something similar in size to a sword.

Standing in the centre of the five women, Emily raised her own rod at the ready. One of the Erilian warriors lunged from behind. There was no way Emily could have seen the rod rapidly approaching her head.

Tomas was about to call out to her, but swiftly, and fluidly, Emily brought her rod about her head and knocked the other's weapon away from making contact. She turned and faced her opponent and made a quick exchange of swordplay with the rod.

Another woman, Karlena, lunged as the exchange with the first Erilian was still in motion. Emily kicked high with her foot and knocked the first challenger off balance. Cold snow met the woman's chin as she landed spreadeagled on the ground.

Emily was already engaged in more swordplay with Karlena as another lunged from behind. Swinging around low to the ground, Emily used her rod to clip both women on the knees, tripping them into the soft ground cover.

"She's a quick learner," David said to Tomas.

"It would appear so," the other replied with a wide smile creeping upon his face.

Emily sent another to the ground as they spoke. She was now exchanging blows with Akasati, who was relentlessly looking for a weakness. Her search was in vain, as Emily continued to block and strike with precision.

One of her thrusts found its mark and smacked the Erilian in the stomach. Akasati fell to the ground hard, dropping her rod to hold her abdomen with both hands.

"Are you all right?" Emily called.

The other women laughed. It reminded Tomas of children at play.

We need to go," David told his friend.

Tomas nodded as he turned towards the woods, monitoring Emily. She was more amazing with every minute that he knew her. The Erilian women would look after her in his absence. They had been training her well whenever they had a chance. Clearly, she was becoming a formidable force in her own right.

He carried his proud smile with him as the men gathered at the tree line.

"Are we ready?" Tarkin called out.

"Ready," came a reply along the line.

"Ready," echoed another.

"Pick up wood," the captain commanded.

As one, the men entered the forest. They chorused the captain's words as they foraged for kindling and timber, so they could keep aware of each other, and build their bravery as a unit.

"Pick up wood," they chanted. "Pick up wood. Pick up wood."

Tomas grabbed an armful of good-sized twigs and sticks. David went for a fallen log roughly the thickness of his torso. He was already dragging it back towards the open ground, as others had just found suitable timber.

A quick look around as the chanting continued informed Tomas that most of the men had done the same as him. A couple of others copied David and paired up to cart larger logs from the woods.

"Back to camp," Tomas called.

"Back to camp," the men chorused. "Back to camp. Back to camp."

David, waiting a small distance from the tree line, counted the men as they exited the woods. His mouth moved and his finger pointed as each man came into view.

"Seventeen," he called. "I count seventeen."

"Aye, seventeen," Jeremy called back from further down the line.

"That's what we went in with," Tarkin nodded. "Whatever we got will have to do us. Let's do as Tomas said. Back to camp."

***

They laid the fire. Jeremy had fished two flint stones from his saddlebags. A quick spark from the rocks was enough to get the kindling alight and, from thereon, as more wood landed over the flames, the hearth was ablaze. The men used two of the fallen trees dragged from the woods as a crude bench. Others simply sat their saddles on the ground or leaned upon them as they sat near the fire.

One of the larger logs lay to the fire's edge, where the heat eventually bit into the large portion of timber. As the night progressed, and the log gradually burnt away, they manoeuvred it over the hottest part of the fire, keeping the flames alive.

Even with the options of dried meat and fish, the simple choice of warm sodden oats was all the travellers wanted for the night's meal. The idea of warm food inside them was clearly the only choice worth making.

Tomas, seated upon his own saddle, had piled some snow into a large pot and placed it onto the hot coals earlier in the night. His intention was to use it for the only thing he really longed for. A hot mug of tea.

As soon as the pot came to the boil, he dipped his cup into the water, holding it by the handle to not scald his fingers. He sat the mug on the snow as he dug into a pouch attached to his saddle for the box of tea.

"Yes, please," Emily said from his side. She was sitting cross-legged on a canvas sheet with Karlena. Tomas silently dipped another mug that was resting on the ground nearby into the water.

"May I have one also?" Karlena asked.

Tomas dipped another cup into the pot. He opened the box of tea, and the scent of the dried leaves wafted into his nostrils where he savoured the aroma for a moment.

"You wouldn't mind making another while you're there, would you?" David asked, leaning over to hand Tomas his mug.

"Make your own," Tomas snarled.

David recoiled and stood back, appearing bashful. Tomas found the vision of the big man behaving in such a way somewhat amusing. He then felt guilt for snapping at his friend for no particular reason.

He held his hand out to David. The big man smiled and handed his mug to Tomas, who then ran it through the bubbling water before placing it at his feet.

"Seems that I'm the tea maid, tonight," Tomas grunted as he mixed the potion of water and leaves in each cup.

Several others felt the urge to enjoy a brew once they had smelt the sweet odour drifting through the air around the campfire. They saw Tomas enjoying his drink and dared not ask him to make them one as well.

Instead, they simply asked if they could share the contents of the box he carried. This was something he had no hesitation in doing. He tossed the small container across the flames to the first man who asked.

"Water's there," Tomas pointed. "Mugs are there. Enjoy."

He closed his eyes as he took his first sip.

The liquid was hot, but not scalding. He cherished it, holding it in his mouth as he swirled it over his tongue. The taste was both sweet and sour at the same time. He swallowed it, appreciating the sensation of warm liquid running down his throat and into his belly.

There is nothing better than this, he thought.

What about Emily?

He considered that as he opened one eye to take in the vision of beauty sitting beside him.

Besides Emily, he corrected himself, *there is nothing better than this.*

***

The thunderous sound of waves crashing upon the rocks was deafening. The wind had picked up and blew Jeremy's hood off his head. He left it to flap behind his neck as he stood by his captain at the top of the encroaching ridge by the water's edge.

Tarkin held his glass up to his eye and scanned both land and sea to the north of their position. The good news was that the coast continued for as far as he could see. The bad news was that he couldn't see the marauders' vessel.

The failing light and deep shadow cast over the water by the mountains made it impossible to discern anything that may float upon the rough surface. He picked out a few large icebergs that rolled slowly over the ebbing tide, but his eyes were heavy and not being very cooperative.

"They're gone," Jeremy called over the wind, "aren't they?"

"I honestly can't see them," Tarkin replied. "They could be right there, but I just can't tell."

The captain folded the spyglass and placed it back in his pocket. He turned and started down the rocky slope.

"Careful, Captain," Jeremy cautioned. "Remember the ice."

"I remember," Tarkin grinned. "I'm not an old man yet."

"Older than me," the other quipped as he placed a hand on the rocks to steady his descent.

"Who's the one with no women," the captain replied. "And who's the one with five in his bed every night?"

Jeremy laughed as they both neared the bottom of the rise.

"I don't know how we're going to get the horses up here," Tarkin mentioned as his feet touched the flat surface of the plain.

"Knowing how many things work for us," Jeremy said, "my guess is that there is probably a nice, smooth path to travel upon just over there somewhere." He pointed back along the ridge towards the mountain.

Tarkin nodded. "You're probably right."

The two men made their way back to the camp in the middle of the open ground. The glow of the fire acted as their beacon as they approached on foot. They had left their horses in the camp where they received a well-deserved rest after carrying them all day.

The captain gave a couple of curious steeds a quick pat as they passed by the temporary yard that housed the horses. Satisfied with the brief human contact, the animals huddled back with the others to keep warm.

Approaching the fire, they first moved by Ivo, who sat by the fire with his back to the horses. Jeremy clasped a hand on the man's shoulder in a friendly gesture. Ivo quickly looked up at him, disturbing him from deep thought. He gave Jeremy a smile and a nod as the other found a place along the side of the hearth to sit down.

"Tea smells good," Tarkin said as he sat on the canvas sheet next to Karlena. She instantly rose to her knees and reached for a mug that sat on the ground near the steaming pot of water.

Using Tomas' technique, she dipped the cup into the pot and placed the vessel on the ground near to where she was sitting. Tomas placed his own mug in the snow and reached into his pouch for the box, but didn't find it.

He was getting so tired his memory was acting up. He desperately needed to sleep. They all did.

"Teabox," he called.

"Here," Oliver called from across the hearth as he reached to the ground by his feet to retrieve the small container. He tossed it over to Tomas, who caught it and handed it over to Karlena.

Within moments, Tarkin had his mug in his hand. The Erilian woman didn't wait to be asked by Jeremy for another mug to be made. He was the type of man to usually get up and do his own work. But the weary look on his face as the light from the fire illuminated his skin made her feel some compassion.

He was always by the captain's side in times of need and always offering advice in times of peril. Jeremy was loyal and cared for the crew just as much, maybe more than Tarkin.

She made him a brew and carried it over to him. He looked at her, confusedly. She had done nothing like this in the past. Reluctantly, and gratefully, he took it from her.

"Thank you, Karlena," he said. "You didn't need to."

"I know," she replied as she returned to the captain's side. "But you looked as if you could use it."

Tarkin smiled.

He wrapped his arm around her shoulders and gently kissed her on the temple.

"That was a gracious thing you did," he whispered.

"He does so much for you," she said. "A cup of tea just doesn't suffice for the gratitude that I should show him."

Jeremy peered into the flames as he sipped his tea. His thoughts travelled to his younger days when he was in love with a dark-haired maiden who lived in a villa near to his home.

He remembered her smile and soft lines at the corners of her mouth. He recalled the touch of her lips and the caress of her smooth hands upon his neck.

Placing his own hands there, as he sat by the fire, he felt only knots in his muscles and an uncomfortable stiffness in his bones. Manual labour on the *Adelandria* was taking its toll.

How he would much prefer her fingers on his skin than the smell of salt, rope, and timber.

But she was gone.

Meaghan.

***

Ivo heard the waves crashing in the distance behind him. He found the sound soothing, relaxing as he stared beyond the flames and towards the forest in the distance.

Deep shadows had obscured the trees as the purple sky dimmed towards black. There were no stars, no moon. Only darkness.

He silently gave a reflection of what had happened earlier in the day. She was there, and they saw her, but few of them could remember her that well. They recalled the presence of her, seeing the woman in white. However, they could not tell of her features. Her beauty.

How could they forget her so soon?

How could they block such a vision from their memories?

Peering into the darkness, hoping to see her again, Ivo focused his essence towards her.

He tried to call her the way she called him. Internally, with the voice of his head.

I'm here. I'm waiting.

But there was no answer.

Ivo knew she was nearby. He could feel her.

He sensed her watching him with her piercing blue eyes. Knowing that she was there, just out of view, made him anxious. He wanted her, and she had called to him.

But now, being so close by, she was silent.

Have you forgotten me?

Don't you want me?

I want you.

I love you.

Still, there was no answer.

He kept his eyes peeled to the dark woods in the distance as thunderous waves continued to crash loudly on the rocks far behind him.

Twenty-Seven

Tomas placed his hand on Emily's waist as she snuggled against him in their tent. He ran slowly his hand along her back, towards her shoulders, until he heard her wince, sucking in a hissing breath followed by a moan.

It was the sound of pain.

"What is it?" he asked her.

"It struck me across the shoulders blades," she explained. "I'll be fine."

He stroked to her neck softly. She closed her eyes and breathed more easily.

"You're really good," he said to her.

"You will need to be a little more specific," she said, smiling.

"With a sword," he told her. "I saw you today, practising with the Erilians."

"Not too good," she replied. "They got a couple of good blows on me."

"I'm very proud of you." He kissed the top of her head.

"For learning to fight?"

"No," he answered. "For standing up for yourself."

"Then I'm proud of myself too," she murmured as sleepiness flooded over her.

"You should be," he said. There was no reply. She was already fast asleep.

He closed his eyes and drifted away into slumber, welcoming the sensation as sleep swept over him like a gentle wave.

***

As tired as he was, Ivo couldn't sleep. He stared wide-eyed at the ceiling of the tent, listening to it softly flapping as the breeze blew up from the shore, across the plains and over the camp.

The other men sharing his tent were asleep. Soft snoring buzzed from David's location at the far end of the tent. The other three men were silent, but he knew they were at deep rest because their conversations had ceased.

He could see the soft orange glow from the camp's fire illuminating the wall of the tent near the entrance. The low drone of the watchmen's voices made their way to his ears.

He wanted to sleep, but could not.

Several times, he had closed his eyes and attempted to block out the stimuli that attracted his attention. Each time had failed and his eyes re-focussed upon the flickering orange light or the whispers of the watchers.

Rolling onto his side to face the back wall of the shelter, something he had done earlier, he closed his eyes and curled his legs towards his body. It appeared darker here, but his ears tuned towards the conversation outside, making the talk seem louder.

His mind swam with emotions of anger and frustration directed towards his body's unwillingness to succumb to the fatigue he was physically feeling.

He rolled over to his other side to be confronted with the luminosity of the flames dancing upon the tent wall.

The others seemed to drift off to sleep so easily. He was just as tired as they were, so why was he having such a great difficulty finding rest?

A man chuckled outside.

Ivo wondered what the joke was. He felt an influx of anger. He didn't need a new distraction to keep him from a much-needed rest.

Sleep!

He screamed the word in his head over and over again.

He wasn't in the mood to heed his own words as he rolled onto his back and stared at the ceiling again.

The canvas covering flapped gently in the breeze as the sound of wind swept past the camp.

He heard his name upon its breath.

A soft whisper filled his mind.

Ivo.

Ivo.

She called to him.

She wanted him.

She needed him.

He sat up and listened, hoping it was her and not just his mind playing tricks on him.

Ivo.

Instinctively, he dressed and quietly withdrew from the tent, leaving his weapons behind.

The men by the hearth didn't notice him as he moved into the shadows cast by the tents and the firelight.

Ivo.

Ivo.

The calling drew him towards the forest. He wrapped his arms around his body as he trudged through the snow towards the foot of the giant mountain the leered menacingly above the camp.

The breeze from the sea pushed him, urged him onwards, as if it was the will of the gods. He was doing the right thing. She needed him, called to him and he was answering.

Ivo.

Her voice sent a warm sensation along his spine and into his loins.

He would serve her as best he could.

As he drew closer, the form of the forest became clearer in the darkness. He could make out the shapes of the trunks and the outstretched limbs of the trees.

Natural archways and corridors became apparent, showing him the way to her as he pressed on. He was at the edge of the forest when a part deep inside himself screamed for him to stop.

He did.

Knowing he should turn back; knowing if he took one step more, he would never see his beloved home again. He would never return to Woodmyst.

As if to entice him back even more so, he heard his name called again.

"Ivo," the voice shouted from behind him.

It wasn't her.

Her voice was soft and enticing.

This voice was rough and deep.

He turned to see who the caller was.

Three watchmen stood at a small distance from him, glaring towards him with confused looks.

"Ivo," one of them called. "Are you sleepwalking? Come back with us."

"She calls me," he slurred, sounding like a drunken man. "I must go to her."

He turned and entered the woods.

"Ivo," they called after him as they watched his form moving among the trees.

"Ivo, come back."

The silhouettes of several other figures stepped from behind tree trunks deeper inside the tree line. The watchmen stepped back tentatively, swords in hands.

They assumed the shadows belonged to more of the straw men they had faced before.

"We should wake the captain," one man suggested.

They turned and fled across the snow back towards the camp.

Ivo.

Ivo.

Her voice was soothing and alluring.

With each step he took, the louder her call became.

Ivo.

Did she burn for him as he did for her? The urgency in her voice seemed to suggest so.

I'm here; he tried to answer her from within. *I'm here, my love.*

She needed him. He knew it. She needed him as much as he needed her.

She loved him as much as he loved her.

Ivo; she called.

I'm here; he answered.

***

"How long ago?" Tomas asked the men as he buckled his sword and sheath to his side.

"Not long," a watcher replied. His back turned towards the open flap of the tent as Tomas and Emily dressed. "We just came back from there and woke the captain first. He told us to wake you and your men."

Tomas pursed his lips. The news of Ivo wandering off into the woods alone was more than disturbing.

"What could he be thinking?" he said to himself as he hoisted his bearskin over his shoulders.

"We'll get him back," Emily said as she pulled on her boots.

"You'll need a weapon," Tomas murmured.

"I have one, sir," the watcher answered.

"Not you," the other corrected.

"The Erilian women have the only swords that I can carry," Emily told him. "All the others are too heavy for me."

"I have an idea regarding that," he said. "I'll need to talk to the Erilians first."

"I see them by the fire," the watcher informed them.

"Good." Tomas turned to Emily, who was strapping on her boots. "Are you ready?"

"Yes," she answered, rising to her feet and throwing her hooded cloak over her form.

"Why would he do such a thing?" David called as they all met by the hearth. "The silly bastard left his sword behind."

Tomas shook his head; he did not know.

"He's bewitched," Karlena answered from the captain's side. "Why else would he enter the woods without his weapons?"

"I need one of your swords," Tomas remarked to her. "I won't leave Emily or you behind. We won't leave anyone behind from now on. I also won't have anyone unarmed. She knows how to handle your swords. Ours are—"

"Yours are too heavy for her," Akasati interjected. "She can take mine. I'm better with my bow."

"Thank you," Emily said as the Erilian handed over her blade.

"We'll need fire," Tarkin called.

"I have my flint rocks." Jeremy patted a pouch that he had slung over his body.

"I mean in the immediate," the captain told him. "The lads told me they saw shadows moving in the trees. If there are more of those straw men waiting for us, we should be prepared.

"All we have is the kindling in the fire," Oliver called.

Simon quickly turned away from the conversation and retrieved the large pot that had steaming water in it earlier in the evening. It was resting on its side near the base of the log the men had been using as a bench.

He grabbed the pot by its sides and scraped it through the hearth, shovelling glowing embers into it. Afterwards, he placed the pot on the ground, and a bright orange glow illuminated the inside as the disturbed embers produced new flames.

The other men watched with curiosity as Simon fetched his saddle from the tent. He turned it upside down and placed it on the snow beside the pot before attempting to pick the metal vessel full of hot coals up with his gloved hands.

He recoiled; the heat penetrated his leather coverings.

"Here," David called, tossing his own gloves to his friend.

Simon took them in the palms of his covered hands and used them to lift the pot onto the inverted saddle. He then stood to full height and tossed the gloves back to David, thanking him for the contribution.

Rhyodia and Akasati had taken the hint. They used their daggers to make strips out of the canvas sheet lying on the ground near the fire. Sharek, Karlena and Rhydra took the strips from the other two women and wrapped them around the arrow tips in their quivers.

"We're wasting time," one crewman hissed.

"We're preparing for battle," Simon corrected him.

"You!" Tarkin pointed at the man who made the remark before pointing to another near to him. "And you. Carry the embers. Make sure they don't lose their fervency."

The second man punched the first in the arm.

Thank you for that.

"What of the horses?" Emily asked.

"They won't serve us well in there," Tomas replied as he peered towards the forest. "They'll feel safer here."

Within moments, the troop was making their way across the snow-covered ground towards the dark woods. The towering mountain loomed over them, seeming to glare at them intensely, mocking their bravery as they approached the shadows beneath the trees.

They paused a small distance from the tree line, peering into the spaces between the tall stems. A thin mist moved over the snow, hugging the ground like a soft blanket.

Hazy puffs drew the attention of the group to several places under the trees.

There was movement.

The forms of men emerged from the darkness, making their way towards the gathering.

Distinctive features became clearer as they drew near.

These were not the straw men that they had encountered before.

There was a familiarity about them that made Tarkin smile as they stepped into view.

Ten men stood before them, lined along the tree line, armed with sword and dagger.

"Where have you been?" the captain asked.

The men stared back blankly.

Tomas scrutinised the figures. They were assuredly the missing men that had disappeared during their journey. But they were also not themselves.

The darkness of night obscured much of what the captain could not see.

But Tomas noticed.

Great, black smears over their clothing and gaping wounds in their bellies, necks and faces had his instant attention.

"Oh no," he whispered under his breath.

"Why no answer?" Tarkin started forward, his hand outstretched to the nearest figure.

Jeremy was quick to note Tomas' caution. He placed a hand on the captain's shoulder, preventing him from venturing forward.

It was only then that Tarkin truly saw the extent of the situation.

"Are they bewitched, too?" Emily questioned, the fear in her voice coming through all too clearly.

"They're dead," Tomas answered, pulling his sword from its sheath.

Twenty-Eight

Ivo.

Ivo.

Her voice drew him onward.

He followed a natural archway formed by the trees. Eventually, he came upon a dark stone wall. It had toppled over in places, revealing gaps here and there, where scarecrows with outstretched arms waited and watched.

They remained unmoving, lifeless, as he passed by them. He continued to follow the edge of the wall for some distance until he came to a passage bordered on either side by stone.

Dark roots and vines, now covered with frost and snow, webbed across the stonework like veins protruding through the skin.

Ivo.

He smiled.

She was so near he could almost feel her breath as she called.

He trudged on, passing through the passage towards an extensive structure with a wide opening that reminded him of a yawning mouth. The longer he stared at it, the more it looked like a living beast preparing to devour him.

Logic told him it was the decaying remains of a gatehouse. Her calls let him know there was no danger beyond the entrance; only her.

He wanted her.

He needed her.

He loved her.

One step at a time, he moved into the mouth and along a dark stone corridor.

A soft voice from within screamed for him to turn around, to flee. It shouted that he was placing himself into perilous danger and that each step he took was towards certain doom.

Her voice was clearer, louder, and more alluring.

Ivo.

Ivo.

He smiled, transfixed.

Intoxicated.

His feet seemed to shuffle forward of their own accord as he neared the end of the dark corridor and an open space surrounded by high walls. A large, rectangular building, resting in the middle of the open area, held the remains of three towers upon each of its corners. A fourth had toppled into the yard many years before and now lay covered with frozen shrubbery and snow.

He recognised the structure as an ancient keep. It was slowly falling apart as time and nature bored their fingers into the stonework.

The large wooden doors of the keep opened inwards, revealing a faint orange glow from a fire deep inside.

It was inviting, and he told himself that he needed to get out of the cold.

His inner voice protested, screaming for him to turn around and go back to camp.

Ivo.

His feet moved him forward.

He knew she was just inside.

He had to be with her.

Moving past the doors of the keep, entering the large room inside, he saw the upper levels had collapsed.

The timber flooring had rotted away and the stairwell that should line the walls was gone.

The ceiling far above was still in place, offering shelter from the outside extremities of snow and rain. Apart from that, it was merely a stone shell of what it once was.

The fireplace at the rear of the room was ablaze and even from by the door, he could feel the heat. He shuffled forward, taking off his thick bearskin coverings and dropping them on the floor.

A thud from behind him echoed through the room.

He turned to see two motionless straw men standing on either side of the large wooden doors, now closed.

"Ivo," she called.

Her voice was no longer in his head.

It was real.

She was real.

"Come over by the fire," she instructed him.

He moved towards the sound of her voice, towards the fire.

She was sitting on a deep chair resting upon a thick rug, facing the flames. All he could see of her was her hand on the armrest. She beckoned with her fingers and pointed to a chair near hers.

"Come and sit," she breathed.

He complied and sat beside her. She moved her hand onto his and removed his glove before tossing it into the flames. Ivo wondered why she would do that, but then she started stroking his fingers with her own. Pretty soon, he forgot he had even had a glove on that hand.

His eyes locked onto hers as she peered into him, seeing him for who he truly was.

"Do you want me?" she asked. Her voice sent a warm shiver over his skin as she stroked his hand.

"Yes," he answered.

"Do you need me?" She leaned closer to him, moving her hand to his cheek.

"Yes." He closed his eyes at her touch.

"Do you love me?" She slid a finger over the top of his ear and slid it slowly to his lobe.

"Yes," he managed, before she pressed her lips against his.

His heart thumped rapidly, uncontrollably in his chest.

She rose to her feet and stood before him.

The firelight revealed the shape of her body through the thin white garments draped over her skin. She guided his bare hand to her breast and the other, still gloved, to her waist.

His loins burned with desire as he rose to his feet, taking her in his arms.

As they kissed, she manoeuvred both of them to the rug upon the floor. She lowered herself onto him, saying his name repeatedly as her fingers removed his clothing.

How he wanted her.

How he needed her.

How he loved her.

***

The creatures lunged forward; swords raised.

Tomas ran in to meet their attack.

He swung his sword upward in a fluid motion, slicing through the groin and chest of the nearest opponent. He then moved past his adversary and swung his blade around to stab it deep into the dead man's back.

The crewman stayed on his feet, unflinching.

"That should have killed him," David called.

"You cannot kill what is already dead," Jeremy barked as he blocked an incoming blow from one of his past comrades.

"Suggestions," Tomas said, still engaged with his challenger.

"Hack them into pieces," Karlena called as she jumped into the fray, swinging her sword wildly. Her blade slid through bone and marrow, limb and socket as she cut one of the dead men into portions.

Dismembered hands, arms, legs, and head fell on the ground. Pleased with her effort, she stepped back to take in her handiwork.

Emily let out a muffled scream as she noticed the eyes of the decapitated head moving about, looking and watching them. The fingers upon the separated hands moved and the torso still bent and flexed in the middle.

"By the gods," David called as he saw the spectacle upon the ground. "It's still moving."

"But it can't fight," Tomas bellowed as he hacked his heavy sword through the shoulder of his opponent. The sword arm of the dead man fell into the snow. It let the blade go and writhed on the ground like a wounded snake.

Tarkin slid his blade across the belly of a dead man with whom he had been exchanging blows. The creature's intestines spilt into the snow and twisted around its feet. As it moved towards the captain for another attack, it tripped over its own innards and fell face-first onto the ground.

As it pushed itself from the snow, Tarkin slashed his sword down across the dead man's neck, removing the head. The dismembered body part rolled a short distance, lolling onto its side where it watched the battle.

The body, however, continued to rise from the snow, sword in hand. It swung another blow towards the captain. Tarkin was in a state of disbelief, but still regained enough self-control to block the blade with his own.

Karlena stepped up behind the headless figure and chopped through both knees of Tarkin's attacker with one swift stroke of her sword.

The dead man crashed to the ground.

It pushed up with its arms and started towards the captain again.

Tarkin stepped back from his foe. He shot a quick glance to Karlena, who raised her sword again; bringing it down on the figure's left shoulder. The captain raised his own weapon and smashed it through the right shoulder.

The torso slumped to the ground, wriggling harmlessly in the snow.

Both Tarkin and Karlena continued to cut the arms into pieces at the elbows and wrists. They weren't sure if it would prevent their enemy from attacking again, but it made them feel better about the situation.

Akasati lit an arrow by dipping the clothed tip into the pot of glowing embers. She took careful aim and hit one of the dead men in the chest.

The flames took hold of his clothing rapidly, and soon his whole body was alight.

It wasn't enough to stop his attack.

Continuing to swing his sword towards the living, the figure pierced a crewman through the thigh. The crewman fell onto the snow, screaming, dropping his sword as he moved both hands to the wound.

The fiery dead man raised his blade to finish the job, but was knocked to the ground. The fallen man watched as both the flaming man and David hit the snow with a thud. Their swords flew off in different directions during the tussle.

The impact and subsequent roll in the snow had doused most of the flames engulfing the dead man. Now steam and smoke rose from his charred flesh as he wrapped his arms tightly around his new adversary from behind.

The dead man gripped David tightly, unable to break free from the corpse's grasp. He jabbed with his elbows and struggled with all of his might as the dead man opened his jaws wide, intending to dig his teeth into the living flesh on David's neck.

Steel crunched deeply into the dead man's skull as Oliver thrust his blade through the figure's head. He pulled on his sword, using it as a handle to direct the dead man's mouth away from his friend.

The figure reached for the sword, gripping his fingers around the sharp blade to remove the intrusion. The steel cut deep into its fingers as it tried to free itself.

David clambered back to his feet and retrieve his sword from the snow. He raced back to Oliver's side and chopped off the dead man's arms.

"Take his legs too," Oliver grunted as he struggled to keep the dead man in place. With two large hacks of his blade, David removed the dead man's legs just below his hips.

"You need to cut them up into smaller portions," the injured man informed them as he continued holding his leg.

"Use the strap attached to your sheath to wrap around your leg," David said to him. "We don't need you bleeding out."

"After that," Oliver put in, "you can cut them into smaller portions. We have more dead men to contend with."

With that, both men of Woodmyst returned to the fight.

Tomas monitored the forest during the skirmish. He watched for any more surprises that might try to attack as they engaged their current enemy.

None came.

Seven of the dead crewmen remained, and over twenty able swords were battling them upon the snow.

Parrying and thrusting blades clashed loudly on the open ground. The din of swordplay echoed across the expanse and into the night air.

They set slashing and hacking blows upon the dead men.

Flesh and bone separated from bodies as the fearless enemies continued to fight the living men and women.

Before long, discarded arms and legs lay on the snow, wriggling and twisting to reach the travellers.

The men gathered portions of the living-dead and piled together a little distance away from the tree line. Simon was unfortunate enough to have one of the dismembered hands grip his wrist as he collected the body parts.

"Get it off me," he hollered.

Sharek dug into the intruder's skin with her dagger. It didn't let go straight away. It was only when she reached in with her own hand that it loosened its grip on Simon, trying to grab her.

She flung the appendage from the end of her blade so that it landed on the pile with the other pieces of dead men.

"Now what?" Oliver asked.

"We burn them," Tarkin replied.

"We don't have the time," Tomas interjected. "We should leave them and burn them when we return."

"I'll do it," called the injured man. He had placed a leather strap around his leg to stop the bleeding and had difficulty standing on his feet. Another crewman standing beside him was supporting his weight. "I'm no use to you in there anyhow."

Tarkin nodded.

"You'll need timber. We'll collect some kindling and start the fire before we leave. It will only take a moment." He looked at Tomas, who was eager to move on.

Tomas agreed with a quick nod. It wasn't fair to leave a man behind without as much as a fire to keep him warm.

"You should leave one able person behind with him," Karlena added.

Tarkin gave her words some thought as he directed the men to gather firewood.

He needed all the able men he could muster to help with combating the witch. There was no way of knowing what lay in wait for them in the dark of the woods.

Yet leaving a wounded man without someone to keep watch was simply inhumane. Someone needed to stay behind to watch over the other.

"You." Tarkin pointed to the man who had acted as a weight barer for the injured crewman. "You stay behind to watch him. Keep him warm and burn these bodies while you're at it."

"Aye sir," the man replied.

"Shall we go?" Tarkin asked Tomas.

"When you're ready," he replied.

Tarkin turned to his men and signalled for them to follow his lead.

Flames ignited upon the open ground as the two men remaining behind watched their comrades and the men of Woodmyst enter the tree line.

"See you when we return," called one of the two men carrying the pot of hot embers.

One by one, the darkness engulfed the travellers as they vanished into the shadows of the woods.

Twenty-Nine

Keeping to what appeared as a natural path, the captain guided the men through a section where the trees were wider apart than the others surrounding them. It seemed too easy; he thought. As if they followed the trail.

"Stop," Simon called from behind the group. He was stooping to look at the base of a tall pine tree. They hadn't come far from the tree line, as Tomas could see the flickering glow of the fire in the distance beyond the dark stems of the pines.

"What is it?" he asked.

"We're going the wrong way," Simon answered.

"It's a path." Sharek pointed with her blade. "We should follow it."

"It's a waterway," he informed her. "Perhaps a stream filled to the brim with snow, but it's no path. Ivo went this way."

"Are you sure?" Tarkin asked, retracing his steps.

"Simon is the best tracker I have ever known," Tomas said, coming to the man's defence.

"Then you had best lead us, Master Bell," the captain instructed.

Simon nodded before entering a thin corridor where the trees arched their lower limbs overhead. Ivo's footprints were clearly visible in the snow. There was no mistaking that he had gone in this direction.

He was glad to hear Tomas refer to him as the best tracker. In fact, his ego almost exploded from the over-inflation. However, a small child with no sense could have followed these footprints.

Simon imagined the captain and the other travellers were too engaged in following the easier route, the wider track, to have noticed the tracks disappearing into the thicker trees to the side of their path.

The dark limbs seemed to loom above him threateningly. A shiver running up and down his spine told him danger was nearby. He turned now and then to assure himself the others were continuing to follow his lead.

He stooped repeatedly to glare towards the dark ground, finding the next footstep before returning to full height and moving on. His biggest desire was to be out of the long passageway of trees and in an area more open.

The dark shrubbery seemed to close in on their position, encroach upon them with their outstretched limbs.

The overhanging branches obscured the moonlight, smothered even further by the thick, swirling clouds. Darkness seemed to fill the very air.

With his sword gripped in both hands, Simon continued to lead the troop through the narrow passage of trees, hoping it would open up to a clearing soon. The depressions of footfalls in the snow continued straight on and steadily spaced in the shadows.

Eventually, they came upon a tall stone wall that forced them to change direction, drawing them to the left. There were sections where the stones had fallen, vanishing beneath the snow that lay over the ground.

Twisted vines had stretched across the wall's surface, now covered in a thin frost. Karlena touched the wall with her sword, causing some of the frozen creepers to break off and fall away like black snowflakes to the ground.

Tomas stuck his head through a gap in the wall.

"Be careful," Emily said to his back.

"It's all right," he replied, stretching his upper body over the broken section. "There's a castle up ahead. I can see a light coming from a window."

He pulled himself back through the gap.

"How far?" Tarkin asked.

"Not too far," he replied before pointing to the tumbled section of the stone wall. "We can't go through there. The ground is steep rock and I couldn't see a way to get in. There are tall walls all the way around. If we continue the way we are going, we will come to a gatehouse."

"We must use caution," Jeremy added. "We don't want to attract any unnecessary attention."

Tomas felt something of significant weight land on his shoulder. He quickly stepped forward and turned around to see a figure emerging from the fallen section of the wall.

Eyeless sockets stared back, and a raggedy uneven mouth twisted into a ghastly grimace as wooden claws reached towards him.

"By the gods," David breathed as he turned in the direction they were heading. Dozens of figures in wide-brimmed hats and long cloaks waited for them.

The straw men had returned.

Not waiting to be attacked, Tomas swung his blade across the scarecrow's neck, sending the creature's head back over the wall and into the darkness beyond.

The body remained rigid and reached out for him with its sharp fingers. His blade slid through the straw man's chest, spilling straw onto the ground.

Akasati was already lighting an arrow by dipping the tip into the pot that two of the crewmen carried. She aimed and hit the open wound Tomas had inflicted upon the scarecrow.

Flames instantly consumed the straw men, but its determination to attack wasn't quenched. It continued to flail and reach out towards Tomas as fire billowed from its body.

Keeping at a safe distance from the flames, Tomas continued to cut pieces away from the attacker, dropping forearms and pieces of torso to the ground.

Ultimately, Tomas piled the remains of the flaming scarecrow in a smoking heap by the broken wall.

The straw men crept forward.

With swords at the ready, the men and women prepared to do battle. Akasati lit another arrow and aimed towards the scarecrows.

The straw men started running towards the troop at a rapid pace.

The battle was about to begin.

***

"I need you," she whispered. The warm glow of the fire caressed her skin as she removed her white garments, letting them fall to the rug beside them. She leant into him, touching her lips against his, parting them with her tongue and pushing inside.

It was new to him.

He had never been this close to a woman in his life.

Elation flowed through him. The idea she would be his first overwhelmed him.

It was an *honour*.

She moved her mouth to his neck and gently, softly bit him where it met the shoulder.

He wanted to be with her more than ever.

He was ready.

She kissed his lips again before recoiling slightly to look at him.

He locked onto her eyes. Her piercing blue eyes.

Captivated and trapped within her stare, Ivo couldn't turn away.

Didn't want to turn away.

He was where he needed to be.

She smiled as she sat upright; tossing her blond hair back over her shoulder, she used her hand to guide him.

Nothing had ever felt like this.

Nothing.

***

Emily hacked a leg off her enemy in one swift blow. The straw man fell upon its side into the snow, where it scrambled to get back into the fight. She seized the opportunity and chopped through hessian skin and straw muscles over and over until a pile of wood and chaff lay in a quivering lump.

"Akasati," she called. "It's trying to reform."

The Erilian warrior flung a fiery arrow into the heap of scarecrow remains, where it caught alight rapidly. She turned to see Emily already in a tussle with another straw man.

The auburn-haired girl swung the curved blade across the straw man's wrist, lopping off its left hand. The claw flexed and fidgeted on the ground of its own accord as Emily lunged with her sword to take the scarecrow's head.

It jumped back to avoid the blow, and its hat was knocked into the air instead. The figure's head turned to see where the hat landed before returning its eyeless stare back to Emily.

This intrigued her. When it lost its hand, it fought on, unflinching. It seemed not to care that a part of it was missing. But it appeared concerned about its hat.

Funny.

It leapt towards her, high off the ground with its mouth wide open and claw extended. She ran forward and fell onto her side to slide underneath its frame.

It landed where she had been standing. She was now jumping to her feet behind the creature, swinging her blade towards its neck.

The head soared through the air, leaving a trail of chaff to float to the ground in its wake. With a dull thud, the hessian sack landed before rolling across the snow.

Emily didn't wait to see where the scarecrow's head landed. She opted to chop the straw man into as many pieces as she could.

As she did so, Akasati had fired several flaming arrows into several attackers. Five of the straw men, fully ablaze, continued to fight wildly.

The men of the troop weren't sure to be thankful to the Erilian woman or not for starting the fires, as now they didn't just have claws to contend with, but flames as well.

Swinging, reaching, stretching their blazing limbs in an attempt to kill the living men, the scarecrows moved towards the troop. The travellers backed away towards the tall stone wall.

They were being cornered.

David risked the flames and the dagger-like claws. He ran forward and stuck his long blade into the gut of a straw man. He then hoisted the flailing scarecrow, still on the end of his sword, over his head with both hands before flinging it into the woods.

Keeping his hands wrapped tightly around the sword's hilt, David pointed with the blade's tip towards the flying straw man. It flew through the sky, reminding him of a shooting star as flames illuminated the dark sky.

It fell hard, right into five other straw men who were emerging from the dark woods.

Flames instantly caught, setting the newcomers ablaze.

"There are more coming from the forest," David called to the others, after seeing the five where his opponent had landed.

"I see them," Akasati called, aiming another fiery arrow towards another straw man making its way towards them.

"It's a distraction," Tomas called. "Ivo is in that castle and we're caught out here with these things."

One of the other flaming straw men fell apart. The fire burnt through its wooden bones and ate away at its joints. Its limbs dropped away until it crashed on the ground in a fiery heap.

Tarkin had noticed it didn't take all that long for the scarecrow to deteriorate in the flames. He surmised it would be more beneficial to battle the creatures if they were all on fire than to dismember them first before burning them, as they had been trying to do.

"Set them all on fire," he commanded. "Every single one of them."

"What are you doing?" Jeremy queried.

"The fire eats them from the inside," he answered. As if to make his point, one of the flaming straw men nearby crashed into the snow as the fire ate through its leg. "Look," Tarkin pointed with his sword.

Akasati was firing arrow after arrow, targeting as many of the scarecrows as she could. It wasn't long before burning straw men filled the forest. The creatures continued to trudge forwards, claws outstretched as they marched through the trees.

Several figures fell to the ground, unable to support their own weight as the flames devoured them. Others breached the trees, only to be met by swords that hacked them into smaller pieces that burnt quickly.

"Now is your chance," Karlena said to Tomas. "We will stay to finish them off. You take your men and rescue Ivo."

Tomas didn't hesitate.

He ran along the length of the stone wall. The other men of Woodmyst followed closely. By the time he had made it to the mouth of the gatehouse, he realised others had joined the raiding party.

Not only did he have the men from his village with him, but Emily as well. Captain Tarkin and Jeremy were near her and puffing from the quick sprint that Tomas had just taken them on.

"What are you doing here?" Tomas asked.

"I want to see this through to the end," Tarkin answered. "After all, she took ten of my men, too. Remember?"

"Not you," Tomas grunted before pointing towards Emily. "Her. Why is she…" He redirected his question towards her, "Why are you here?"

"Because you are here," she replied.

"True love," David quipped.

"Besides," she said. "It's no more dangerous here than it is back there. I could be killed just as easily in either place."

"Now kiss the woman, you fool," David snickered.

"Quiet," Tomas snapped. "Ivo is in there. We need to get him back safely. Who knows what she is doing to him."

***

Thrusting her hips back and forth over his, she moaned and called his name over and over. Her palms rubbed his chest, occasionally squeezing his muscles, pushing her fingernails against his skin.

It was more pleasurable than painful.

He gripped her thighs and waist with his hands, feeling her smooth skin with his fingertips, absorbing everything that he could from her.

Her thrusts became more intense as she quickened her pace. Her moans changed into loud exhaling breaths.

She leant into him again and kissed his neck, his ear, his lips. Her tongue pushed inside him again. He welcomed it and met it with his own.

He held her there for a moment.

Rising again, she continued moving, moving, moving.

He felt an uncontrollable release.

His body shuddered and his eyes closed as pure ecstasy and elation flowed over and through him.

She kept moving upon him, even though he had nothing more left to give her.

Her hips continued to thrust back and forth, as he felt his arms being pulled away to his sides and weight applying to his ankles.

Upon opening his eyes, he saw the hessian faces of four straw men, each holding one of his limbs against the rug on which he lay.

She seemed oblivious to them, continuing to thrust herself upon him, smiling, moaning.

"My lady?" he whimpered.

"Don't you want me?" she breathed.

"Yes," he sighed.

"Don't you love me?"

"I do."

She leant into him again and kissed him.

"I love you, Ivo," she whispered in his ear.

He smiled after hearing her words.

She loves me.

He kept smiling as she buried a dagger deep into his chest, sawing into his ribs.

I love her.

His eyes closed as she ripped the wound open with both hands before retrieving his heart from the cavity, cutting the valves with her blade.

She lifted it to her lips, where she slowly licked the dark moisture from its surface. It pumped rapidly in her hands, spraying blood over her naked flesh as she bit into it.

The doors thudded loudly.

Something was trying to get in.

The four straw men released Ivo's body and made their way to the entrance to the keep.

The doors thudded again as she tore a chunk of the heart away with her teeth. She chewed it, tossing the rest of the pulsating mass into the flames behind her.

Lifting herself from Ivo's body, she smeared his blood over herself, paying careful attention to her loins.

The doors thudded again, bursting inwards and allowing a cold gust of wind to fill the room.

Tomas ran in first, sword high. His eyes landed immediately upon his friend lying in a pool of his own blood on the floor by the fire. He then saw the naked woman covered in blood by the flames.

"You bitch," he snarled.

She laughed softly, eyeing the next man to enter the room.

Tarkin stopped dead in his tracks, taking the scene in and not wanting to believe his eyes.

Ivo was dead. He could not change that, but the woman responsible was right in front of him and he was ready to run her through with his blade. The only obstacles that he could see standing between himself and her demise were the four scarecrow warriors standing in his way.

"Witch," he called to her. "You have killed my men, my friends. Do you know who I am?"

"Captain Dakmel Tarkin of the *Adelandria*," she slurred. "Self-proclaimed hunter of the Sovereign."

"And you are his Mistress," Tarkin said back.

"*His?*" she snickered. "I am the Sovereign's Mistress, yes."

"What is your name?" the captain asked.

She laughed, backing away towards the side of the fireplace.

"Your name," Tarkin barked.

"Sumaiyya," she hissed. "Hello, Father."

Thirty

"Sumaiyya?" Tarkin stared wide-eyed in disbelief.

"It's a trick," Jeremy said from his side.

The captain lowered his blade and stepped further into the room towards her. Her blonde hair and blue eyes were like his daughter's.

Could it be? After all this time?

"Dakmel," Tomas called, but the other wasn't listening.

Tarkin dropped his sword on the stone floor. It rang loudly as it hit the hard surface, resonating throughout the room. He passed by the four straw sentries, continuing towards the naked woman.

"Sumaiyya?" He held his hands out to his side, a non-threatening gesture. "Where have you been? I've missed you." Tears welled in his eyes.

"You know where I've been," she spat angrily.

His eyes moved to Ivo, lying naked and covered in his own blood by the fire.

"Why have you done this?" he asked. "How could you do this?"

She smiled as she slunk away towards the darkness beyond the firelight.

"I have his seed and his blood inside me," she breathed. "I will bear his child. It will be the master of all. Even the Sovereign will bow to my son. I feel him growing already." She ran a hand over her bloodstained stomach.

"Your mind is twisted," he said, reaching towards her. "Remember our home. Try. Remember the fun we had."

She stopped moving and became silent, still draped in the shadows beyond the firelight.

"Do you remember?" he asked her softly as he drew near to her.

"I remember Takmel pushed me over," she whispered. "I remember you picked me up and put me on your knee and held me until I stopped crying."

"Yes," he said. He stepped closer to her.

"Captain," Jeremy called, fear in his voice.

"I remember you tucking me into bed at night and kissing me on the forehead. I remember Mama cooking lamb with sweet spices, and potatoes."

Her voice changed, becoming sad. Soft sobs came from the shadows.

"I remember, Papa," she said. "I remember everything." She reached a hand out to him.

Jeremy shook his head.

Don't do it.

Tarkin took her hand in his and pulled her back into the light, holding her against him as she sobbed.

"I remember, Papa," she blubbered.

"I know," he said. "I've missed you, Sumaiyya."

"I've missed you too, Papa." She pulled back to look into his eyes, tears streaking down her cheeks. "I love you."

The dagger plunged deep into his back, piercing through his ribs and into the tissue beyond.

He gave a long, exhaling breath as it knocked the wind from him.

She stuck him again and again.

"I remember how they forced themselves inside of me while you watched, Papa," she yelled. "*They* showed me true love. *You* let them kill Takmel. *You* let them give true love to Mama. *You* let them, Papa. *You* let them."

Tarkin fell to the floor before the fireplace, blood spilling from the many wounds that she inflicted.

"No," Jeremy screamed as his captain twisted in agony on the floor.

The witch retrieved her garments from the floor and disappeared into the darkness again.

Jeremy bolted forward to aid his fallen commander, but one of the straw men stopped him. It hit him in the stomach with the palm of its wooden claw. The first mate of the *Adelandria* landed in a heap on the floor.

"Find the witch and kill her," Tomas barked.

The men of Woodmyst moved towards the scarecrows. Their blades swung and hacked at the straw warriors, sending pieces of wood and straw across the stone surface.

Jeremy climbed back to his feet, rubbing his stomach. He and Emily raced towards the fireplace as the others continued to skirmish with the straw warriors.

"Captain," Jeremy called as he dropped to his knees by the fallen man's side.

"Jeremy," he replied, gargling, as blood filled his throat.

Emily cradled his head in her lap, hoping that by elevating him a little, she could help him speak more easily. "I've not long. She is my daughter. She is my Sumaiyya."

"I know, Captain," he replied, not wanting it to be true. Deep inside, he had always hoped that Tarkin's daughter would have met a far better fate through death than to become a servant of the Sovereign.

His interpretation of a female servant of this fiend was a woman existing for no other reason than to please the men under the Sovereign's control. But it would appear that Sumaiyya had become a genuine believer, trained in the dark arts and, ultimately, a formidable weapon for their enemy.

"Find her," Tarkin gargled. "Save her if you can."

"I'll do my best," Jeremy replied.

"The *Adelandria*," the captain breathed. "The *Adelandria*. She is yours, Captain."

His eyes closed, and his breath escaped him. Emily sobbed as Jeremy lowered his head, filled with deep sorrow.

"Goodbye, Papa," her soft voice murmured from behind Emily.

The auburn-haired girl turned to see Sumaiyya leaning her back against the stonework of the fireplace. She had donned her white garments, now stained with the wet blood she had smeared over her body.

Emily jumped to her feet, blade in hand.

"You bitch," she called, swinging her sword towards the woman in white.

The witch moved with unnatural speed, dodging the blow.

Steel met stone.

Sparks and flint burst from the stone where the witch had been leaning.

She now stood beside Emily, only an arm's reach from her.

The witch pushed her against the stonework where the sword had struck. The force from hitting the fireplace knocked the sword from Emily's hand, sending it skating loudly across the floor.

Jeremy moved towards the witch, intending to strike her down. She repositioned Emily so her face was against the stone, her arms behind her back and held in place by the witch's body.

Sumaiyya brought her dagger into view by pulling Emily's auburn hair away from her neck and over her shoulders. The small blade, still dripping with Tarkin's blood, pressed against the girl's throat.

Tomas bolted towards them, ignoring the straw warrior he'd been battling. Jeremy held up his hand, signalling the other to stop.

"The Sovereign wanted this one," Sumaiyya said. "There is something about her. Something special. I wonder if she could have been like me."

"Let her go," Tomas ordered.

Sumaiyya extended her tongue and licked Emily's lobe as she gave a soft chuckle.

Emily winced in disgust.

"The prophets marked me," Sumaiyya replied. "From that moment, I belonged to the Sovereign. This one is meant for something more.

"They looked for you," she said to Emily. "Searched for you. Never, had they travelled so far into the mountains, so far away from the sea.

But that's where you were. That's where the Sovereign said that they would find you. And they did."

"We could use some help," David called as he hacked through the body of a straw man, eyeing another that was reforming itself upon the floor nearby.

"The prophets weren't quick enough," Sumaiyya continued. She tore Emily away from the stonework and made her face toward Tomas. "This one beat them to it. You belong to him now."

"I said, let her go," Tomas shouted.

"The Sovereign has no use for you," the witch breathed, before turning her attention to Tomas. "She will never bear your children. I don't intend to let her live long enough.

"Your sister, however," she whispered into Emily's ears. "She will be with the Sovereign soon. Maybe, the prophets have lain with her just as they once did with me."

Emily thrust her head back as hard as she could, connecting with the witch's chin. Sumaiyya relaxed her hold just enough for the girl to free her arms and rapidly strike the other with her elbows.

The witch stepped back, surprised at the sudden outburst.

She quickly dashed into the darkness and out of view.

"After her," Tomas called.

"Help us first," Simon bellowed as a scarecrow lifted its frame from the floor to re-join the fight.

Tomas was suddenly torn.

He could give chase after the witch, who was responsible for much of what had happened to them over the past few days, or help his friends.

Peering into the darkness where Sumaiyya had vanished for a seemingly long time, he wrestled with his choices.

His loyalty to his friends won him over, and he dashed across the floor to assist them.

"We can give chase," Jeremy called after him, referring to Emily and himself.

"No," Tomas replied. "I do not want to risk either of you. We confront her together. All of us."

Jeremy looked into the darkness beyond the firelight and considered disregarding Tomas' words. The thought was only fleeting as he turned towards the skirmish near the doors and headed into the fray.

Emily started after him, keeping her eyes upon the shadows.

Something moved in the corner of her eye, towards the ceiling where a small window looked out upon the overgrown forest beyond, from where one of the upper levels of the keep used to be.

She spun her head to see something white disappearing through the portal and into the night. At least, she thought she saw it.

She gave a quick shake of her head, bringing herself back to reality, as she directed her attention to the straw men in the room.

"The fire," Oliver called. "We need to get them into the fire."

"I have a better idea," Tomas replied. "David, grab the captain. Oliver, take Ivo. We're leaving."

The two men gave Tomas a quizzical look as they ran across the floor towards the two bodies by the fireplace.

"What do we do?" Simon asked as he chopped the arm from one of the straw men.

"Take that," Tomas called.

"What?"

"Pick up that arm and take it to the fire," he replied, nodding to the discarded arm of a strawman. "Bring it back here and set these bastards alight."

Simon hacked a leg from his opponent, sending it sprawling to the floor. He then seized the opportunity to grab the discarded arm and scramble to the fireplace, passing his two comrades on the way.

"Where do we go?" Oliver called, Ivo slung over his shoulder.

"Outside," Tomas replied as he sliced the belly of his attacker open, straw intestines spilling over the floor.

Simon didn't take too long in retrieving the flame. He was already bolting back across the floor as both David and Oliver exited through the doors of the keep. The first to receive the flame's kiss was his opponent, which was still lying on the floor, reaching for its dismembered leg.

The fire engulfed the straw man quickly.

Not stopping to admire his work, Simon moved to the next scarecrow. Emily was so engaged in hacking at it with her blade that it surprised her to see it burst into flames. Simon grabbed her and moved her on as he made his way to the next straw man.

Jeremy saw the others approaching and stepped out of the way as Simon stuck the creature with the flaming appendage. He was about to move over to Tomas in order to complete his task.

"Out of the way," the other commanded as he kicked his foe as hard as he could with the heel of his boot. The scarecrow flew into the air and crashed into another that was fully alight with fire. "Throw that into the room," he instructed Simon, pointing to the burning straw arm still in the man's hand.

Simon lobbed the flaming limb towards the rug that rested in front of the fireplace. The fire caught in places and spread to the chairs positioned at the sides of the mat.

"Let's go," Tomas shouted to the other three.

They ran for the doors.

"Simon," Tomas called as he closed one of the large wooden doors. Simon took the other in his hands and pulled the monstrosity shut.

With both doors closed, the men turned and ran into the yard between the keep and the gatehouse, where both David and Oliver waited with the bodies of their fallen friends.

They watched as smoke billowed out of the upper windows of the structure and through the cracks of the large doors before them. Flickering orange light radiated from deep inside as fire consumed everything flammable.

"Do you think she is still in there?" Jeremy asked.

"I don't know," Tomas replied.

"She isn't," Emily told them. "She left through an upper window. I saw her."

"Why didn't you say something earlier?" Oliver questioned.

"We were engaged in battle," Tomas replied. "There was nothing we could do. She has gone."

"We'll see her again." Jeremy frowned. "She'll run to her master. If we don't see her before we get to him, we'll catch her on the way."

"So, you'll be joining us then?" Simon asked.

"The captain may have met his end here," Jeremy said, looking down upon the remains of his commander, "but we have not yet fulfilled his mission. We must kill the Sovereign. This is something that I must see completed, for the captain. For my crew. For me."

Loud footfalls in the gatehouse caused them to tense up and turn, ready for another attack.

It was the Erilian women and remaining crewmen of the *Adelandria*.

"The straw men are gone," Karlena informed them with a smile. "We burned them to ash." Her eyes fell upon the two bodies lying in the snow. She recognised her beloved immediately and fell to her knees, where she wept uncontrollably.

"No," Rhydra screamed, running forward and falling upon him at his side.

The other women moved towards him, tears streaking down their faces as the men stared with disbelief at the lifeless form of their leader.

The men of Woodmyst stepped back, drawing nearer to the body of their fallen friend on the snow. A half-circle formed around the two departed warriors as the keep burned before them.

Large flames burst through the roof of the structure as smoke billowed into the dark sky.

Gentle snow drifted from the clouds, landing silently on the ground around them.

The travellers mourned their loss together.

They gave themselves time to remember all of their fallen.

They remembered their friends and family, victims of evil intent.

They remembered their captain, his words, his guidance, his friendship.

They remembered their mission.

They remembered their calling.

Epilogue

The sloshing waves broke against the hull as the vessel moved through the rolling sea. The sails were full, and the wind was strong, pushing them onward towards the north.

It wouldn't be too long before they would reach port.

Perhaps a day or two.

The scarred man scratched at his beard as he examined the maps laid upon the table inside the chart house. He traced a finger along the intended route before raising a mug of rum to his mouth.

He gulped the contents as if he was dying of thirst.

"More," he barked to a crewman standing nearby, holding his mug out to be refilled.

The crewman obliged by pouring from a large jug, refilling the scarred man's mug. The man gulped the contents dry again and then thumped the cup onto the map in front of him before staggering towards the door.

He stumbled through the entrance and onto the upper deck, where another burly figure manned the wheel.

"Sir." The wheelman nodded as the scarred man staggered by, heading for the stairs that led to the lower decks.

"Keep her steady," he ordered. "Don't lose sight of the shore."

"Aye," the other replied, returning his eyes to the horizon ahead.

The scarred man descended the stairs and entered a small alcove to the rear of the vessel that housed another stairwell that took him to the hold deep in the ship's belly. There, he found the many cages that lined the walls of the hull. Each cage contained several prisoners.

Women and young girls.

He eyed each of them as he passed by. Any of them would do, but he wanted one in particular.

She cowered in the back of a cage, behind some older girls. He unlocked the cage with keys hanging from his belt and opened the door.

"Move," he barked to the others.

The girls parted, allowing him access to his desired target.

She had tucked her legs up to her chin as she tried to bury herself into the wall.

Grabbing her by her auburn hair, he forced her to her feet. She screamed in pain, feeling as if her scalp were tearing from her skull.

The other girls screamed also, frightened out of their wits. The women in the cages nearby cried as they knew the fate of his chosen prey.

"Come on," he grunted as he dragged her from the pen. He slammed the door behind him before locking it shut.

Keeping her fist around her hair, he directed her back along the way he had come from, up the stairs and to his cabin below the upper deck.

She whimpered as he pulled her this way and that, manoeuvring her towards his bunk.

"It would be easier if you simply submit this time," he breathed into her face.

The smell of rum was strong, almost sending her into a dizzy spell.

He flung her hard against his bed and stared at her for a long time, devouring her with his eyes, before closing the door behind him with a soft thud.

The ship creaked soothingly as it rolled over the waves.

The wind continued to blow from the south, pushing them onwards, towards their destination.

It wouldn't be too long before they would reach port.

Perhaps a day or two.

She hoped.

She prayed.

About The Author

Robert E Kreig was born in Newcastle, Australia and grew up in its outer suburbs.

He has always had a love for books, particularly well-told stories involving action, adventure and fear.

Some of Robert's favourite authors as a young reader included J. R. R. Tolkien, Stephen King, Orson Scott Card, Ray Bradbury and Frank Herbert. As he grew into adulthood, the list continued to lengthen, adding more influential writers such as George R. R. Martin, Matthew Reilly, Nathan M. Farrugia, Dan Brown, James Patterson, Michael Connelly and Lee Child just to name a few.

Inspired by movies like Star Wars, King Kong, Jaws, Jason and the Argonauts and other great adventure pieces, Robert listened to the voices in his head and entertained the strange visions dancing through his mind to assist him with writing his fantasy series The Woodmyst Chronicles.

Robert has penned ten books for the series which follow the lives of many characters, particularly focussing upon a family who must face many trials before the epic conclusion. Clashing swords, strange creatures, flying dragons and sorcery inhabit the world surrounding Woodmyst.

Other Books By This Author

LONG VALLEY

In the small community of Long Valley, nestled comfortably beneath snow-capped mountains, people quietly go about their business. Everybody knows everybody and there are no worries to give mind to.

But something has awakened.

A tragic accident near the valley's army base sparks a number of terrifying events, placing the local civilians in mortal danger.

A contagion is subsequently released into Long Valley, infecting pets, livestock, wildlife and people.

It's up to the local law enforcement and a small band of citizens to try to keep the town safe.

In the end, it becomes a struggle for survival as the people of Long Valley are overcome by the urge to feed.

THE WOODMYST CHRONICLES

From a faraway land...
...comes a new adventure.
The Woodmyst Chronicles is the story of a small community that faces the hardest of trials in a world filled with darkness, violence and magic.

Books In This Series...
THE WALLS OF WOODMYST
THE SONS OF WOODMYST
THE HEIR OF WOODMYST
THE WARLORDS OF WOODMYST
THE HUNTRESS OF WOODMYST
THE SHADOW OF WOODMYST
THE BRIDES OF WOODMYST
THE GODS OF WOODMYST
THE WEAPONS OF WOODMYST
A FAREWELL TO WOODMYST

http://www.robertekreig.com/

http://www.whitekeepbooks.com/

www.ingramcontent.com/pod-product-compliance
Lightning Source LLC
Chambersburg PA
CBHW020336120726
47904CB00002B/432